MARIJUANA
BEAR

MARIJUANA BEAR

DALE THACKER

Botetourt Nace Press
Troutville, Virginia

Printed in the United States of America
First Printing, 2025

ISBN-13 (Trade Paperback): 979-8-9923495-2-8
ISBN-13 (eBook): 979-8-9923495-3-5

Botetourt Nace Press
dalethacker.com

MARIJUANA BEAR

CHAPTER 1

Introduction to Benjamin

The morning after his very first hibernation, Benjamin crawled out of his den to find swaying trees and more than a foot of snow still on the ground. After being denned up for over three months, he was looking forward to all the adventures he would have in the year ahead.

Before hibernation, Benjamin had learned to do all the things bears do. Since a lot of a bear's diet is plant-based, Benjamin had to find food to eat. Blackberries and raspberries were his favorite treats, but he also loved blueberries and strawberries. Acorns—especially the yummy white oak acorns—were a great source of food in the fall. Corn was filling and tasty, provided his family could find a large cornfield to eat in. The only problem was that it could be hazardous to their health—if, for example, a farmer caught them eating his corn.

Benjamin also learned how to scavenge for food. When deer hunting season started in the fall, the bears could hear lots of bangs and pops from the hunters' guns. But they found that if they waited for at least an hour after the shooting stopped, they could head in the direction of the shots and find the piles of guts the hunters left behind. Hearts and livers were Benjamin's favorite parts to eat.

Deer season was scary enough, but when bear season came in, hunters would turn their hounds loose to track down the bears and chase them. One time, the hounds almost caught Benjamin, but he was able to scamper up a tree and stay out of reach. Fortunately, his dad, Oliver, showed up just in the nick of time. With a few hard smacks, he sent the dogs scurrying away with tails tucked. Benjamin had never been so scared in his life.

Benjamin's mom, Sophia, was really good at catching small game. Rabbits were her favorite. But while they were delicious, they just weren't enough for a family of four, so she would also capture other animals, like possums. These were easy to catch because when they got scared, they just played dead, making for easy pickings. Benjamin had become quite skilled at capturing possums himself. Sophia would also capture raccoons, which were great eating with lots of fat. If there's anything bears love, it's fat. Most people think bears eat their prey raw, but they actually cook their food, just like humans do.

The streams nearby were loaded with native brook trout. They were a treat, but because they were so small—usually about seven inches long—they were really more of an appetizer. The year before, Benjamin had caught one a whopping thirteen inches long.

Sophia was still sleeping in the den with Oliver and Benjamin's little sister, Lucy. She and Benjamin were inseparable. They had so much fun together. They would play fight a lot, and even though Lucy could hold her own against him, sometimes Benjamin would let her win, although he would never tell her that.

Hearing sounds, Benjamin looked over and saw Lucy coming out of the den. Her face lit up when she saw the snow. When they had denned up, the snow was just beginning.

They were both happy to see each other again, and they decided to go on an adventure down to the stream. The snow on the hillside had frozen over, and as they walked down, Lucy started sliding downhill. *Wow, she's sliding so fast*, Benjamin thought as she picked up speed. *I want to try!* He joined in the fun. It was like sledding with no sled. Luckily, they missed all the trees on the way down, but at the bottom, they slid straight into the deep water of the stream. Fortunately, bears don't feel the cold very much.

Right away, Benjamin caught an appetizer: a nine-inch native trout. The "sushi," as he called it, was delicious. His waist had gotten skinny after their three-month hibernation, and until that moment, he had no idea how hungry he was. Seeing Lucy splash from one side of the pool to the other trying to snag her appetizer made him laugh. He was impressed—well, maybe a little jealous—when she came up with the biggest native trout he had ever seen, at least eighteen inches long. It was a whole meal. Benjamin was happy with his nine-incher since it was larger than the average size last year. But he was still hungry, so he dove in and caught two more seven-inch trout. Then it was time to head back to the den to see if Mom and Dad were awake yet.

As the cubs walked up to the entrance of the den, Oliver sauntered out. He looked so thin. Back in the fall, he weighed over five hundred pounds, but now he'd be lucky if he were four hundred.

"Dad, I wish you saw the native trout I caught!" were the first words out of Lucy's mouth. "It was *huge*, over eighteen inches!" She threw Benjamin a taunting look as she spoke.

This made him so mad, he started a fight with her. They had never had a real fight, only play fights. But this one was serious. Oliver had to step in and break it up. He then asked the cubs to apologize to each other. Oliver was happy they had made up. For Benjamin, it felt good telling his sister he was sorry. They really did love each other.

"I was so hungry, Dad," Benjamin said. "Those trout tasted so good." He turned to Lucy. "I'm proud of you for catching such a large native trout, Sis." Secretly, he was hoping he would catch a fish even bigger than hers someday.

"Welcome to the life of a bear, Son," Oliver said. "When we go into our dens every year, we're fat and happy, but we come out hungry enough to eat a moose."

Oliver was a skilled hunter of big game. He would go out hunting by himself and bring back does and fawns for the family to eat. On occasion, he would drag home a buck, warning everyone not to eat the antlers.

Sophia was now crawling out of the den. She, too, looked thinner. If she had been 250 pounds when they denned up, she looked more like 200 now.

She looked straight at the others. "I hope y'all have been behaving."

"Yes, Mom," Benjamin said. "We went sledding down to the stream and Lucy caught an eighteen-inch trout! I was so proud of her. But I was also mad and jealous about it so we got in a fight and then Dad made us apologize to each other, but I feel so much better now after making up. And I'm gonna— well, never mind." He was about to tell her that he planned to catch a fish bigger than Lucy's, but he thought better of it.

The four of them made their way down to the stream and found different pools to fish in so they could each catch a good meal. Benjamin swam the farthest upstream and caught several trout that were all six to eight inches long. Then he spotted a huge one and dove in after it. He came up with a twenty-inch, beautifully colored native trout, and it was delicious. But he decided to be humble about it and not let anyone know about his catch.

With full stomachs, the family regrouped and headed back to the den. After all the excitement, a short snooze was in order.

CHAPTER 2

The Neighbors

They woke up the next morning with bellies still full from all the fish they had devoured the day before. Sophia and Oliver asked the cubs if they wanted to walk the mile and a half to their next-door neighbors' den to see if they were awake yet.

Today seemed a little warmer. As they walked through the snow, it didn't have as hard of a crust as it did yesterday, and Benjamin broke through the crust on most of his steps. All the trees were bare in this white oak forest, and they could see several hundred yards ahead. The trees swayed gently against a pale-blue sky.

Benjamin observed the wildlife as they walked. He saw a red fox and several very large-bodied deer. None of them had antlers. Oliver said they were probably bucks that had lost their antlers, which happened a lot around this time of year. There were also quite a few squirrels, which were hard to catch because they were so fast and would scamper up trees before the bears could get too close.

Just then, they spotted a turkey about fifty feet away.

"Y'all stay here," Sophia said. "I'm going to sneak over and catch this turkey to give to our neighbors."

They knew that George, the father of the family of bears they were visiting, had been killed during last year's hunting season, which was why Sophia really wanted to bring a small meal to Angel, the mother bear, and her cubs, Luna and James.

Sophia snuck right up on that twenty-five–pound tom turkey and killed it with one smack of her paw.

When they arrived, they were happy to see that Angel was awake from her hibernation. "I brought y'all a fresh meal!"

Sophia called out.

Angel said they had been awake for two days now and hadn't been able to forage for food, so she was grateful to get the turkey. She said Luna and James had left early in the morning to look for some food and hadn't returned yet. When she pointed at the tracks they had left, Benjamin and Lucy ran off, excited to go find them.

಄

Oliver and Sophia stayed behind with Angel. Oliver dressed the turkey by gutting it and removing all the feathers while Sophia and Angel talked. Angel was very sad. She said she missed George now more than ever and explained that being so sad and depressed made it hard for her to go out and hunt for food. Sophia said she and her family would help Angel out for as long as she needed.

಄

The cubs caught up with James and Luna, who were also feeling very sad. They said they missed their dad so much and just wanted to get away from the den for a little while to clear their minds. Benjamin suggested they play a game called rough and tumble. Using a stick, he traced a large circle on the ground, and everyone stepped inside. The object was to wrestle the others out of the circle, and the last one left in the circle was the winner.

The two sow cubs paired up and began wrestling, followed by Benjamin and James. Lucy was the first to be pushed out, and Benjamin was next. Then, James and Luna wrestled each other. James was pushing hard, and just when Luna was almost out of the circle, she outsmarted her brother by falling to the ground and letting his own momentum carry him out of bounds. They were both beaming, Luna because she had won the game, and James because the game had taken his mind off his father's death.

"I think we need some food now," James said. "I appreciate the turkey you brought over, but for the three of us, it would just be an appetizer."

Benjamin had an idea and grinned at the thought. "You guys want to go to Possum Hollow?" That was the next holler over, famous for its abundance of possums. He loved catching possums. If he just scared them a little, they would roll over and play dead. It was like shooting fish in a barrel.

The cubs caught two apiece and took them back to Angel's den. Angel was so proud of them and happy they had brought more food.

"Mom, where's Dad?" Benjamin asked.

"He went out big game hunting," Sophia said. "He's hoping to bring a big deer back."

While they waited for Oliver to come back, they dressed the possums and got them ready to cook. Benjamin was excited. Possums were almost as delicious as a hot cup of porridge.

Just as they finished, Oliver showed up with a big-bodied deer with no antlers. Benjamin could see the circles where the buck had dropped its antlers.

"I also got a doe," Oliver said, smiling at the cubs. "It's over in the next holler. Follow my tracks and you'll find the doe." He gave them the job of bringing the doe back to the den. Last year he hadn't given them jobs like this, and Benjamin guessed it meant they were growing up and would have more responsibilities now.

They played and roughhoused with each other as they walked to the holler. Benjamin was glad to see that for at least a moment in time, James and Luna were happy and not feeling down about the loss of their dad.

They found the doe and took turns dragging it back to the den. Even though it was only a mid-sized doe, this was the first time any of them had dragged any type of large game. It was exhausting, but also fun.

"Y'all did a great job bringing the doe back," Oliver said

when they returned. "But the work isn't done yet. We're now going to cook this doe for supper. Ben and James, I'll help you dress the deer and get it ready. Then, Sophia, Angel, Lucy, and Luna will cook the meal. Benjamin felt proud the cubs were getting so much responsibility.

After the meal, Cliver stood up. "Get ready, cubs," he said. "It's about time to head back to our den."

"Stay the night," Angel said. "Our den is big and there's plenty of room for all."

"Oh, I don't know. We should—"

"Come on," she insisted. "We'll have a great time."

The bears stayed up late. The cubs played cards and board games while the older bears sat and talked. Angel said this was the best day their family had had since losing George. She shed happy tears watching all the cubs sitting around the fireplace, playing and laughing and having the best time.

Benjamin was enjoying the time with family and friends. He just hoped the happiness would last after they left.

CHAPTER 3

The Bad News Bears

The next morning, Angel was up early, singing and humming while she prepared a breakfast of possums and porridge. She appeared to be much happier than yesterday, which made Oliver and Sophia happy. When the cubs woke up, they set the table and got it ready for their delicious breakfast. Oliver said the blessing, and the two clans dug in like a bunch of hungry bears. Afterward, everyone chipped in to clean up the table and tidy up the den. Angel thanked them for a great time as Benjamin's family headed out the door.

Trudging through the snow back to their den, the bears came across plenty of game. Benjamin was able to kill a couple of possums, and Sophia caught a rabbit and another turkey. Oliver came across two yearling deer: a small doe and a button buck. He was able to catch both. Sophia brought the turkey, rabbit, and two possums back to the den while Oliver dragged the button buck and Benjamin and Lucy hauled the doe.

"I like fishing better," Lucy said, out of breath. "When we get home and drop this stuff off, I'm going to get some native trout."

Just before they reached their den, a commotion erupted. Someone was yelling words Benjamin had never heard before.

"Fuck you, bastard," came the gruff sound of an older bear's voice. Benjamin couldn't see who was speaking.

Then a younger voice: "You're a son of a bitch, Oliver!"

The younger bear used more words Benjamin didn't know, but he heard the word "shit." *That one I know*, he thought. *Bears shit in the woods every day.*

"Dad, what do those words mean?" he asked. "Who is saying all that?"

"That's Samuel," Oliver said. "He's a three hundred–pound bear. The other one is his son, Maverick. He's two years old."

Oliver explained that a year ago, a group of hunters had killed Charlotte, Samuel's mate, and illegally killed his daughter, Emma. She was still a cub and didn't meet the minimum weight to be legally hunted.

"Samuel and Maverick are just like Angel and her family," Oliver said. "They're very depressed and sad. I tried to help them out just like we did with Angel and her family, but after two months, they never really seemed to appreciate us like Angel's family does."

Oliver recalled that things started getting better once he got in touch with Caesar, Angel's granddad, who gave Oliver a possum bag of marijuana to give to Samuel. Caesar sold marijuana in different-sized bags: The smallest was the rabbit bag, then possum bag, turkey bag, and deer bag. The largest one was the bear bag, which was enough to keep a normal user supplied for a three-month period. After Samuel got the marijuana, he seemed to calm down.

"I never believed in marijuana," Oliver said. "But after witnessing that, I saw it could be helpful in extreme circumstances."

Caesar let everyone know he only sold the highest-quality marijuana. That meant it was never laced with any other drug, such as fentanyl, ketamine, cocaine, or PCP, any of which could be very hazardous to a bear's health. And he wouldn't provide marijuana to anyone who wanted to use it recreationally. It was only for severe depression or extreme pain. He cautioned everyone about other dealers who sold laced marijuana, which could cause severe medical issues like psychosis, breathing difficulties, and even death, depending on what it was laced with. He also recommended that anyone who used marijuana from an unreliable dealer have a supply of Narcan, a nasal spray that could save a bear's life in an emergency.

But Samuel, after a few months of using Caesar's marijuana, had found another bear who was selling it much cheaper. Boy, did the forest remember that night. Samuel was going around whooping and hollering with every breath. He was psychotic. Nothing he said or did that night made any sense. "I'm the purple alligator the dragon slayed," he had shouted at one point. And later: "I will put the sky into the lake." If anyone confronted him, he would yell and curse and say he was going to kill them. After that night, any bears that heard him coming would just hide and let the dang fool go his way.

Benjamin spoke up. "Dad, we need to do something to help him out."

"Your heart is in the right place, Son, but there's no helping Samuel. He'll have to hit rock bottom and be willing to reach out for help. Until then, we just ignore him and stay out of his way."

They remained out of sight in a small gully until they could no longer hear them, then continued to their den with the fresh game. But just in front of their den, they heard Samuel again. He was behind them but heading their way.

"This is bad news," Oliver said. "Looks like Samuel saw all this food we have. He'll want it for himself, so we'll have to give it up."

"But you're so much bigger, Dad," Benjamin said. "Why not fight for our food?"

"That's true, but I can tell by the way he's acting that he's been smoking laced marijuana. It's bad stuff. It gives him super bear strength. I saw him get shot five times once, and it didn't stop him. I may be able to take him due to my size, but it's just as likely he would win. He may even kill me."

"That's not fair," Benjamin said. "It's our food!"

"I agree, Son. It's not fair at all."

Samuel stepped into Oliver's path. "You damned son of a bitch, Oliver. It's been a long fucking time since I saw you last."

"Not long enough, Samuel," Oliver said. "What brings you by today?"

"You bastard, you know what brings me by. The deer, the possums, the rabbits, the turkeys. I'm here to take them off your hands."

Oliver took a step toward Samuel. "We harvested them, Samuel. They're ours."

"Don't make me hurt you today, Oliver. You know what I'm capable of."

"Yes I do, Samuel. I don't want anyone to get hurt. Just take the food."

As they walked away with the dead animals, Oliver heard Samuel tell Maverick, "You see how it's done? One day, when you confront those bastards and take their food, you'll make me proud."

Sophia was crying. "I remember before they lost Charlotte and Emma," she said, dabbing her eyes. "They were our good friends, just like Angel and her family. It's that laced marijuana that makes them act like this. I'm glad you didn't confront him, Oliver. Everyone remembers the time Lucky got in his face when he was in a rage, and Samuel just slaughtered him. I miss Lucky. He was such a great bear friend."

Sophia entered the den and let out a piercing scream. The others rushed in and found their den had been ransacked. There was no food left. Everything had been turned over and broken. They had no doubt it was the work of Samuel and Maverick.

"I'll get started cleaning this up," Sophia said.

Lucy looked around. "Dad and I will help you."

"I'll go down to the stream and catch us some fish for supper," Benjamin said, grabbing a basket on his way out of the den.

Fortunately, the fishing was good, and Benjamin returned with a full basket of trout. By then, the den had been cleaned up for the most part.

"Wow, look at all that fish," Sophia said. "I hope everyone is hungry. I'm going to fry up the best fish supper we've ever had!"

When Oliver yawned after dinner, they all realized how tired they were and agreed it was time for bed.

Before they turned in, Benjamin gathered the family and said a prayer. He wished that Angel and her family would heal and be okay. He also prayed that Samuel and Maverick would find peace and joy in their lives.

"Amen," they said together, then wished each other goodnight.

CHAPTER 4

Springtime

It was now spring, and the weather was beautiful. There was a slight crispness to the early morning air. The trees, with different shades of green showing up all over, were no longer bare.

"These fresh leaves are so delicious," Benjamin said to Lucy as he pulled off another handful.

"Yes, they are, but these flowers are so sweet. Yum!"

As they enjoyed the fresh leaves and flowers, Lucy happened across a large beehive. "Come over here, Brother! I found some honey."

As she dug in, the bees swarmed about her in a cloud. Fortunately, bees don't have the same effect on bears as they do on humans, so she hardly noticed.

"Save me some!" Benjamin called out.

"It's a big hive, Ben," she yelled back. "There's plenty for all!"

After they ate to their hearts' content, they fetched a large container to bring all that deliciousness back to the den. They were careful not to harm the bees so they could produce even more scrumptious honey for them.

Sophia was pleased to see the honeycomb and ten gallons of honey the cubs had brought home.

"We must have eaten a gallon of honey each, Mom," Lucy said. Sophia told them they would probably be sick from eating that much honey. She was right. They both felt just *blah* for the rest of the day.

Sophia used frozen berries and some of the honey to make four large cobblers, then poured the rest of the honey into smaller containers to store for later. For supper, she fried up some possum along with some morel mushrooms she had collected earlier.

When Benjamin woke up the next morning, Sophia had set a gallon of honey near the front door. "Let's go visit Angel and her family," she said. "I want to take her some of this honey."

Benjamin and Lucy were beside themselves. It had been a couple of weeks since they'd seen James and Luna. Wanting to bring them some fish as well, they grabbed a basket and headed down to the stream. The pools were loaded with native trout, and in less than half an hour, the basket was overflowing. Back at the den, they cleaned the fish and placed them in a large bag to take to Angel's.

Excited about the day ahead, they grabbed the honey and the fish and headed to see their friends. As they walked, Oliver told the rest of them to go on ahead while he tried to find a deer to bring to Angel and her family.

"Can I go with you, Dad?" Benjamin asked. "Can you teach me to be a big game hunter?"

Oliver smiled, happy his son wanted to stay with him and participate in the hunt. "Bear country is steep, Ben," he said. "I've found if I run a deer up into the rock cliffs, it's much easier to catch."

Soon, they found two yearlings. Oliver pointed in the direction they needed to go to trap the animals.

"I'll be right behind you, but this is your hunt," Oliver said.

"Dad, I'm afraid they'll get away from me!"

"Well, that's why it's called hunting. I've been outsmarted by many deer."

Benjamin took the lead as the deer ran up toward the steep rocks. One of the deer cut to the right, and Oliver said he would take that one. Benjamin continued chasing his. When it reached the rocks, he swiped at it with his paw. That didn't kill it, so he swiped again. When that didn't work, he bit the deer's head with his massive jaw, and at last it dropped dead.

A few minutes later, Oliver came over and congratulated

Benjamin on his first big game kill.

"Thanks, Dad. Well, I guess we can take these deer to Angel now."

"One deer," Oliver said. "Yours. Mine got away from me." Benjamin was surprised that his dad didn't get his deer, but he was learning such was the nature of hunting.

"I'm so glad y'all are here," Angel said when they knocked on her door. "We've been a little down lately, and this visit is just the pickup we needed."

"What's been going on, Angel?" Sophia asked.

Angel rolled her eyes. "That Samuel and his son, Maverick, came by a few days ago and took some of our food. They didn't tear the place up, they just yelled a few swear words and left." She sighed. "Believe it or not, that was the most pleasant meeting we've had with them in the past year. It just sucks they took our food."

Benjamin gestured at the deer. "Look here, Angel. I brought y'all this yearling doe. And I caught it all by myself."

Sophia leaned over and whispered to Benjamin how proud she was of him for his first deer kill.

Benjamin looked around at the other cubs. "Want to go out hunting and find some game to bring back?" Lucy, Luna, and James lit up. They were all for this adventure.

"Let's go to Possum Hollow!" James said.

But Luna had other ideas. "I know where there are several yearling deer," she said once they had left the den. "Ben, you got your first deer today. Maybe we can all go and try to get our first deer, too."

The cubs were excited about this. "Ben, you come with me over to the next holler," Luna said, "and James and Lucy can go into this holler."

"Sounds good," James said. "But I've never killed a deer. Tell me how you did it, Ben."

"Just get down below the deer, then run them up to the steep part of the mountain. They'll have a hard time getting over the rocks. That's when you go in for the kill."

James smiled. "Sounds easy enough."

CB

James and Lucy made their way down into the holler and spotted a yearling right away. The chase was on. They pursued it all the way up to the rocks, then James gave it a powerful blow, knocking it down, and told Lucy to go in for the kill. She leaned over and sunk her teeth into the yearling's head.

"Great job, Lucy," James said. "Let's take this deer back to the others now."

Lucy looked at James all googly eyed. "You're so strong and awesome, James."

Together, they dragged the deer back to the den, laughing and giggling. They could tell they were acting differently around each other now.

James stopped and turned to Lucy. "You're a special bear, Lucy. I'm so glad we've come to be such good friends."

Lucy smiled. "Why don't you come over to my den sometime? I know a great fishing spot. The native trout is so much fun to catch! Fresh sushi is the bomb. It's a delicacy, you know."

James couldn't wait. His area of the woods had good hunting for big and small game, but no place to fish.

CB

Over in their holler, Benjamin and Luna spotted two yearlings.

"I'll take the one on the left," Benjamin said, "and you get the one on the right."

Luna looked worried. "I don't think I can do this, Ben."

"You've got this. I know you can do it. Just remember to get in below the yearling, chase it up into the rocks, then go in for the kill."

"Well, okay. If you think I can do it, then I can do it."

They ran down into the holler and got below the two deer, and the chase was on. Luna was fast. She caught up with her deer before it even got to the rocks, and with a big smack of her paw, she broke the animal's neck. Benjamin chased his deer up into the rocks, and with a blow to the head, his deer was dead, too.

"Today was such a good day," Luna said as they dragged their deer back to the den. "I don't feel depressed anymore. Showing me I'm stronger than I thought meant so much to me."

They heard voices in front of them and realized they had almost caught up to Lucy and James. *They're giggling and laughing*, Benjamin thought. *They're not acting their normal selves. What's going on?*

Luna knew what he was thinking. "I've read enough romance novels to know those two are falling in love, the way they're acting." She laughed.

When they returned to the den, the cubs showed off the three deer they had caught. The older bears were surprised.

"I thought y'all were going small game hunting," Oliver said.

"We were," Benjamin said, "but then Luna said she knew where we could find some yearling deer. Since I know how to big game hunt now, I taught the others how to do it."

He lowered his voice and leaned over to tell Lucy they had heard her and James laughing and giggling. "I've never seen you two like that."

"Yeah," she said, blushing. "We had fun together today."

Oliver looked at his watch. "Well, time to head back to the den," he said. "Come on, cubs."

"Y'all stayed the night last time you were here," James said. "You know you're always welcome. Y'all might as well stay."

Oliver looked at Angel. "We don't want to wear out our welcome ..."

"Nonsense," Angel said. "That would never happen."

Lucy looked relieved. "Whew, thank you. I don't know about the rest of you, but I didn't want to go home tonight."

The next morning after breakfast, they told Angel goodbye. James and Luna were coming back to their den for the day. James was looking forward to spending some time with Lucy, who had promised to teach him how to fish. As they all walked home, James and Lucy hung back a ways. All Benjamin could hear were their giggles and snorts.

"That's just sickening," he said to his mom.

Sophia laughed. "Someday, Benjamin, you'll understand."

When they got back to the den, everyone went in except Lucy and James. "Would you like to go to the stream with me, James?"

"I'd love to."

They walked down the hill, side by side. At the bottom, Lucy pointed at the stream. "This is the deep pool I've been telling you about. It's loaded with native trout. Are you ready to learn to fish now?"

"You know, I'm a little tired right now," James said. "Can we just sit here on the bank for a while before we start fishing?"

Lucy liked the idea. They sat there telling stories, holding paws, giving bear kisses by rubbing each other's noses, and of course, laughing and giggling.

"My dad taught Ben how to hunt, you know," Lucy said. "Ben really looks up to him."

James got quiet, and Lucy could sense he had withdrawn.

"Are you okay, James?"

He looked at Lucy with tears in his eyes. "I just miss my dad."

Lucy felt horrible, and for a few moments, she didn't know what to say.

"It's okay," James said. "It's nothing you did. I just have these moments sometimes." He moved closer to Lucy. "Hold me tight. That will make me feel better."

They gave each other a huge bear hug and just held onto each other.

Afterward, they were getting hungry and decided it was time to go fishing. Lucy dove into the pool and came out with an eight-inch native trout.

"Here, James," she said, handing him the fish. "This is some of the best sushi you've ever had."

"Well, it will be the first sushi I've ever had, but I'll try it." He took a bite, and his eyes widened. "That is yummy. It's really just an appetizer, though."

"Well, let's catch some more! It's easy. Just dive in and swat at the fish with your paws. Your claws will catch and hang onto the trout as you swat at them. On his first try, he snagged a beautiful, ten-inch trout.

"Wow, that's fun!" James said. For the next thirty minutes, they fished and ate until James had had his fill. "This is so much fun, Lucy, but I couldn't eat another trout if I had to."

Back home, Lucy and James told Oliver and Sophia how much fun they'd had fishing down at the stream. Lucy also told them about James's moment of silence. This prompted James to explain how much he missed his dad.

Later, when Oliver saw James playing games with Benjamin in the living room, he had an idea. "Looks like you two are having the best time playing together," he said. "Almost like y'all are brothers. When I was a young bear, my best friend and I became blood brothers. We each made a small cut on our paw, then held our paws together to let the blood mix."

James lit up when he heard this. "I would love to be your blood brother, Ben!"

In the way Oliver had described, Benjamin and James became blood brothers. Afterward, James thanked Oliver for the idea. "You know, Oliver, since Ben and I are blood brothers," he said, "that almost makes you my dad."

Oliver smiled. "I'm honored to be your almost-dad, James."

James and Luna spent the night, and the next morning, Benjamin and Lucy walked them home.

James sang to himself as he walked. "I haven't been this happy since losing my dad," he said. "It's all because of you, Lucy, and your family. Y'all are the best. I just feel good when I'm with you."

Lucy put her paw on his shoulder. "You make me smile, James, and I'm the happiest when I'm with you."

"Thanks for walking me home. I can't wait to see you again." He and Lucy leaned in and rubbed noses.

As they hiked back to their den, Benjamin turned to Lucy and smiled. "I guess you and James are becoming a thing, huh?"

"Yes, I believe we are, Brother. How about you and Luna?"

"I like her a lot, but we're just friends." He gave her a playful push. "Anyway, Sis, I'm happy you and James have hit it off so well."

CHAPTER 5

Early Summer

By early summer, the flowers had turned into fruit. There were so many delicious strawberries in the meadows, and the growth was so thick, the bears couldn't walk without stepping on them. At the edge of the woods lay the blackberry and raspberry bushes, covered in luscious, black-and-red fruit. Deeper in the woods, blueberries grew on low bushes that were at just the right height for bears to forage on them.

With so many choices, Benjamin didn't know which ones he wanted. So, he and Lucy ate all of them—and kept eating until it felt like their bellies might pop.

"I'll help you pick a basket of all the different types of fruit, Lucy," Benjamin said, "and we can take the basket over to Angel's." He nudged her and giggled. "I don't think you would mind seeing James, huh? Even though y'all were just together yesterday."

"Can I tell you something, Ben?"

"Yes, of course."

"I think I'm falling in love with James."

Benjamin smiled. "I've noticed."

"I just feel so much joy when we're together. It's like nothing else matters."

"Yep, the old love bug has bitten the two of you," Benjamin said, chuckling. "I'm very happy for you, Sis. I'm also happy that James is my blood brother."

With a full basket of berries, they set off through the woods, chatting with each other and feeling happy.

Just then, a gruff voice: "Fuck you, Ben."

Oh no, it's Samuel! Maverick was with him, and they

stepped out in front of Benjamin and Lucy, blocking them from walking. Benjamin noticed that Maverick didn't seem to be in his usual, terrible mood, which was probably a good thing.

"Maverick?" Samuel said, glancing over at his son. "Is there anything you want to say? Anything you want to do?"

Maverick hesitated. "No! I told you, Dad. I don't want to live like this anymore."

"I'll deal with you later, Son." Samuel turned his attention to Benjamin and flashed an evil smile. "Well, well. I see you picked me a basket of berries." His smile disappeared. "Hand them over right now, and we won't have any problems."

As father and son walked off with the basket of berries, Benjamin could hear Samuel hissing at Maverick.

"Damn it, Maverick, you were supposed to handle this."

"I told you, I don't like being mean to our fellow bears anymore."

"Fine! This basket of fruit is all mine." Samuel stormed off and left Maverick behind.

Maverick sat down on a rock and started crying. Seeing this, Benjamin walked over to him.

"I stood up to my dad," Maverick said, wiping away tears. "It really felt good. But I also feel so empty now, with him walking away from me."

Benjamin sat down next to him. "Maverick, I know your dad loves you deep down. He hasn't been the same since you lost your mom and sister. I remember how hard it was for y'all. My mom and dad tried to help you out for several months. Then, when Caesar gave y'all the possum bag of marijuana, you were doing much better. But ever since your dad got ahold of that laced marijuana, it hasn't been good for you or anyone else in this neck of the woods." Benjamin snapped his fingers. "I just had an idea! Y'all were at your best when you were getting your marijuana from Caesar. What if I could get some for you?"

"I wish it were that simple," Maverick said. "Samuel has gotten used to this way of life, and he doesn't want to change.

Just the other day, he told me he loves being the worst bear in the woods."

"That's so sad. In any case, I think if he was off the laced marijuana, he wouldn't feel that way. We're on our way over to Angel's den right now. Why don't you come with us?"

When James saw Lucy, he smiled from ear to ear. Then he saw Maverick and looked confused. Benjamin filled James in on what had just happened, and James agreed it was a sad situation.

"I wish we could help Samuel out," James said. "It sounds like Maverick is ready for a change."

"I have an idea," Benjamin said. "It's clear that Samuel doesn't want to change on his own, so what if we help him change?"

"But how can we help him if he doesn't want to change?" James said.

"Well, our first step is to get some marijuana from Caesar, your granddad. Then, Maverick will replace all of Samuel's laced marijuana with Caesar's pure marijuana. Once the laced stuff is all out of his system, Samuel will stop being so mean and nasty."

They agreed it was a good plan, especially Maverick. "I haven't had any hope since we started smoking the laced marijuana. But now I do, thanks to your plan."

When they entered Caesar's den, Benjamin explained the plan. Caesar asked Maverick how much marijuana Samuel had right now. He said Samuel had just bought a deer bag but still had two or three possum bags lying around.

"I won't charge you anything for this," Caesar said, handing Maverick the marijuana. "If your plan is successful, the forest being at peace again is all the pay I need. Good luck."

Outside Angel's den, Maverick stopped. "I'm heading back home, guys. Wish me luck with the plan."

"I'll go with you, Maverick," Benjamin said. "Wait here for just a minute. I'll be right back." He slipped into Angel's den, where Luna was now awake and getting ready to help Angel prepare supper. He explained their plan to them.

"I hope it all goes well," Luna said.

"Me too. I'm sorry for bringing Maverick over, but I saw it as a chance to help him."

"With any luck," Angel said, "you will have helped the whole forest with your kindness."

As he left the den, Benjamin caught James out of the corner of his eye saying goodbye to Lucy and giving her all kinds of sickening bear kisses.

As they walked, Maverick seemed happy. "I really hope I get my dad back," he said. "We were both very depressed, but we were doing better each day until we started smoking that laced marijuana. I never liked what it did to me, but I wanted to please my dad. I really hope he doesn't catch me making the switch."

"Good luck, Maverick. I'm proud of you for doing this."

Maverick's eyes teared up. "That's the first time in a long time anyone has been proud of me," he said. "The closest I get is when my dad says he would be proud of me for doing something bad to the other bears."

"You know, Maverick, James and I just became blood brothers. I'd like to be blood brothers with you, too." Benjamin told him what they had to do, and Maverick was excited about the idea.

"I lost my sister, so it would be great to have a blood brother." They cut each other's paws and held them together, making it official.

He thanked Benjamin for his help and headed home.

ભ

Maverick was hopeful, but also worried that he might get caught switching out his father's marijuana. When he got home, the first thing he did was apologize to Samuel.

"Well, I hope you've got your damned shit together now," Samuel barked. "And I hope in the future, you'll stay by my side and do what I tell you to do."

"Yes, sir," Maverick said. "I plan to be right there by your side." Figuring this was his chance, he walked through the den, furtively replacing each marijuana stash with the exact same amount of the new marijuana. He was just about done, but the last stash was in a cookie jar on a shelf very close to where Samuel was. When his father looked the other way, Maverick emptied the jar and had just started putting the new marijuana in when Samuel hollered at him.

"What the hell you doing in that cookie jar?"

Maverick froze. Thinking quickly, he turned around and said, "I'm ... getting me some of your marijuana, Dad. You know, so we can go out and raise some hell tonight."

"Oh, good," Samuel said. "Roll us two big cigars, boy. You're making me proud, and I want to celebrate."

This was the first time Maverick had smoked in the last two weeks, and it was the first non-laced marijuana in months. He wondered how his body would react. But he was even more nervous about the effect it would have on Samuel. Would Samuel have so much residual PCP in his body that this huge cigar from Caesar would have no effect on him? Would he still expect Maverick to raise hell with him tonight?

After the third deep puff, Maverick was already feeling less anxious. *It's working on me*, he thought. *And Dad looks a little more relaxed than usual, too.*

Samuel examined the cigar he was smoking. "For some reason," he said, "this cigar isn't having the same effect it normally does. I'm feeling way too calm." Maverick felt himself tense up. "Roll me another double, boy, and while you're at it, get you another one, too, so we'll be ready to rip these woods apart."

He's calmer, Maverick could see, *but still having bad thoughts*. He was worried, but also optimistic, seeing Samuel calmer than he had been in months.

After they had finished their second smoke, Maverick was as calm as a cucumber. He had no angry thoughts and wouldn't be able to hurt a spider if he had to. He looked over at Samuel, who was out cold, snoring away.

The next morning, Samuel woke up and looked around. He saw Maverick.

"Son, I haven't felt this good in a long time," he said, his voice groggy. "But what I don't understand is why I'm so calm. Why didn't I want to go out and wreak havoc last night?"

"I'm glad you're feeling so good, Dad. Why don't I fix you another cigar? It was because of those two cigars last night that you felt so good."

"Roll me two, why don't you."

"How about just one for now, Dad? In fact, I think we should try to wean ourselves off this marijuana. I think we're both strong enough to do that."

Samuel stared at him for a few moments. "Okay. I'll try. Right now, I feel stronger than I have for a long time. But I can't just quit cold turkey, you know."

For the next two weeks, Samuel smoked less each day. When his supply ran low, he told Maverick to go out and get him some more marijuana.

"Sure, I'll go and get it. You're doing amazing, Dad." Maverick rolled him a small cigarette to smoke while he was gone. "You just sit here, and I'll be back shortly."

He returned with a possum bag of marijuana and told Samuel it was all he'd been able to get.

"That's perfect," Samuel said. "I'm not going to smoke any of it anyway, unless I feel so depressed that I have to. But having you here with me is really the only thing I need right now."

"I'm proud of all the hard work you've done, Dad," Maverick said. He didn't want to continue lying to his father, but should he come clean about what he'd done? How would the old bear react? He decided to tell the truth, and out it came in a flood of words.

Samuel was surprised. "Son, I have only one thing to say to you right now." He spoke slowly. "I'm ... so ... very ... proud of you. And I'm so sorry for how I've been acting."

"Dad, I'm so blessed to have you back," Maverick said, choking up. "I've missed you so much. You used to be the best dad in all of the Appalachian Mountains. When we lost Mom and Emma, I also lost you."

Maverick and Samuel sat there in a bear-hug embrace the rest of the evening. Before he drifted off, Maverick had but one prayer: that Samuel wouldn't start using the laced marijuana again.

CHAPTER 6

Late Summer

The late summer air was hot and sticky, but also full of love. *Whatever that means,* Benjamin thought. *All I know is the love bug hasn't hit me yet.* Lucy, on the other hand, was absolutely glowing all the time. She and James found every excuse they could to be together. If she wasn't at his place, James was at hers. Benjamin loved it when his blood brother came over, but the problem was he wanted to spend all his time with Lucy. Benjamin had to admit he felt a little lonely sometimes.

That day, Benjamin decided to go over to Samuel and Maverick's den to see how they were getting on.

"Hey there," Samuel said when he saw Benjamin. "Thanks again, by the way. I'm so grateful you had the idea to switch out the marijuana."

"How are you doing these days?"

"Well, I still miss Charlotte and Emma, of course. We both do. But it's getting easier every day."

Benjamin loved seeing these two not angry and mean anymore. He and Maverick had become close friends and blood brothers. They loved to go hunting, fishing, and foraging for food together. It was nice having Maverick as a friend, because it seemed like now that James was in love, he didn't have time for his blood brother anymore.

"Why don't we go over to Angel's?" Samuel said. "I'd like to thank her for Caesar's marijuana."

As they walked to Angel's den, Benjamin stopped by his own den to tell his parents where he was going. But as he walked in, he heard the bed creaking, and his mother was making strange, loud noises. He decided not to disturb them. He was old enough to know they were making some new brothers and sisters for him and Lucy, which was an exciting thought.

Samuel wanted to pick some fruit along the way to give to Angel's family. "We can also get her a deer and some small game," he said. "I want to repay her for all the bad deeds I've done."

They gathered a basketful of fruit, then went to find a deer. Several minutes later, they found two standing down in the holler. The bears ran them up into the steep rocks and killed them both. Benjamin and Maverick volunteered to drag the deer while Samuel walked in front of them, carrying the basket of fruit. Before they reached Angel's den, Samuel happened upon a turkey, which he swiftly killed.

"I think this is a pretty good start on repaying Angel and her family," Samuel said.

Angel was the only one home when they arrived. Samuel gave her the basket of fruit and the turkey and told her it was for her family. As he spoke, he broke down and apologized for everything he had done. "I know my behavior was totally inexcusable, Angel—"

"Well, yes, that's true," she said. "But I understand why you were so horrible to us. Losing your mate and young daughter at the same time is more than any bear should have to endure. I know how hurt I was losing George. It was almost unbearable. I was able to get through my loss without turning to marijuana, but I know it helped you. Even though you were doing better, you were still hurting. Then you ran into another dealer who was evil and unreliable. You and Maverick started using his laced marijuana, and that changed your brains and the way you both thought."

She looked at him and smiled. "With all this said, Samuel, I'm not holding you responsible for your actions. All this started because a bear hunter took your young daughter cub illegally. If you had only lost your mate, as I did, you probably could have gotten through this without turning to the laced marijuana. I can tell you are very sorry for what you put our great forest through. For these reasons, I totally forgive you for everything you did."

Samuel gave Angel a big bear hug. This took Angel by surprise, but she was even more surprised by the fuzzy feeling she got when he hugged her.

She looked up and saw Benjamin and Maverick coming in with the deer they had caught. "What do we have here?"

"We were able to get you two deer," Benjamin said. "This should help feed your family for a while."

"Yes, it sure will," Angel said. "Thank you so much!"

"Where's Luna?" Maverick asked.

"She's with Caesar today."

"Great. Benjamin and I will go over there. I want to thank him for the deer and possum bags of marijuana he gave us. I want to tell him how much it's changed our lives and let him know we're weaned off of it now. But most of all, I want to thank him for giving me my dad back."

They headed over to Caesar's den. Luna's eyes lit up when she saw them coming.

"Hi, Maverick!" she called out, then looked at Benjamin. "Oh, you're here, too."

For the first time in his life, Benjamin felt jealousy. *Luna has always acknowledged me first*, he thought. *Does this mean she has feelings for Maverick now? I've never wanted to be anything more than friends with her, so why do I feel so hurt about this? Could I be starting to have more serious feelings for her?*

Confused, Benjamin decided not to say anything about the way he was feeling. Luna and Maverick were his friends, and he didn't want to cause any friction, so he pretended nothing was wrong.

After talking to Caesar, the cubs headed back to the den, where they found Samuel and Angel sitting in the kitchen talking.

"I'm so glad you all came over today," Angel was telling him. "And I'm even more glad we have had this talk. It means so much to me."

"It means even more to me," Samuel said. "It really helps me heal after losing Charlotte and Emma."

As she sat there, Angel couldn't help but notice what a sexy bear he was. But it was the first time she'd had these thoughts since losing George, and she wasn't ready to tell Samuel how she was feeling.

Benjamin now knew for sure that Luna and Maverick were starting to have feelings for each other. Coming back from Caesar's, they were giggling and laughing together in the same way James and Lucy had been for a while now. Even though he felt left out, they were his friends, and he would support them if they decided to become a couple. Besides, he knew Mrs. Right would come to him when he least expected it. *I guess I'm growing up a little*, he thought, *even though I feel a little silly having these thoughts now.*

Angel insisted everyone spend the night. The cubs played cards all evening. Maverick and Luna were clearly trying not to let anyone know they had feelings for each other. Angel and Samuel stayed in the kitchen and talked until it was time for bed.

The next morning, Luna and Maverick were nowhere to be found. Wondering where they had gone, Benjamin stepped outside and walked around. He found the two cubs rolling in the leaves, with Maverick on top of Luna.

Looks like they'll be starting their own family now, Benjamin thought. *It hurts, but I've never had feelings for Luna until now, so I can't blame anyone but myself.*

Before they could see him, he snuck away and went back to the den. When Samuel and Angel woke up, they asked him where Luna and Maverick were. Benjamin said he hadn't seen them.

"They must be outside somewhere," he said. "They were gone when I woke up."

But all Benjamin could think was, *Why do I feel so alone now?*

CHAPTER 7

The Moves

A short while later, Maverick and Luna came back to the den. Angel took one look at Luna and knew something was different.

"Luna, you're glowing. What's going on here?" she asked.

Luna blushed. "I'm in love. It was like love at first sight. I know that sounds silly, but I have never had such strong feelings for anyone. I know it wasn't really love at first sight since I've known Maverick for a while, but literally until yesterday, when I saw Maverick over at Caesar's, I'd never looked at him this way."

Maverick was standing off to the side as Luna told Angel the story. He, too, was blushing.

"Okay, I can't hold it in any longer," Luna said. "Mom, guess what? You're going to be a grandmother!"

Angel fainted and fell to the floor. Concerned, Samuel rushed over to check on her. As she came to, she looked admiringly up at Samuel. "And you," she said. "You're going to be a grandfather! Congratulations, you two."

"Yes," Samuel said, helping Angel up off the floor. "Here's to you both."

Benjamin had to summon the strength to congratulate them. "I'm so happy for both of you," he finally said. *If only I'd had feelings for her earlier, she could have been mine.*

But Benjamin kept his thoughts to himself. Luna had always been his friend, and he wanted her to be happy. From the looks on their faces, they were very happy and very much in love.

"Let's have a celebratory breakfast for the new couple," Angel said.

Samuel moved closer to her. "I'll help you make it."

While breakfast was being prepared, Luna, Maverick, and Benjamin went out for a walk. As they walked, Benjamin felt more and more like a third wheel.

As if reading his mind, Luna spoke up. "I hope this doesn't change anything between you and me, Ben. You'll always be my best friend, even if Maverick and I are a couple now."

"Yes, Luna, and you will always be my best friend, too."

⊳

As they made breakfast, Angel brushed up against Samuel every chance she got. Her feelings for Samuel were getting stronger. But Samuel was showing nothing that made Angel feel the attraction was mutual. So she came up with a plan. She asked Samuel to get the native trout out of the refrigerator for hors d'oeuvres. Then she stood in just the right spot where she'd be nose to nose with him as he turned back around.

It worked. Their noses met, and Samuel rubbed Angel's nose. Angel blushed and returned the nose rub.

Samuel stepped back. "I'm so sorry. I shouldn't have rubbed your nose."

"Why not? I kind of liked it," Angel said, smiling and batting her eyes.

Samuel looked down. "I guess I did, too. Angel, I've ... I've been having feelings for you for a while now, but I've been afraid to say or do anything about it. I've been such a horrible bear, and I didn't think anyone could ever have feelings for me."

"You're a damn sexy thing, Samuel. Get your ass over here and give me a big bear hug." Samuel took Angel in his arms and held her tight.

"What are y'all doing?"

They both stepped back and saw Luna standing there. They blushed.

"Ahem, well, Luna, it looks like you and Maverick aren't the only ones acting on your feelings this morning," Angel said.

When Benjamin and Maverick saw what was happening, they congratulated the new couple.

"This is very new, y'all," Angel said. "It's not like we're a couple yet."

"Well, if you want to be a couple, we can be," Samuel said.

Angel beamed. "I for damn sure want to spend the rest of my life with you."

There was so much love and joy in the room. There was also plenty of food, and the bears enjoyed a feast fit for a king.

When they finished eating, Benjamin felt a little down, and Luna sensed it. "I know a sow will come along for you very soon, Ben."

He sighed. "I know, I'm sure she will."

"And what a lucky sow she will be. You are the most amazing bear out there. Truly."

Not long after, Benjamin headed back to his den, where Oliver and Sophia were fixing lunch.

"You're home a little earlier than we thought," Sophia said. "James and Lucy are down by the stream fishing."

Benjamin told his parents of the day's happenings. Sophia and Oliver were happy for the new couples.

"Sounds like you've had a few big days," Sophia said. "How are you doing with all this?"

"Luna has always been my best friend, and I never thought of her as anything more than that." A tear rolled down his cheek. "It wasn't until I saw Maverick and Luna start with the googly eyes and giggly giggles that I realized I may have had feelings for her. I thought we would always be best friends."

"And you will be," Oliver said. "Best friends support each other through anything."

"I know, and of course I will support the two of them."

Sophia smiled. "I know you will." She wiped the tear off his cheek. "You're such a great bear, Benjamin. I'm so blessed to have you as my son."

☙

A big discussion about dens was happening back at Angel's, and it had started when Samuel told Angel she could move in with him.

"Well, I could," Angel said, "but how about you move in with me instead? This is a larger den than yours."

"I love this den," he said. "But the best part of this den is you, Angel. In that case, Maverick and Luna, why don't you two move into my den? It would be a great starter den for your new life together."

Maverick and Luna stood there with the biggest bear grins, knowing they were getting their own den to start their new bear family.

"Let's go over to our new den, Luna, and we can fix it up to your liking."

As they headed out the door, Samuel told them to just put his belongings in one place and help themselves to all the food and furnishings.

"Oh, Maverick, this is just perfect," Luna said as they walked to their new den. "Just think, yesterday morning we knew nothing about any of this. We had no idea we'd be starting a family together."

They spent the next few hours cleaning and moving Samuel's belongings to one area. "Okay, let's take your dad's stuff over to him now," Luna said, "and I can get the last of my belongings to bring back here."

"Good plan," Maverick said. "Then we can come back and not be concerned that Samuel might come over to get his stuff while we are doing what bears do on honeymoons."

"Oh yes," Luna said. "We can do it all night long."

By the time they arrived at Angel's den, Luna's belongings had been moved to one place. But they left James's room alone since he had no den to move to yet. Angel said she knew James and Lucy would soon find a den to start their family.

Luna looked around. "Wow, y'all have really tidied this place up!"

"Yes," Angel said. "It's amazing what you can get done when you're joyful and happy." She looked at Samuel and grinned. "This was only possible because of you being strong enough to get off the marijuana."

"We're heading out," Luna said. "By the way, we're starting our weeklong honeymoon, so don't come a-knockin', 'cause the den will be a-rockin'."

Once the cubs had left, Angel turned to Samuel. "You know, we need to get our den a-rockin', too. We haven't had time alone together. Why don't we start our honeymoon now?"

A shit-eating grin spread across Samuel's face. "Let's get this den a-rockin', baby."

CHAPTER 8

Lucy's New Den

"With all the love in the air and couples moving to new dens," Oliver said, "Lucy and James are going to need their own den, too. And I know of the perfect one."

"Where is it?" Lucy asked.

"It's just across Stone Coal Gap Road. It's large and spacious, perfect for starting a new family."

"I've seen it," Benjamin said. "Last week when I was out hunting. It's low on the mountain and close to the creek. And I know how much you love to fish, Sis."

Sophia said she couldn't picture where it was.

"In that case," Oliver said, "let's make it a family outing. We can help Lucy and James carry their stuff over there."

After Lucy and James collected their belongings, they all headed to the new den.

"I'll lead the way," Benjamin said. "I know how to get there."

They followed Benjamin down the mountain, where he led them across Stone Coal Gap Road.

Benjamin turned around. "We're almost there," he said. "It's in this holler, less than a quarter of the way up this ridge."

"A word of warning, cubs," Oliver said. "Don't wander too close to the road during hunting season because the dogs will pick up your scent."

"And then they'll chase you up a tree," Benjamin said, remembering his own harrowing experience.

"Exactly," Oliver said. "You'll hear the hunters say their dogs are 'treed.' That means the dogs are under the tree, jumping up and barking at you. The dogs will stay there until the hunters come and put leads on the dogs, tell them they did a good job, and take them away. Now, during training season, the hunters can't shoot you, they can only chase you, but it's still scary."

Lucy and James looked at each other, concerned.

Oliver went on. "But in December, kill season starts. That means if you're in the tree, they'll shoot you. They're not supposed to shoot a mother with cubs, but some hunters are unethical, so be careful. Remember, they shot Emma, and she was just a tiny cub."

They all murmured in agreement about how terrible that was.

"One more thing," Oliver said. "Bear hunters will often walk the top of the mountain looking for bears. Just stay off the top of the mountain, and you should be okay. Understand?"

"Yes, sir," James said. Lucy nodded.

At last, they arrived at the new den. "What do you think?" Benjamin said as Lucy walked in.

"It's nice and spacious," she said. "This will be perfect for our new family. But it smells a little musty."

"We'll get this place cleaned up," James said. "And then we can finally have our honeymoon." He looked around at the other bears. "When y'all leave, don't be coming back until our honeymoon is over in one week, all right?"

The others winked at each other and agreed to stay away.

"Before we leave, we need to make sure y'all have plenty of food," Oliver said.

"Lucy, how about we go down to the stream and fish?" Benjamin said, remembering how much fun they used to have fishing for native trout. "I know of a few big pools we can fish in."

Lucy lit up. "Okay! I have two baskets we can take down to the stream to put the fish in."

Oliver placed his paw on James's shoulder. "We haven't done much hunting together, James," he said. "Let's go find ourselves a deer and maybe some small game."

"Sounds good. Benjamin has always talked about what a great hunter you are."

☙

Within minutes, Oliver and James were outside and ready to start their hunt.

"Let's go straight up this holler," Oliver said. "Hopefully we'll find a couple of deer and we can run them up into the steep rocks."

As soon as they started up the mountain, they happened upon a flock of turkeys. Oliver was able to catch three while James got two.

"That was fun!" James said. "My first turkey kill."

"You did a great job, James." He pointed at the entrance to a small cave. "Let's leave these turkeys in this cave opening for now and we can get them when we come back."

They continued up the holler, where they spotted two deer. The hunt was on. They ran the deer up into the steep rocks, then went in for the kill.

"Wow," James said, looking at the dead deer. "I see why Benjamin says you're such a good hunter."

☙

Sophia didn't want Lucy and James to be doing housework on their honeymoon, so while the others were out, she cleaned and organized their den for them. She swept and mopped the floors, scrubbed the walls, and wiped down the furniture with lemon oil. Then she hung a few pictures on the walls to make the home feel cozier. She knew the couple would be happy with their new den. She took a deep breath. The lemon oil smelled amazing.

☙

"I've missed this, Sis," Benjamin said as they fished. "I remember sliding down the hill and watching you catch the largest native trout ever in these parts."

"I know how jealous you were about me catching that fish," she said. "But what you don't know is that I saw you catch that even bigger trout. I knew you were just being humble, wanting me to think I had caught the largest one. And you never told me, even after all this time. You're a good bear, and I'm lucky to be your sister."

"I love having you as my sister," Benjamin said. "I would love it if you caught a trout that was two feet long and over eight pounds. I only want the best for my sis!"

"I would love that, too. But I don't care if you always have the record. You're an awesome brother, Ben, and I love you."

"I'm glad you and James are mates. I can't wait to be an uncle and play with your little teddy bear cubs."

Soon, they had two baskets full of native trout, and they got out of the water.

"Thanks, Brother," Lucy said. "It's been great spending the day with you and the rest of the family."

"Great, huh?" A mischievous smile spread across his face. "Since you're enjoying it so much, I'll come by tomorrow."

Lucy glared at him. Her voice became gruff and much deeper than Benjamin had ever heard. "Don't you dare come by for at least a week, Benjamin. You let me enjoy my honeymoon!"

He giggled and told her of course he wasn't going to come over.

Lucy's voice returned to normal. "Well, why don't we head back to the den and see what Mom's up to? We left her there all alone."

Benjamin could smell how clean the den was before they even entered. When they walked in, they were shocked to see it totally organized and spotless from floor to ceiling.

"I hope you like what I've done," Sophia said.

"I don't like it, Mom," Lucy said, then smiled. "I

love it!"

"I'm glad you love it." Sophia's smile faded and she started crying. "I feel like I'm losing my little girl."

Lucy hugged her. "Not at all, Mom. While we hibernate this winter, the family will grow, and come spring, you can spend time with your grandchildren."

Sophia wiped the tears away and smiled. "I'm going to be a grandmother! I'll spoil them as much as I can. I can't wait. And I'll be having more cubs myself this winter, too."

Just then, Oliver and James burst into the den, dragging their wild game into the kitchen and leaving a dirty trail through the living room.

Sophia erupted. "What the hell are you doing, Oliver? I worked hard to clean this den. Take all this game outside right now! And when you come back in, I want you and James to clean up this mess you've made."

Oliver and James both looked down. "Yes, ma'am," they said in unison.

As soon as they were outside, Sophia turned to Lucy. "Take note of what just happened. That's what you have to do to keep your mate in line."

"Wow, Mom, I've never seen this side of you before!"

"I know," Sophia said. "That's because I don't show this side of myself when you and Ben are around."

"I think I'll need to take some lessons from you so I can keep James in line."

When Oliver and James came back in, Sophia handed James a broom and Oliver a mop. "Y'all better make sure this den is spotless—just the way it was before you dragged all that wild game in here."

"Yes, dear," Oliver said. "I'll make sure it's clean."

James looked at Oliver and did a double take. "Why did you cave to her, Oliver? When we were outside, you said you were going to ... how did you phrase it? 'Set her straight.'"

"Oh, did he now?" Sophia said, throwing Oliver a look of death. "Thanks for letting me know."

"Well, you have a big mouth, James," Oliver muttered

under his breath. "Thanks for nothing."

Once they had thoroughly cleaned the den, Oliver and James went back outside to clean the deer and turkeys. Benjamin, Lucy, and Sophia all burst out laughing.

"Wow, Mom," Benjamin said. "I didn't realize you wore the pants in this family until just now."

"Why don't y'all spend the night?" Lucy said. "We can celebrate our new den."

"Are you sure?" Sophia asked. "We don't want to interfere with your honeymoon."

Lucy shook her head. "We appreciate y'all and what you've done for us, so let's be a family tonight and have a great celebration."

James and Oliver came back in with all the game cleaned, bagged, and ready to freeze.

Oliver placed the bags in the freezer and joined the others. "Well, guess we'd better get moving, so y'all can enjoy your honeymoon."

"Actually, Dad, we decided that tonight is going to be a celebration with the whole family," Lucy said.

James didn't look happy. "Lucy, I thought we were going to do it all night long."

"James, show some appreciation for our family. If not," she lowered her voice, "you'll be cut off for the next week, sir."

"Okay, yes, ma'am. Let's get this celebration started, then."

Sophia winked at Lucy. "You're a fast learner. Oliver? Ben?" She walked into the kitchen. "Can you come in here and help me prepare the meal?" They marched in after her.

 𝕮𝕾

James and Lucy decided to go for a walk while the others made supper.

"My life is perfect," Lucy said as they hiked down to the stream. "I have you, my family, and our new den. Best of all, when we wake up from hibernation, we'll have our very own family."

James gave her a bear hug and rubbed her belly. "I can't wait to be a papa bear," he said. "And I can't wait for our honeymoon to start."

They made their way back to the den.

CHAPTER

The table was set for supper, and the countertop was piled high with food.

"Come on in here, Lucy and James," Sophia said. "Dig in! Y'all are the guests of honor."

Once they had filled their plates to the point of overflowing, as you would expect hungry bears to do, Benjamin said he would go next. "I'm about to starve to death, guys."

When everyone had their food, Benjamin gave the blessing, saying a prayer for their new den and life together. Lucy thanked him and told him he was the best brother. They spent the evening enjoying the big feast and the companionship of family.

The next morning, Benjamin woke up first, followed by Lucy. She talked about how lucky she was to have him as a brother and Oliver and Sophia as parents.

"I hope this family will always be this happy together, and that no harm will ever come to any of them," she said.

When Oliver and Sophia woke up, they packed everything up and said it was time to head back to their den so Lucy and James could start their honeymoon.

As he walked out the door, Benjamin couldn't resist. He turned around and waved. "See you guys tomorrow!"

Lucy stuck her tongue out at him and shut the door.

CHAPTER 9

Lost Without Lucy

Oliver and Sophia had never been happier. Every day, they were just glowing, knowing that Lucy would soon be making them grandparents. Sophia would hum and sing as she did housework, and Oliver couldn't stop talking about how much fun he'd had hunting with James.

But without Lucy around, Benjamin was feeling down. The den seemed so empty. He also felt left out with Oliver and Sophia constantly talking about Lucy and James. And he missed Luna more than ever, knowing she and Maverick were starting their own family. *I'm beating myself up for not making a move on Luna*, Benjamin thought. *She is such a good bear.*

"Is everything okay, Ben?" Sophia asked, seeing him sitting on the floor. "You're not your usual energetic self. You must be missing Lucy and the rest of the cubs now that they're starting their own lives together."

"Yes, and I feel hopeless right now. Maverick is over with my best friend, who I now know I was falling in love with."

Sophia gave him a big bear hug. "I know there's a young sow out there looking for you right now. Y'all will meet one day, and you'll both be so very happy."

"Thanks, Mom. That makes me feel better. I'm going for a walk now." He wasn't really feeling better, but he didn't want his mother worrying about him.

He also didn't want his parents to know where he was going: Caesar's den. A little marijuana, he knew, would help him feel better.

On the way, a deer almost ran him over, but Benjamin

was so depressed he didn't see it. Even though it would have been an easy kill, he had no interest in doing much of anything. He hated that feeling, especially since he had always been such a happy bear. But he knew—or at least hoped—that Caesar would be able to help him.

Off in the distance. Ben heard familiar voices. He looked and saw Luna and Maverick having a picnic lunch under a tree. He tried to slip by without being noticed, but Luna saw him.

"Hey, Ben! Come over here and join us for a picnic!" Luna called out.

As much as Benjamin wanted to pretend he didn't hear her, he shouted back. "Hey, Luna! Okay, I'll be right there." *I must put on my happy face,* he thought, *so they don't see how depressed I am right now.* He walked over and sat down with them.

"The food smells delicious," Benjamin said.

"Dig in," Maverick told him. "There's plenty."

"You look good, Ben," Luna said. "How's it going?"

Benjamin decided not to let on how terrible he was feeling. "Just great," he said, telling her about Lucy and her new den, how Oliver and James had gone hunting together and made a mess that Sophia scolded them for, and how he and Lucy had gone fishing together. He felt better as he told the stories, but what he was really thinking about was how beautiful Luna looked.

"And then," Benjamin said, "Lucy told James she'd cut him off if he wasn't more respectful to our family. Can you believe that?"

Luna chuckled loudly at this. "I actually can," she said. "My brother can be a handful sometimes. Good for Lucy." That made Benjamin smile.

Their lunch together was delicious and satisfying. In the background, a squirrel was chirping, a buck was grunting, and all the birds were singing. For the first time today, Benjamin was feeling happy, but he knew this feeling might not last. Even though he pulled it off this time, would he be able to hide his depression next time?

He said goodbye to Maverick and Luna and continued on his way to Caesar's. The farther he walked, the more he got back inside his head, and the faster the depression came back.

Then, another voice. "Come on over, Ben!" It was Angel. She was with Samuel down by a pond Benjamin never even knew existed. He put his happy face back on as he headed down to the pond.

There, Benjamin saw something he'd never seen before: Angel and Samuel were sitting by the water holding fishing poles in their paws. He'd seen humans use these, but never bears.

"I have one!" Angel screamed as her pole bent over. "It feels like a big one, too!"

Fascinated, Benjamin watched her reel in the fish. It was a different kind of fish than the ones he was used to. It had rosy, pink sides, a dark, olive-green back, and a belly as white as snow.

"What a beautiful fish," he said. "What is it?"

"A rainbow trout. Look here. You can tell it's male because of its elongated jaw."

Samuel handed Benjamin a ruler and a scale. "Would you like to do the honors?"

At twenty-six inches long and nine pounds, it was truly enormous. Benjamin had never seen such a fish.

"This pond didn't originally have trout in it," Samuel said, "but old Farmer Brown stocks the pond with rainbow trout. Just be careful, though. He's got a twelve-gauge automatic shotgun, and he'll fill your ass full of birdshot if he catches you fishing here."

"Birdshot?"

"It's a very small type of ammunition humans use to hunt birds and other small game," Samuel explained. "And it hurts. I know because I've been shot twice now with it. In fact, just last week at this very pond, Farmer Brown caught me fishing and shot me from twenty-five yards away."

Benjamin winced. "That sounds painful!"

"It is. It won't kill a bear, though, unless the human is really close to you. At close range, the pellets don't have a chance to spread out, so it's like being hit with a slug."

Just then, Samuel's pole doubled over. "Hey Ben, this one's yours. Just hold on to the pole, then turn that handle to reel in the fish."

The fish jumped out of the water a few times, flipping over each time. Benjamin was having a blast, but it was hard to hold on to the fish. Finally, he was able to reel it in.

Benjamin grinned. "I got a nice rainbow trout!"

"You sure did, Ben," Angel said. It turned out to be twenty-two inches long and six and a half pounds, the largest fish he'd ever caught. Today was turning out better than he'd hoped. As Benjamin was leaving, Samuel told him he had an extra pole back at the den that he was welcome to use. That made him even happier.

Benjamin was feeling good after his fishing expedition. Bears really got shortchanged on their fishing method, he decided. The human way was so much more fun.

When he got to Caesar's den, Benjamin told him how depressed he'd been that day. He mentioned the deer that almost ran into him, the picnic, and fishing with Samuel and Angel.

"And now," Benjamin said, "I don't feel nearly as depressed anymore."

"It's normal to have highs and lows with depression," Caesar said. "But keeping yourself busy is really the best medication."

Oh no, Benjamin thought. *Is he not going to give me any marijuana because I told him I'm not depressed right now?*

"Okay, here's the deal," Caesar said. "When you are feeling down, I want you to first try some kind of fun activity *before* using any of this turkey bag of marijuana I'm about to give you."

"That's a deal I'm happy to accept," Benjamin said. "How much do I owe you?"

"You're a good bear, Benjamin. This first bag is free."

"Thank you, Caesar. I promise I won't misuse any of the marijuana."

On the way back to his den, Benjamin thought about how Samuel and Maverick had started out using Caesar's marijuana. It was helping, but then they got mixed up with the shady dealer who was selling them marijuana laced with PCP. And everyone knew how bad that was for the whole forest.

Benjamin swore to himself he would never use anything except Caesar's pure marijuana. *I'll always be a force for good*, he told himself. *Starting now, I am Marijuana Bear.*

CHAPTER 10

Early Fall

Benjamin had good days and not-so-good days. On the good days, he was happy and loving life. On bad days, he would go out and talk to his neighbors and family. He preferred to do this than go straight to marijuana.

There were days when this worked perfectly, and he could get himself out of his head. But some days, all he could think about was Luna. *I truly missed out on a golden opportunity with her*, he thought. *If I had recognized my feelings for her earlier, I wouldn't be going through this right now*. But even when he was very depressed, he refused to let anyone know about it.

Sophia and Oliver could see he wasn't happy at times and often asked if he was okay. His answer was always yes. He just didn't want anyone to worry about him. Walking down to the pond with the fishing pole Samuel had given him was almost always what he needed to get him out of his own head.

Feeling depressed today, he walked over to see Lucy. She was so busy working on her relationship and new family that she didn't recognize how emotional and out of sorts her brother was.

So instead, he decided to go over to Angel's. They were having a blast remodeling their den, trying to make it perfect for their new family. Not wanting them to know how depressed he was, he told them he was just stopping by to say hello, but he didn't stay long.

With each den he visited, his depression got worse. At this point, he was desperate, feeling so down and depressed he was actually thinking of harming himself. Benjamin's next stop was to see his best friend, Luna, and blood brother

Maverick. He hoped they would have time for him.

Before he could knock, he realized the den was a-rocking. The sounds he heard left no doubt Maverick and Luna were making wild, passionate love. *Damn you, Maverick. That should be me.*

He was just about to barge in and confront Maverick when he realized he had a better option: fishing. He had his fishing pole, so he could just head to the pond to catch some rainbow trout. The human way of fishing was so much more fun than the bear way, and he knew it would get him out of his head for sure. *I am so depressed right now. I'm all alone. I desperately need help to get out of my head.* He didn't want to hurt himself, but such were the thoughts that were running through his mind.

Down at the pond, the fishing was great. After landing a 22-incher, an 18-incher, and a whopping 23-inch rainbow trout, he was actually feeling happy for the first time today.

Then came a deep voice from behind him. "You fucking bears, coming here and stealing all my fish! I should just fucking kill you right now!"

Oh no, it's Farmer Brown! As Benjamin reached for his pole, *BOOM!* He felt pain like he'd never felt before. His ass was on fire. *That son of a bitch just shot me!* Benjamin was more pissed off than he had ever been in his entire life. He charged at Farmer Brown, who raised his gun and pointed it directly at him.

"Make my fucking day, you damned thieving bear," the farmer hissed. "Take one more step toward me, and you are *fucking dead*, you hear me?"

Benjamin knew if he took another step, Farmer Brown would shoot. He was close enough that the birdshot would hit him like a slug, and he would be killed. He turned to run away, but that bastard needed the last laugh, and he pumped another round of birdshot into Benjamin's ass from thirty yards away.

I will kill that son of a bitch the second I get the chance, Benjamin vowed. As he limped back to his den, the anger slowly gave way to the worst depression of his life. With this much depression and anger, he knew he couldn't go back to his den and face his parents. Instead, he sat down on a rock, took out the bag of marijuana and rolled himself a cigarette. Smoking it calmed him down a little, but his ass was still in so much pain from that fucking Farmer Brown's birdshot.

He rolled two more cigarettes and was soon in much less pain. His depression was improving. Since he had started using it, the marijuana had really helped him with his pain and depression. But even though he was now Marijuana Bear, he still swore never to use the laced stuff. Everyone hated the way it had affected Samuel and Maverick. The forest was a very dark and unhappy place during that time.

He continued to his den in a better mood, but his ass still hurt unlike it had ever before. *Two rounds of birdshot really sucks*, he thought. *Farmer Brown, he's a dead man. I'll make sure of that.* His anger caught him by surprise, and Benjamin decided he needed one more cigarette—no, a double cigar—before facing Oliver and Sophia. He sat down and focused on happy thoughts as he smoked. One of those thoughts was Luna. Even though he knew he couldn't have her, he could still dream.

Feeling calmer, Benjamin entered the den, where Oliver was helping Sophia fix supper.

"What have you been up to?" his mother asked.

"I went around to visit everyone," he said, but didn't tell her he hadn't really spent much time with any of them. "Then I went down to the pond with the fishing pole Samuel gave me. I caught three nice rainbow trout, but then I met Farmer Brown, who threatened my life and put two rounds of birdshot in my ass. Man, it hurts so bad."

"Oh my gosh, Ben! Are you okay? You know, I've heard marijuana can help relieve pain," she said. "We keep a small amount here just for situations like this. Would you like me to roll you a cigarette?"

"Um, sure. I guess so. I've never had marijuana," he lied. "I mean, I know how bad it was for Samuel and Maverick."

"Well, this isn't laced. It's some of Caesar's own marijuana."

"If you think it will help with the pain, then go ahead and roll me one." He didn't want them to know about his depression or that Caesar had already given him some marijuana.

Benjamin smoked the cigarette his mother had rolled. Afterward, he felt as calm as a cucumber and most of the pain was gone. Sophia told him to let her know if he needed more.

"This is ridiculous," Oliver said. "I'm going over to kill that Farmer Brown."

"No, Dad! He has a gun, and he'll probably kill you." Benjamin was concerned for his father's safety, of course, but he also wanted the pleasure of killing that son of a bitch all to himself.

Benjamin lay down for a nap and slept until noon the next day. He couldn't remember ever sleeping that long in his life. He had sweet dreams of hooking up with Luna and having a family of their own. They were just dreams, he knew, but he also knew that sometimes dreams came true, and that gave him hope. Still, he had no plans to stir up trouble for Maverick and Luna. He would be as supportive of them as he had always been, even if it hurt.

Feeling much better, Benjamin ventured over to see if Lucy and James were home. He knocked on the door and Lucy opened it, very happy to see him.

"Sorry about yesterday," she said. "It was just a hectic day. James is off hunting right now. Want to go fishing?"

"I'd love to," Benjamin said. "And guess what? I have two fishing poles we can use. It's the way humans fish, and it's so much fun." I told her about the pond loaded with rainbow trout.

"Can we go there?"

"Not today. Let's just catch some native trout from the stream." He told her all about his bad luck the day before: going around visiting everyone because he was so depressed, hearing Luna and Maverick making love, catching three rainbow trout before being shot by Farmer Brown, and smoking several marijuana cigarettes only to have Sophia roll him another one when he got home.

"I'm sorry for all that," Lucy said. "Now I feel so bad I didn't take time for you yesterday. But wait ... did you say *Mom* rolled you a marijuana cigarette? I never knew she had any in the den!" She frowned. "No one messes with my family. I'll go kill Farmer Brown right now for shooting you."

"Thanks, Sis, but please don't confront him. I don't want you injured or killed. He is a mean man. All we want is a few fish. There's no reason for violence. I'm sure Farmer Brown will get what's coming to him soon enough."

CHAPTER 11

New Friend

Benjamin woke up to a delicious breakfast his parents had prepared. After they ate, he made an announcement.

"I'm going out," he said, "and it might be a day or two before I return. I woke up happy this morning and decided that since Luna isn't available, I will go out and find myself a sow friend and mate, someone I can spend my life with. This will keep me happy in the long term, instead of just a temporary fix."

Oliver and Sophia were happy to hear this. They wished him luck, and Benjamin set out.

He already knew there were no available sows where he lived on North Mountain, so he decided to cross over Stone Coal Gap Road and start his search there. Since Lucy and James lived nearby, he made a stop at their den.

"Ben, what a surprise! I haven't seen you in a week," Lucy said. "James has gone out in search of game to fill the freezer. I'm not so sure he'll have any luck, but he assured me he would."

"I think he will," Benjamin said. "Dad taught him well."

Benjamin told his sister what he was up to, and she asked if he'd like to take a fishing break before continuing his search. He didn't have his pole, so they couldn't fish the human way, but the bear way ended up being much faster. In less than forty-five minutes, they had filled two baskets with native trout.

They took the fish back to the den, and Benjamin headed off.

"Ben!" Lucy called after him. "Be on the lookout for James when you're out there, won't you?"

He raised his paw and kept walking. No sooner did he make it up to the steep part of the mountain than he spotted James off to his right, close to the rocks. He was standing near two deer he had killed. *I guess Oliver did teach him well*, Benjamin thought with a smile. He went over and congratulated James on his deer. James told him he had also caught two rabbits and a turkey and left them in the same cave he and Oliver had used the day they went hunting together.

"I'm out here searching for a sow to be my mate," Benjamin said, "but I can help you get these deer back to the den before I leave."

"I have all day to get these deer back, Ben. Go find yourself a sow. Having someone really makes all the difference. Now that Lucy and I are together, I've never been happier."

Benjamin continued on his way. He knocked on the door of the first den he came to and was pleasantly surprised when a young sow bear answered.

"Hi," Benjamin said, grinning. "I'm out here looking for—"

"Who is it?" came the deep voice of a boar bear from inside the den.

"Uh ... hello? I'm Benjamin," he stammered. "I'm just ... out meeting all the neighbors." He decided not to mention he was on a mission to find a sow.

The young couple invited him in for supper and told him he might as well spend the night and head out in the morning. He accepted the offer and was glad he did. They had possum and greens for the main dish, and for dessert, they brought out a blueberry pie. It was delicious, and Benjamin had to stop himself from eating the whole thing.

Before turning in, they sat around and talked, and Benjamin asked where their closest neighbor was.

"Well, Tom's den is just one holler over and down pretty low," the boar told him. Benjamin said he'd visit in the morning.

He slept well that night and woke up the next morning to the smell of turkey, eggs, and another aroma he couldn't quite place. As they sat down to eat, they told him it was called sausage.

"I've never had it. What is it?"

"It's ground hog meat with sage, red pepper, and other seasonings," the boar said.

Benjamin took a bite. "It's delicious." He shoved another forkful into his mouth. "I mean, I've heard of wild hogs, but I didn't think there were any around here. Where does the meat come from?"

"There's a farm over the top of the mountain that has hogs. Maybe twice a year, I'll slip over and get one. I have to be careful, though, because one time I got a twelve-gauge slug right in my hip. Believe me, those slugs penetrate deep. It was a good thing I didn't get shot in the shoulder, or I'd be on their dinner plates."

Benjamin was learning that a bear's life could be difficult and painful. After breakfast, he thanked them for their hospitality and headed off to Tom's den, hoping Tom would have a daughter—a daughter who would fall in love with him.

Benjamin hiked over to the next holler then dropped down low. Tom's den was just where they said it would be.

Benjamin introduced himself, and Tom invited him in. There was no one else in the den. Tom was lanky and looked unhealthily thin, almost like he had just come out of hibernation.

Benjamin was concerned. "Are you okay, Tom?"

"No, but thanks for asking." He sat down.

"Is there anything I can do to help?"

"Yes. Give me my Lula back."

"I don't have your Lula. I don't even know what that is!" Benjamin was confused.

"I know you don't have my Lula." Tom sighed. "Last winter, my mate, Lula, was killed. She was carrying my soon-to-be family. I've been so upset, I've hardly left this den. Every now and then I'll go out and kill something, but only when the hunger gets unbearable. Otherwise, I just sit here waiting to die."

Those were feelings Benjamin could relate to. He told Tom about Caesar and how much he had helped him. "I'll tell you what," he said. "I have almost a full turkey bag left. Let me roll you a large cigar and you can try it out."

Tom thought for a moment. "I don't know if I should. I've never done anything like that before."

Benjamin told him about the promises he had made to Caesar: to smoke only when he was very depressed, to always try other activities before using marijuana, and to never use it recreationally.

He finished rolling the cigar and handed it to Tom. "I think you're way past the point where other activities will help. Try this."

"Okay," Tom said "If you think it will help, I'll give it a try. I don't really want to die, I just don't have anything to live for."

Before Benjamin lit the cigar, he made Tom agree to the same rules regarding marijuana use. Then he started toward the kitchen. "You look hungry. Let me get you a bite to eat."

"The pantry is bare," Tom said, drawing a puff. "I might kill a possum this week to tide me over, though."

"You're going to need more than that, Tom. I'll go out and get you something to eat."

He grabbed a basket and walked down to the creek, which wasn't far from the den. The creek was loaded with native trout, and it only took Benjamin ten minutes to fill the basket. Then he headed straight back.

"Hey, Benny, did you get me anything to eat? I'm so hungry."

"Yeah, smoking can give you the munchies. Plus, you've been starving yourself, Tom. I hope you're feeling a little better now. You know, when you're less depressed, you're more likely to—"

"That's enough talk." Tom reached his paw out. "Now give me that basket of fish."

Benjamin watched in astonishment as Tom devoured every one of the fish in that ten-gallon basket. He had never seen a bear eat so much so fast, not even when coming out of hibernation.

Tom belched. "Excuse me," he said. "That was good."

"How are you feeling?"

"I'm full for the first time this year," he said. "But I still miss my Lula and the family she was about to give me."

Benjamin rolled him a double cigar and handed it to him.

"Have one with me, Ben."

"I can't. I'm not depressed right now, and I promised Caesar I wouldn't smoke unless I was."

Tom sighed. "Honestly, I don't know if I'll ever get to where I'm not depressed."

"Let me tell you a story that might make you feel better." Benjamin told him about Luna, and how he had missed out on having a relationship and family with her. "Now, she's spending the rest of her life with my blood brother Maverick."

"You're right, that does make me feel better," Tom said. "For the first time since that dreadful day when I lost my Lula." He looked up at Benjamin. "What's a blood brother?"

Benjamin explained the concept, then assured Tom he'd be right by his side until he was no longer depressed. But there was a hidden benefit for Benjamin: making sure Tom was taken care of would be therapeutic and give him a purpose in life.

Benjamin rolled another cigar for Tom and told him he'd be back shortly. "I'm going fishing again, and maybe I'll do a little hunting to help fill your pantry."

Benjamin caught a deer and collected another basket of fish. When he returned to the den, Tom was in bed snoring. He ate a few of the fish for supper, then cleaned the deer and the rest of the fish and placed them in the freezer. He left the backstrap out for their morning breakfast.

Since their marijuana supply was running low, he knew they would need to make a trip to see Caesar tomorrow. He hoped Tom would go with him. Today had been good for Benjamin, making him feel like he was helping someone. He was happy to have Tom as a new friend.

The next morning, Benjamin rose early, but he wanted to wait for Tom to wake up before he started fixing breakfast. At eleven, Tom was still snoozing. At noon, he decided to prepare lunch and hope the smell would wake Tom up.

A few minutes later, Tom shuffled into the room. "That was the best night's sleep I've had in a long time." He yawned. "By the way, thank you for everything yesterday. What time is it?"

"It's lunchtime already. You slept through breakfast."

He sniffed the air and licked his lips. "Is that backstrap you're frying up? My favorite."

Benjamin served the backstrap with some greens, and the two bears feasted. Tom was looking forward to meeting Caesar and excited to get out of the house.

Before they headed out, Benjamin rolled him another cigar. As depressed as Tom had been, it would help to have marijuana in his system for as long as possible.

The bears crossed over Stone Coal Gap Road and arrived at Samuel and Angel's den. When they didn't answer the door, Benjamin figured they were visiting Luna and Maverick. Seeing Samuel's fishing poles sitting outside, he left a note saying he was borrowing them and would have them back in a couple of hours. He wanted to show Tom the pleasures of fishing the human way.

No sooner did Tom's line hit the water than he got a bite, and Benjamin showed him how to reel it in. Tom had a nice-sized rainbow trout on the hook. They didn't have a ruler, but it looked to be about twenty inches long.

"That's a beautiful fish," Tom said, then took a closer look. "What a large and strange native trout."

"They're rainbow trout," Benjamin said. "Farmer Brown stocks them in his pond."

After catching a few more trout, Benjamin got nervous. He didn't want to stay too long and have another run-in with that damn Farmer Brown, so they packed up and took the poles back to Samuel's.

As they continued on their way to Caesar's, Tom looked over at Benjamin. "Yesterday I was just sitting there waiting to die, but now with you as my friend, I have hope. I can't thank you enough for everything you've helped me with."

"You're welcome. I'm so happy to hear that."

"Seriously," he continued. "I haven't had so much fun catching fish since I lost Lula. I miss her so much, but now I see that with your help, and a little added help from Caesar's marijuana, I can get some joy back in my life."

It warmed Benjamin's heart knowing how much he had helped his new friend.

When they arrived, Benjamin introduced Caesar to Tom. They sat down in the living room, and Caesar listened patiently as Benjamin told him about how Tom had lost his wife and unborn cubs, how depressed he had been since last winter, and how the small amount of marijuana had already helped him a great deal.

"You've really had a tough year," Caesar said. "I'm going to fix you up with a nice deer bag of marijuana." Caesar started explaining the conditions for using it, but Benjamin stopped him, saying he had already explained it to Tom, and he had agreed to abide by the rules.

Tom was almost in tears at how willing his new friends were to help him. Thanks to them, he said, he would be able to get his life back.

"If you're up for it, Tom, I'd like to take you by to meet my parents, Oliver and Sophia."

Tom said he would be honored. He admitted he was a little nervous, so Benjamin rolled him a small cigarette to smoke while they walked over to his parents' den.

"Who's your friend?" Sophia asked. "He doesn't look like a sow friend."

"Mom, Dad, this is my new friend, Tom. I met him when I was out looking for a sow. I'm glad I did, because he was just sitting in his den, waiting to die. I brought him some food, and today I introduced him to Caesar, who gave him a deer bag of marijuana."

"You're a good bear, Ben," Sophia said. Oliver and Tom both nodded in agreement.

"Honestly, meeting Tom has been good for me, too. It's nice to have a new friend, and having a new purpose in life is helping me a lot. Today, I even showed him how to catch rainbow trout using a fishing pole!"

Sophia frowned. "You didn't go back to Farmer Brown's pond, did you?"

"Yes, but trust me, this time I was keeping a watchful eye out for him."

As Oliver and Sophia prepared supper, Tom went on about how nice they were. "You're a great friend, Ben. I know I haven't known you for that long, but I would love to be your blood brother. I mean, if you would like to."

"I'd be honored," Benjamin said, and they made a miniature ceremony out of it.

With yet another blood brother, Benjamin found himself wondering if things could possibly get any better. He didn't think they could. Did that mean they could only get worse?

CHAPTER 12

Chase Season

Fall was here, and the trucks rumbling up and down Stone Coal Gap Road made Benjamin nervous. But it was the dogs barking in the back of the trucks that really terrified him. He knew he couldn't keep crossing roads like he had been, or the dogs would catch his scent and give chase. Benjamin had nightmares of being chased up a tree and torn to pieces by hounds. He was a larger bear now, but a group of dogs could still chase him and have him treed in no time.

Mostly he feared for the safety of his family and friends, mainly Lucy and James, since they lived across the road. But he also worried about Maverick, his blood brother, and Luna, his best friend. And now, he had a new friend to worry about: Tom, who also lived across the road. He knew they couldn't check on each other because that would involve crossing the road and leaving their scent for the dogs.

Late one night, Benjamin was at home considering sneaking across the road to go live with Tom. That way, he could watch over him while also being able to keep an eye on Lucy and James. It was a hard decision, and he kept going back and forth. On the one hand, Sophia and Oliver had each other, so he wouldn't be leaving anyone on their own. On the other hand, he had to hope that when he crossed the road, the hounds didn't pick up his scent. In the end, he decided it was best to live with Tom.

Tears ran down Sophia's cheeks when Benjamin told her. "I hate the thought of having an empty nest," she said.

"We knew this day was coming," Oliver said, "and Ben is an amazing bear. He always has other bears on his mind and wants to help them out."

"I know. But it's going to be hard without him around."

"I'm not sure if Tom will even want me to stay with him," Benjamin said. "But once I'm on that side of the road, I can at least go back and forth between Tom's and Lucy's."

"Okay, Benjamin,' she said, wiping away tears. "You have my blessing. I'm just thankful it's chase season and not kill season."

"Believe me, Mom, I wouldn't be doing this if it were kill season. If the dogs run me up a tree, I'll just have to sit there until the hunters come and pull their dogs back. Then I can go on my merry way."

"Don't leave yet. I'm going to send you off with some of my berry cobblers, two for Lucy and two for Tom. By the way, we're almost out of honey. Could you keep your eyes out for a beehive when you're out there?"

By the time the cobblers were ready, it was after dark. Benjamin headed down the mountain, crossed over the road, and made his way up to Lucy and James's den.

Lucy was surprised and happy to see him, but also worried. "Ben, come in. Why are you taking a chance of the hounds catching your scent?"

"I waited until after dark, so all the hunters would have gone home. My scent shouldn't be very strong by morning."

"Are you feeling better, Brother? I know it's been hard."

"Yes, so much better. And it's been weeks since I've used any marijuana at all. I'm still mad at myself for Luna, but at least she's happy, so I've accepted them being mates. Maverick has had a rough life, so I'm glad he has Luna to keep him happy."

James walked into the room and said hi.

"Oh, guess what?" Lucy said. "James and I have been fishing a lot. We even got ourselves two fishing poles because we love using them so much. It's so relaxing. Maybe in the spring, we can all go to the pond."

"I can't wait for spring! The three of us will have a blast fishing together. Well, listen. I better head over to Tom's now."

"Why don't you spend the night? It's been so long."

"Yes," James said. "Stay with us tonight. I miss my blood brother!"

The next morning, Benjamin woke up early and got ready to head over to Tom's. But Lucy wouldn't let him leave until after breakfast. She had been teaching James to cook, and he was about to prepare deer tenderloin and eggs.

"We can sit here and reminisce about old times while James makes breakfast," she said.

Benjamin chuckled. "Does this mean the honeymoon is over? You have all this time for me now."

"Well, it's not over because we have our whole lives ahead of us. Family is important to us, so we want to enjoy everyone's company when they come and visit."

James set their breakfast, still sizzling, on the table and told them to dig in.

Benjamin was happy to oblige and took a bite. "Wow, this is delicious. You trained him well, Lucy."

After breakfast, Benjamin stood up and gathered his things. "Oh, I almost forgot! I have two berry cobblers that Mom made for you." He handed them to Lucy. "Have you seen any beehives around? They're almost out of honey at the den."

"I haven't seen any, but I'll keep my eyes open."

Benjamin had just left Lucy's den when a truck pulled up and stopped right where he had crossed the road the night before. Several dogs jumped out, barking as loud as they could.

"We got a track that crossed the road right here," one of the hunters said.

Oh no, my scent is still there. He realized with horror that his scent would take the dogs right to the front door of Lucy's den. *I need to do something.*

He ran down to the road and met the dogs head on. When they spotted Benjamin, they ran straight toward him. He smacked one of the dogs hard. *Damn, that felt good.* Then he took off running away from Lucy's den. Recalling his dad's advice to run up into the rocks when being chased by hounds, Benjamin ran toward the steepest rocks he could find. He'd be able to climb the rocks, but the dogs wouldn't. As he scampered up the rocks, the dogs fell well behind.

The voices coming from the road sounded familiar to Benjamin. "Looks like we lost another one to the rocks, Dale," one of the voices said.

"Yeah, Rob. I just wish our dogs could get up there."

Whew. Benjamin's heart was racing. *I survived this one, but I have to be more careful. I can't be crossing roads anymore.*

He continued on his way to Tom's den, hoping he wouldn't run into any more dogs today.

Tom didn't answer when Benjamin knocked, so he went inside and saw that Tom wasn't home. He was concerned at first, but the den looked good, and it didn't seem like anything was wrong. He was very tired, so he lay down and took a little bear nap.

It wasn't long before Tom came home and woke him up. "Welcome, welcome, blood brother!"

"Hey, Tom. I brought you two berry cobblers that my mom made."

"Yum, yum, yummy, thank you," he said. "I didn't think I'd see you again until after chase season."

"I got to thinking, it might be a good idea to stay with you until after chase season, if you don't mind."

Tom loved the idea.

"I wanted to go back to my den and get my stuff first," Benjamin said, "but I got chased by some hounds earlier today, so I don't think I should cross the road again."

"Don't worry, my friend. I have anything and everything you may need here. I even got a deer bag of marijuana from Caesar just before chase season started. I didn't want him to just give it to me this time, so I brought him two large does for it. He doesn't think I'm ready to come off it yet, but I'm down to one or two cigarettes a day now."

"That's great news! What else have you been doing since I last saw you?"

"Been trying to find me a sow. No luck so far, but hey, we got this whole mountain range we can stay on without crossing any roads. Are you still looking for someone? Let's go sow hunting together!"

Benjamin was excited. With any luck, they could find two beautiful sows, one for each of them. For the next two days, they stayed out all day long, looking for available sows. None seemed to be around.

"You know what's interesting?" Tom said toward the end of the second day. "I haven't smoked so much as one cigarette for the last two days. Having a good friend around really helps with this depression stuff. I owe you a lot."

"No you don't," Benjamin said. "You being my blood brother is all the payment I need."

On the way back to Tom's den, Benjamin spotted the biggest beehive he had ever seen. He told Tom about his mother's request for honey.

"I have some five-gallon buckets we can use to harvest all this honey for her tomorrow. Let's get a good night's sleep and plan on collecting honey in the morning, then go sow hunting again after that."

The next morning, Benjamin and Tom had filled almost seven buckets with honey when they picked up the faint sound of barking dogs. As the barking got louder, a young sow crossed just above them, running for her life, the hounds right behind her.

"I'm going up there," Benjamin said. "I'm going to get the hounds to chase me."

"Not without me, you're not!"

"All right, Tom, let's go rescue this bear." They bolted up to where the sow had crossed and waited for the hounds. They swiped at the dogs, sending them flying through the air.

They ran off, and the hounds gave chase. Benjamin spotted a tree that was leaning into another tree at a forty-five–degree angle. Wanting to teach the dogs a lesson, he ran right up that tree while Tom followed. For a few moments, they sat in a nook where the two trees met and stayed there while the dogs scampered up after them. Before the dogs could reach them, the bears slid down the other tree, leaving the dogs stuck and unable to climb back down.

"Brilliant!" Tom said. "And listen, they're not barking anymore. Now they're sitting up there whimpering."

The two bears climbed to the top of the next ridge so they could watch when the hunters found their dogs.

"Y'all gotta see this," the first hunter yelled when he arrived. "All our hounds are fifty feet up in the damn tree!"

Benjamin and Tom howled with laughter from their spot on the ridge. Since the dogs couldn't chase them now, they walked down to where the hunters could see them and growled just to let them know they'd won this match.

"Let's go find our damsel in distress, Tom."

It took a few minutes to find her, but she was very appreciative they had helped her out. They invited her to spend the night in safety at the den.

When they had a chance to talk the next morning over breakfast, they found out her name was Sue.

"Hello, Sue. This here is Tom, and I'm Benjamin."

"I'm glad to meet y'all," she said. "Thanks again for helping me."

"Where do you live, Sue?"

"Three mountain ranges over from here. I've been all alone since losing my mother and father almost a year ago."

"Well, you're welcome to stay with us for as long as you need."

"I would love to," Sue said, then smiled. "Thank you. I have been very lonely."

CHAPTER 13

Sue

Tom was thrilled to have Sue staying with them. Benjamin wondered how the competition to win her over would play out.

Not so fast, he thought. *Tom needs her more than I do. I have my whole family and their mates. All Tom has in life is his blood brother. I must make sure Sue is his.*

If he hadn't shown up in Tom's life when he did, Benjamin reasoned, Tom would dead by now. But with Caesar's help, he had nursed him back to a joyful life. As much as Benjamin would have loved a mate, he wanted Tom to have Sue—if she was even interested, of course. As Benjamin vowed to do whatever was necessary to get her interested in Tom, they all lay down for a good night's sleep.

The next morning, while Sue was still sleeping, Benjamin put the first part of his plan into action.

"Tom," he said, "I think you should fix breakfast for Sue."

Tom eyed Benjamin suspiciously. "And where will you be while I'm doing all the work, Ben? Are you planning to make a move on Sue?"

Benjamin was taken aback but understood Tom's reaction. "No, I'm going out to do a little hunting."

"Oh, okay."

Benjamin could see the wheels turning in Tom's mind, probably formulating a plan to make a move himself.

☙

From her bed, Sue could smell the food cooking. She was now

fully awake, so she followed the scent into the kitchen.

"Smells delicious, Tom."

Tom wheeled around and smiled. "Good morning, Sue! Hope you're hungry."

"Where's Ben?"

"Oh, he's just out hunting while I make breakfast."

Sue's eyes widened. "Wow. Ben is so strong and brave to go out hunting by himself."

Tom frowned. He wasn't happy with the way this was going. Thinking he could win her over with a delicious breakfast, he grabbed a plate, piled it high with tenderloin and eggs—and a generous helping of porridge—and set it down in front of Sue.

She looked at the food, then up at Tom. "Shouldn't we wait for Ben to come back before we eat?"

"No! I mean, aren't you hungry?" Tom sighed. *Ben, Ben, Ben, always Ben*, he thought. *Why not Yes, Tom; Great, Tom; You're the best, Tom?*

They ate mostly in silence, then he served her a dessert of berry cobbler.

"Everything was really good, Tom," Sue said after she had finished the last bite. "Especially that berry cobbler."

"Thanks." Tom wasn't about to tell her it was Sophia who had made it. "Anyway, Sue—"

"Where the heck is Ben, anyway? He should be back by now."

C3

When Benjamin came in dragging a twelve-point buck, Sue walked right over to him. "I'm so impressed, Ben. What an amazing hunter you are. So strong, so brave. So ... handsome." She ran her paw along his arm.

"I'm really just helping Tom out," he said. "Tom's the gourmet chef here."

"Yes, we had breakfast, and it was really good. And he

makes a mean berry cobbler, by the way."

That Tom had accepted credit for the cobbler didn't make Benjamin mad at all. As far as he was concerned, whatever it took to get Sue interested in Tom was fair game.

"And I have plans for an even better lunch," Tom said, his eyes on Sue.

"That's great, Tom. What will you be doing, Ben?"

"I was about to go fishing," he said, thinking that would give Tom and Sue more time to get to know each other.

Her eyes lit up. "I love fishing!" she said. "I'll go with you."

Benjamin paused. "Oh ... well, wouldn't you rather stay and help Tom with lunch? You can learn some of his gourmet recipes." He turned to leave, but Sue ran in front of him.

She looked him in the eyes. "I *really* love to fish, Ben."

Benjamin sighed, then looked at Tom, who was in the kitchen getting some pots and pans out. "Uh ... yeah, sure. Okay then. Let's go." He told Tom they'd be back shortly, and they headed out.

ಞ

Tom was depressed again, and he had to take a break from cooking and sit down. *Ben is outsmarting me*, he thought. *First, he tells me to fix breakfast while he goes out to hunt. Then he comes back, not with a small yearling that we can eat right away. No, he hauls in a massive, twelve-point buck, and Sue falls all over herself complimenting him. Then he tempts her with a big fishing adventure. She loves fishing—of course she wanted to go with him!*

He rolled himself a double cigar and smoked it. *I'm just Ben's slave. Everybody wants a brave hunter and fisherbear, not a damned cook. Why is Ben doing this to me? He's my blood brother!*

Tom felt a little better after smoking the cigar but rolled another for good measure. Now much calmer, he thought about what he needed to do to win Sue over. He came up with the perfect plan: instead of plain old fried fish, he'd fix up a fancy, flavorful trout dish along with some gourmet sides. *My scalloped potatoes are second to none,* he thought with confidence, *and when I serve up some greens with bacon, she'll recognize what a prize she has in me.*

಼

Down at the stream, Benjamin spent his time in the deepest pools, filling the basket quickly. Sue was enjoying watching him fish. Once again, she told him how strong and brave he was.

"You know, Sue, Tom is stronger than I am, and he's a much better cook, too. You might not know this, but he's also a master hunter and fisherbear."

"That's nice," Sue said, "but I kind of like *you.*"

Benjamin was lost for words. As much as he wanted a mate, he wanted Tom to have a mate even more. He'd have to change his approach, he thought as they took the fish back to the den.

"Lunch is ready, guys!" came Tom's voice from the kitchen.

Benjamin sniffed the air. "It smells delicious in here, doesn't it, Sue?"

"Just wait until you taste it," Tom said. "It's better than it smells."

Tom served Sue's meal first, arranging the food on her plate just so, as if they were at an expensive restaurant.

Sue took a bite, then looked up at Tom, who was staring at her, waiting for her to say something. "It's not bad," she said. "But honestly, I prefer plain old fried fish." She noticed the crestfallen look on Tom's face. "I'm sorry. It really is delicious, but I prefer simpler food. And I'm a bear. What I really want is a full plate, not a plate that looks like a beautiful painting. You know?"

Tom nodded. "Okay, then. I'll keep my cooking simpler, and I will always fill your plate from now on."

After lunch, Tom came up with another plan. Since Sue loved a big, strong hunter, he'd go out and hunt for their food this time while Benjamin prepared supper.

Benjamin thought that was a great idea. He knew right away what he would make: deer brains and tripe, the worst-tasting meal he could think of.

"Sue, why don't you go with Tom so you can see how a master hunter operates?"

"I think I'll stay here," she said. "In fact, I may take a little bear nap."

By the time Tom got back, the room was filled with an odor so foul, all he could do was throw his paw over his nose. "Ugh," he groaned. "Ben? What the hell is that god-awful stench?"

"You're both going to love it," Benjamin said, coming out of the kitchen. "What did you bring us?"

"A yearling doe. A nice, small yearling doe. Is Sue awake?"

"I am now!" Sue came around the corner. "Mmmm, that smells amazing, Ben."

When they sat down to eat, Benjamin was careful to make Sue's portion the smallest. He handed it to her.

"That's the best-looking plate I've ever seen," she said. "I can't wait to dig in."

Benjamin handed Tom a plate, but he didn't take it. "Actually, I don't think I'm hungry anymore."

Sue cleaned her plate, then grinned. "That was absolutely delicious."

Neither Tom nor Benjamin could believe what was happening. Benjamin knew he needed to do something, perhaps something extreme. But what? Then he remembered the time Angel placed herself right where Samuel was, so that when he turned around, they rubbed noses.

Seeing Tom sitting in the living room smoking a double cigar gave Benjamin an idea. As soon as Tom finished it,

Benjamin rolled him another one. He needed Tom to be as sleepy as possible for his plan to work.

After smoking, Tom stood up. "All right, I'm going to bed now."

It was time to put the plan into action. Benjamin walked with Tom to the bedroom and helped him into bed. When Tom was fast asleep, Benjamin turned off the light and climbed into bed as well.

"Sue?" Benjamin called. "Come and get into bed with me."

Sue was excited that Benjamin wanted to sleep with her tonight. She was starting to think he wasn't interested in her.

"Don't turn on the light because it will wake Tom up. Just come into the room and get in bed with me."

Sue walked into the room and slipped under the covers. "Wow, you have more muscles than I thought," she said. "You just wait, big boy, I'm going to rock your world tonight."

But it wasn't Benjamin she was with, it was Tom. Benjamin had helped Tom into his bed, and he had taken Tom's.

With Sue's paws all over him, Tom woke up in total disbelief. He didn't know why this was happening, but he knew he was enjoying it. After the third time they made love, Benjamin quietly got up and went into the other room, where he spent the rest of the night trying to sleep over the sound of the squeaking bed.

The next morning, when Sue realized she had slept with Tom, she didn't tell him she had intended to sleep with Benjamin instead.

"Damn, you are one hell of a good lover," was all she said.

"You're not so bad yourself, Sue. And it looks like we may be having a family this winter."

Benjamin was already up cooking bacon, and the scent drew them out of their room and into the kitchen.

"Sounds like y'all had a good night?" Benjamin said.

They looked at each other, laughed, and nodded.

"Come on, lovebirds, let's have some breakfast."

After breakfast, Sue told Benjamin she was surprised. "So you *can* cook, Ben. That last meal you cooked, let's just say I've had week-old roadkill that tasted better than that shit you fed me."

They all laughed. "Brother, I am so sorry," Tom said. "I thought you were trying to move in on Sue, and I wasn't happy about that. But now I know you had my back the whole time."

"Truthfully, I've been alone so long, I wasn't thinking of this as a competition," Benjamin said. "I just wanted to do whatever was needed to make Sue yours."

They agreed they were still blood brothers and that nothing could ever separate them.

Benjamin stood up. "I'm going back to Lucy and James's den for the week, so y'all can have your honeymoon. But after last night, I'm not sure you need any more lovemaking." He chuckled.

"If this den's a-rockin', don't come a-knockin'," Sue said with a big grin. "I'm just kidding. As far as we're concerned, you're part of the family, and you're welcome here anytime."

CHAPTER 14

Late Fall

With training season over now, the bears felt comfortable crossing roads again. Benjamin was excited to visit everybody. First stop: James and Lucy's den.

The white oak acorns were so thick that he was able to gorge himself along the way. It was very important this time of year to put on at least four inches of fat to get through the upcoming hibernation. Under some trees, the acorns were literally on top of each other, so it didn't take Benjamin long to fill his belly and continue on his way.

Lucy's den was empty, so Benjamin let himself in. He was just about to lie down and wait when he got a big surprise: Tom and Sue showed up.

"I thought y'all lovebirds might still be shacked up," Benjamin said.

"After our honeymoon, I told Sue she needed to meet everyone, so here we are."

"This is where my sister, Lucy, and my other blood brother James live. They're not here right now, though. Probably out stuffing themselves with acorns like I just did. We can hang out until they show up."

"This is a nice den," Sue said, looking around. "Bigger than ours, anyway."

They didn't have to wait long before Lucy and James returned carrying two baskets full of fish. Benjamin introduced them to Tom and Sue.

"We went out this morning and gorged ourselves on acorns," James said. "Then we decided we needed more protein, so we went fishing."

Sue was amazed at how many fish they had caught.

"Sometimes we use fishing poles, just like humans do," Benjamin told Sue. "Whenever we just want to fish for fun."

"I've seen fishing like that before, but never with a bear," Sue said.

Benjamin said it had been almost a month since he'd seen Lucy, and he wanted to spend some time with her. So Tom and Sue borrowed their fishing poles and headed down to the stream to relax. Tom said he would teach Sue how to fish with a pole.

After they left, Benjamin sat down and talked with James and Lucy about everything that had happened this past year and how different everything was now. They talked about all the new couples and their new dens.

"Have you had any luck finding a sow, Ben?" Lucy asked.

He told them the story of how he and Tom had saved Sue from the hounds that were chasing her, and how he had tricked them into sleeping together.

Lucy laughed, then turned serious. "I know how much losing Luna hurt you, Ben. Are you sure you're okay with Tom and Sue being together?"

"This is what I wanted," Benjamin assured her. "I was so grateful to have Tom in my life and to feel like I had a purpose. Tom was just sitting there waiting to die, and I couldn't let that happen. Now, he's so happy, and I'm happy that he's happy. I already have a huge support system, and not only do I get to spend the winter with Mom and Dad, I get to be the first to see our new brothers and sisters when Mom has cubs!"

When Tom and Sue came back up to the den, Sue showed off the eighteen-inch native trout she had caught, along with several smaller ones. She couldn't stop talking about how much fun she'd had.

"One day, we'll sneak over to Farmer Brown's pond," Benjamin said, "and you can catch some really big rainbow trout."

Sue seemed into the idea. Benjamin warned them they'd have to keep an eye out for Farmer Brown, because he wouldn't hesitate to shoot them with birdshot, which not only hurts like crazy but could even kill them if they got close enough. "Last time, he threatened to kill me if I took one more step toward him."

Her eyes widened. "I see," she said. "Oh well, it sounded like fun, anyway."

The next morning, Benjamin awoke to a smell he wasn't familiar with. He walked out of his room and said good morning to Lucy. "What am I smelling, Sis?"

"You know what that is, silly. It's bacon and eggs!"

"Well, yeah. But what's the other smell? It's delicious."

She grinned. "I learned to make a human food," she said. "Sourdough bread. You know how we find scrap bread lying around sometimes? Well, now I know how to make it fresh, which is even better. I like to drizzle honey on it when it's still warm."

Benjamin couldn't wait to dig in, but Lucy told him to mind his manners and wait until their guests joined them.

When Sue woke up, the aroma that permeated the den brought back memories of her mother, who always made the most delicious sourdough bread.

"That smells amazing, Lucy," Sue said. "Is that sourdough bread?"

Lucy looked surprised. "Yes, how did you know?"

Sue explained that she had many childhood memories of her mom baking the best sourdough bread.

"If you like it," Lucy said, "I'll give you a sourdough starter and the recipe I use."

Tom soon joined them, and everyone dug in. Knowing the bread would be a big hit, Lucy had made a loaf for everyone. She also brought out small bowls of honey to drizzle on the bread. They all tried it with the honey and without, and none of them could say which they liked more. Each way had its own, equally good taste.

After breakfast, the bears were stuffed. Lucy gave Sue

the recipe and sourdough starter.

"Thanks so much, Lucy," she said. "My goal is to fatten Tom up before it's time to hibernate."

Tom laughed. "That is, if you don't work all that fat right back off, like you tried to do our first night together."

"Are you complaining, Tom?" Sue said, winking at him.

"No, ma'am. No complaints here."

Benjamin asked Sue if she would like to meet his parents.

"You've got to meet them, Sue," Tom said. "They are amazing bears. Oliver is over five hundred pounds. He makes everyone feel safe and secure."

Oliver was out hunting, as they found out when they got there. Sophia said he would probably be gone all day. Sue already liked Sophia and wanted to stay, but Benjamin suggested visiting Samuel and Angel for a few hours and returning once Oliver was home.

Angel was cleaning out the den when they arrived. She told them Samuel was down at the pond catching some rainbow trout.

"There are several poles down there," Angel said. "Y'all can go on down and enjoy some fishing with him, if y'all want."

"I would love to," Sue said, "but I'm scared that Farmer Brown will show up and kill us."

"Let's go," Benjamin said. "We'll have four pairs of eyes watching out, and it will be so much fun."

She agreed, and off to the pond they went. Samuel was happy to see them, and Benjamin introduced him to Tom and Sue.

"Check out all these fish I caught," Samuel said, showing them twelve rainbow trout, each ranging from 14–20 inches long.

Sue's eyes widened. "Those fish are huge!"

Samuel motioned toward the pond. "Get your poles out, y'all, and get your lines in the water. You'll catch some, too."

Sue caught one right away. It was the biggest one of

the day at 22 inches. She squealed with delight. Then her pole bent in half like a horseshoe.

Benjamin had never seen a pole bend that far, and he knew she had a massive fish on the line. Just then, it leaped out of the water, splashed back in, and thrashed about. Benjamin was hoping the line wouldn't break, but Sue managed to reel the fish in. When they got it off the hook, it measured a whopping 33 ½ inches long and weighed over 15 pounds.

Just then: *BOOM! BOOM!*

Tom screamed out in pain, holding his ass, which was now full of birdshot. With all the excitement, the bears had forgotten to watch for Farmer Brown. They grabbed the poles and the fish and sprinted out of there, heading back to Angel's den, as Farmer Brown shouted curse words after them.

When she saw what had happened, Angel got her tweezers out and plucked all the birdshot from Tom's rear end, while Sue held Tom's paw to comfort him.

"How do you feel, Tom?" Angel asked.

"It hurts, but it's not as bad as the slug I took last year. That was worse."

Once Angel had removed all the birdshot, she applied yarrow to his wounds to stop the bleeding.

"Now, who's hungry for lunch?" she said. "I prepared a feast!"

After lunch, the bears stopped at Luna and Maverick's den. If Maverick was happy to see his blood brother, Luna was even happier. She asked who the sow was.

"This is Sue, Tom's mate." Benjamin told them the exciting story of how Sue had come into their lives and how he had helped Tom get together with her.

"Wow," Luna said. "Ben, you've always been such a good bear. I miss when we used to hang out all the time as best friends."

Benjamin nodded. "Me too, Luna. But we're still great friends, you know."

"What a story," Maverick said. "Nice to meet you both. Tom, you look like you're in pain. How are you doing?"

"I was doing pretty well until I got shot at the pond," he said, forcing a chuckle.

Luna fetched some herbs to help Tom with his pain. She had learned how to stop bleeding and prevent infection from her mother, Angel.

"Y'all must spend the night," Luna said. "I'll fix supper." She walked into the kitchen.

Sue followed. "I'll help you, Luna. If you'd like, I can make sourdough bread. I got the recipe and a starter from Lucy."

"Sour what, now?" Luna said, puzzled. "Whatever that is, I've never had it before."

"Sourdough bread," Benjamin said. "It's a little piece of heaven, Luna. You'll love it."

Luna fixed deer ribs and greens while Sue baked the bread. Within minutes, the whole den was basking in the aroma of a delectable feast. After eating, they were all so full it didn't take long for them to fall fast asleep.

The next morning, Benjamin planned to make one more stop before heading back to Tom's den. He wanted Sue to meet Caesar. She knew about the marijuana they had procured for Tom when he was depressed, and she wanted to thank Caesar for saving the love of her life.

Caesar was happy to meet Sue, and he told Tom how proud he was that he was able to recover from the trauma in his life.

"I owe it all to you, my friend," Tom said. "Without your marijuana, I wouldn't even be alive today. But I am alive, and I'm in a lot of pain today from that damned Farmer Brown, who shot me. I think I'm going to need a little something." He asked for a possum bag of marijuana and paid Caesar for it.

Caesar handed him the bag. "You know, Farmer Brown can be grumpy," he said, "but he really isn't a bad guy."

"Well, I think Tom's ass begs to differ," Benjamin said. "But thanks for everything. Catch you next time, Caesar."

They left and headed back to Tom's den.

CHAPTER 15

Kill Season

It was early on the first Monday of December, the official start of bear season in Virginia. Starting today, hunters could legally kill any bear over a hundred pounds.

On this frigid morning, Oliver was away from his den foraging when he heard several hounds open up barking from across Stone Coal Gap Road. To Oliver, it sounded like it was coming from on top of the mountain above Lucy and James's den. Terrified they would tree James or Lucy, which would mean certain death, he sat there listening, trying to figure out where the hounds were going.

He could distinctly hear two dogs. Neither was putting off a lot of mouth, but he could tell one of them was coming down off the top, heading toward Lucy's den. He was hoping another bear had crossed the top of the mountain and that was who the dogs were chasing, but that was unlikely. The dogs must be smelling James and Lucy. He had to do something, and quickly. But what?

Oliver knew how these hounds were. They hadn't hunted since chase season, and they couldn't wait to pull some hair and lick some blood. Every hound loved the taste of bear blood, and a kill on the first day would lift their spirits.

"I hope this is a legal bear," Oliver heard a voice say from the top of the mountain. Another voice: "Yeah, let's get this season started off right."

A truck rumbled down Stone Coal Gap Road. Panicked, Oliver ran out in front of it. As he stood in the middle of the road staring down the driver, Oliver recognized him. It was the hunter they called Rob. Oliver knew him to be an ethical hunter, so he wouldn't shoot any bear that was under a hundred pounds, but the problem was that both Lucy and James were well above that by now. Whichever one got treed would be killed on the spot. He ran back into the woods and found a place where he could hide and watch the road.

Rob spoke into his radio. "Guys, I just saw a bear that had to be over five hundred pounds. He ran out in front of my truck then back into the woods. I think he's down in the creek now."

The radio crackled and a different voice came on. "I fell up here, and I think my leg is broken. It hurts like hell, but don't worry about me. I'll fix me a crutch and make it down later. For now, I'm giving my dogs to the other guys. Go kill that big son of a bitch for me."

"Buddy," Rob said, "I will kill this bear for you."

Oliver watched as all the hunters made their way down the mountain, except for old Cripple Leg. As they assembled in the road, the dogs were raising so much hell, Oliver couldn't hear himself think.

Rob directed the other hunters to walk down the road, pointing to the spot where Oliver had run back into the woods. Oliver watched the hunters and their six dogs get nearer until the hunters cut them loose. The dogs ran into the woods, splashed into the creek, and swarmed him.

But Oliver wasn't about to go down without a fight. He gave one of the dogs a hard smack. With a yelp, the dog fell down, dead. Oliver took off up the mountain with the remaining dogs in pursuit, while Rob picked up the dead dog and carried it away, shouting into the radio to Cripple Leg. "I am going to make *sure* this bear dies!"

Oliver made his way up the mountain as fast as he could, but the dogs were catching up. When one of them was within reach, he smacked its head, picked it up with his teeth, and flung it off to one side. The rest of the dogs moved in on Oliver, spoiling for a fight, but he mustered the strength to pull away and run off.

Oliver realized the hunters had already made it to the top of the mountain before him. They found the second dead dog and informed Rob over the radio. His voice came back, angrier than ever, in a stream of obscenities. Then he heard Rob talking to someone named Dale, another name Oliver recognized.

"Rob, they're coming straight down the mountain now," Dale said. "Go kill this damn bear that's been killing your dogs!"

The hounds closed in on Oliver and attacked him. With one violent swipe, Oliver flung one of the dogs over twenty-five feet through the air and into the trunk of a massive tree.

He knew Rob was coming for him but didn't know where he was. With three dogs still chasing him, he had no time to think and didn't know which direction to run in. He stepped out into a logging road, and to his horror saw Rob just fifty yards away, aiming his .45-70 rifle right at him. He fired the gun. Oliver was hit but still determined to get away. Rob fired twice more, hitting Oliver both times. When Rob went to lever the next bullet, he realized his rifle was empty.

This is my chance, Oliver thought. Angry as hell, he charged directly at Rob. A look of panic came over Rob's face, knowing he was about to be killed.

"Die, you son of a bitch!" It was Dale, who had come up behind Rob. He lifted his .30-06 rifle and took aim at Oliver. He fired.

Ↄ

High up on the mountain, Benjamin and James sat together, crying. James had gone to get Benjamin when he realized Oliver was in trouble, but by then it was too late. All they could do was helplessly witness Oliver's death.

"I'm glad that son of a bitch is dead," they heard Dale say.

"Me too," Rob said. "He killed three of my dogs. I almost shit my pants when that bear came at me. Did you see how big he was? I'm so glad you had my back today, or I'd be dead meat."

As Rob and Dale waited for the others to come help with Oliver's body, they sat there petting the three dogs that were still alive, telling them what good dogs they were.

Benjamin was seething over the murder of his dad but tried to stay calm and keep his anger at bay. "James," he said, "go back and protect Lucy until I return. I need to stay here so I can be close to my dad for as long as possible."

Benjamin watched in horror as Rob and the others field dressed Oliver by pulling out his guts, heart, and lungs. He considered sprinting down and tearing them all to shreds, but he thought better of it. They had guns, and he knew they would shoot him dead before he could even get near them.

Several more hunters showed up, each telling Rob this was the biggest bear they had ever seen killed and congratulating him like he was some kind of fucking hero.

I'm so angry, Benjamin thought. *I just need to chill out before my head explodes. I wish I had some marijuana right now. Even better if it was laced with PCP. That would change the game.* But the thought of using PCP-laced marijuana scared him. He never wanted to be like Samuel back when he was terrorizing everyone. The forest was such a dark place for everyone back then.

The hunters dragged Oliver's body to Rob's truck. Benjamin knew exactly where they were taking him: Rob's clubhouse. *I must go there*, he thought. *I need to be with my dad as long as I can.* He knew he would be safe because it was after sundown, and it was illegal to kill a bear now. As much as he hated Rob and Dale, he at least knew they were ethical hunters, and they wouldn't kill him. He had been to Rob's house before—on occasion, his family would go raid Rob's chicken coop, so he knew how to get there.

Benjamin beat them to the clubhouse and sat on the hillside waiting for them. A few minutes later, they drove up and unloaded Oliver's body before dragging it into the clubhouse.

"It's been a long day," Rob said. "Let's weigh this thing

and call it a night. We can skin it tomorrow." From outside the door, Benjamin heard them using some kind of machine that made a lot of noise.

"Okay, the scale has been zeroed out," one of them said. "Before we raise the hoist back up, I want each of y'all to put five bucks on how much you think this thing's gonna weigh."

"Field-dressed weight?" Dale said. "I'll go with 450 pounds."

"380," said another.

Hearing them take bets on his father's weight, Benjamin had never been so angry and hurt in his life.

Several other guesses were ventured before Rob delivered the verdict: 420 pounds. The clubhouse erupted in laughter.

"420 pounds?" Dale said. "What is this, the Marijuana Bear?"

The laughter only got louder.

CHAPTER 16

Marijuana Bear

As the laughter continued, Benjamin could take it no longer. He broke the door down and burst into the clubhouse.

"Y'all think it's so damn funny you killed my dad?" Benjamin shouted. "Well, guess what? His name was Oliver. Right now, my mom is waiting for him to come home. Her name is Sophia. My sister, Lucy, has lost her dad now, too. All of you and your sick sense of humor, laughing and calling him Marijuana Bear. He never touched marijuana in his whole life! But because you ripped his guts out and the weight of his body happens to be the slang term for marijuana, you gave him this disrespectful nickname. I should kill each and every one of y'all right now."

The hunters stared at Benjamin in stunned silence, mouths open.

Rob spoke first. "What's your name?"

He took a deep breath. "Benjamin."

"Benjamin." Rob walked across the room and opened a drawer. He took out a plastic bag of marijuana and some paper, rolled a large cigar and a small cigarette, then walked back and offered the cigar to Benjamin as the others watched.

"I'm so sorry for taking your dad's life," Rob said. "Please, sit down and smoke with me." He flicked his lighter and lit Benjamin's cigar. After Benjamin took his first puff, Rob lit his own. They sat down.

Benjamin felt calmer after a few minutes, but he was still very sad. He was also angry at the entire hunting group for killing his dad. For the next several hours, they smoked while the others sipped beer and hard liquor. Then, Rob stood up and motioned for Dale to come outside with him.

"Benjamin," Rob said when they came back in, "Dale and I feel really bad. You've had enough heartache this season, and it's only the first day. So we've come up with a plan to protect you and your family." From another drawer, he took out three blaze-orange ribbons and told Benjamin that he, his mom, and his sister could wear them around their necks. His hunting group wouldn't shoot any bears wearing the ribbons, and he would ask other hunters to honor them as well.

Benjamin took the ribbons in his paw. "Thank you."

"Of course, we can't guarantee your safety from other hunting groups, but my group will honor the ribbons," he said, looking around. "Ain't that right, fellas?" The men nodded. One lifted his beer can in acknowledgement.

The door opened, and in hobbled another hunter who had been injured. *Looks like he got what he deserved for trying to kill my dad,* Benjamin thought.

The injured man stopped and stared when he saw Benjamin. *What's the matter?* Benjamin wanted to say. *Never seen a bear sitting around smoking marijuana with your buddies before?*

When he got over his shock, the man asked Rob to roll him one, too. Benjamin stayed long enough to smoke one more cigar. He felt calm but still sad. There was a huge hole in his heart. He was hoping James hadn't stopped by to tell Sophia the news yet, because he thought she needed to hear it from her own son.

As Benjamin stood up to leave, Rob handed him what was left in the marijuana bag, saying it wasn't much, but he knew Benjamin would need it.

In the crisp night air, Benjamin strolled home in a drug-induced haze, the bright moon lighting his path. He still felt angry, but the marijuana had calmed him so much that he no longer wanted to kill everything he saw.

He felt he had no purpose now, like he was simply existing and nothing more. His dad had been his world, but he was gone now. Tom had his new mate, Sue. He felt so alone.

"Where have you been?" Sophia asked when Benjamin walked in. "I've been worried sick about Oliver. He's been gone for hours, and I'm afraid the worst might have happened."

"He's dead, Mom. I saw his lifeless body." Benjamin told her about the dogs and the hunters that had killed Oliver, and how he had met them at their clubhouse and smoked with them.

Sophia couldn't believe what she was hearing. "You were ... let me get this straight. You were *smoking marijuana* with your father's *murderers*?" She raised her voice. "What the hell were you thinking?" She took a deep breath. "You know what? Get out. If you can sit and smoke with those murderous bastards, I don't need you here. Get out of my den right now."

"Mom, I—"

"Get the *fuck* out, Benjamin!"

He nodded. As he turned to leave, Benjamin left the two cigars he had rolled on the counter, hoping his mom would pick them up and smoke them. He knew Sophia was hurting and needed someone to blame, and Benjamin was the only one around. He didn't want to go far from his grieving mother, so he made himself comfortable next to a rock just outside the den.

But he couldn't sleep. All he could hear was Sophia crying from inside the den the whole night. At the first hint of morning light, he went back in.

She looked up, her eyes swollen and face soaked with tears. "Benjamin," she said. "I thought I had lost you, too. I was horrible to you last night, Son. I was in so much pain, and I had to take it out on someone. I'm sorry I unloaded on you. You are the most loving and caring bear I know."

He told her he had been right outside the den all night, unable to sleep. He could hear her bawling her eyes out but was afraid of how she would react if he came back in.

"Yes, thank you," she said. "I just needed some time. Thanks for the marijuana you left me, too. It helped take the edge off."

Benjamin showed her the orange ribbons. "One of the

hunters, Rob, gave us these ribbons to wear around our necks so his group knows not to kill us. He said his group would honor them, and he's also going to try to get other groups to honor them as well."

Sophia took the ribbons. "Well, that's actually nice of Rob, trying to protect us."

"One of those is for you, and one is for Lucy."

She asked about James, and Benjamin said he only had enough for immediate family. He rolled Sophia the last cigar and told her he was going to Caesar's to get some more deer bags.

Benjamin knew Rob wasn't hunting today but hoped he had gotten word out to the other hunting groups about the ribbons. Still, he had to stay alert for any hunters or hounds he saw and not spend any more time than necessary outside. Unfortunately, that meant no fishing at the pond on the way to Caesar's.

When he arrived, Caesar could see Benjamin was not his usual happy-go-lucky self and asked what was wrong. He was shocked to hear Oliver was gone. "I looked up to your dad so much," Caesar said. "He was so strong and smart, and he really helped me out more than a time or two."

"My mom's in bad shape, and I know Lucy will be, too, when she hears the news." Benjamin asked him for two deer bags of marijuana.

"I'll give you four," Caesar said. "I'll probably have to visit Farmer Brown soon. But with that much sadness and depression in your family, I know you'll need all of it. I won't charge you for it." He sighed. "I'll miss that old son of a gun Oliver."

Farmer Brown? Benjamin thought. *Why does he need to visit Farmer Brown? Is that who he buys his marijuana from?* He remembered Caesar saying Farmer Brown wasn't all that bad of a guy.

With more questions than answers, Benjamin kept his thoughts to himself. He thanked Caesar and left.

On the way to his den, Benjamin stopped by Luna and

Maverick's to tell them the news. They were heartbroken. He gave his own orange ribbon to Luna and explained what it was for.

"But it's meant for you, Ben. You should keep it," she said.

"You're giving birth soon, Luna. Those cubs are going to need their mother." He turned to leave. "I have a big day ahead of me. I need to take some of this marijuana to my mom, then bring some to Lucy and James." He knew Lucy would have already heard the news from James.

Back at his den, Benjamin set aside one of the deer bags for Lucy and kept three for him and Sophia. Feeling in need of a cigar, he rolled two and they each had a smoke to calm down.

After dark, Benjamin headed over to Lucy's. By now, the traffic on the road had slowed down, so he wouldn't be in as much danger. He also remembered his dad telling him to go a different route this time of year. *Turn right when leaving the den*, Oliver had said, *and before reaching the road, walk up the creek and use the culvert to pass under the road. On the other side, stay in the creek for a while before leaving it. That way, the hounds won't be able to pick up your scent.* Oliver had been a brilliant old bear.

When Benjamin arrived, James was holding a sobbing Lucy in his arms. He said she had been like this ever since he told her the news. "I've tried to console her," he said, "but nothing I do helps."

"I'll roll us three big cigars to smoke," Benjamin said.

Lucy shook her head. "I don't want any of that stuff, Brother," she said. "I don't want to end up like Samuel and Maverick. I'd rather die than live that life."

"I agree, Lucy," Benjamin said. "But it's Caesar's marijuana. It's pure, so there won't be any side effects."

It helped. She felt better afterward, even though she was still angry at the world. He rolled her another cigar, plus two cigarettes for himself and James.

"Will you two be okay?" Benjamin asked. "I should be

getting back to Mom soon, since I'm the boar of the den now."

"We'll be okay," James said. "But I have a better idea. How about Lucy and I come back with you? We can all be there for each other."

Benjamin liked the idea. Before they left, he went over the special route they needed to take to get back to the den.

Sophia was overjoyed to see them and happy they were all okay. Benjamin was happy to be with his family, too. But he thought about the other bears. He knew Luna and Maverick were okay. Samuel and Angel must be okay, otherwise Luna would have said something. Hopefully Tom and Sue were okay, too. And what about that young couple that lived near Tom?

All he could do was hope everyone he knew would make it through hunting season.

CHAPTER 17

Tom and Sue

The next morning, Benjamin told Sophia of his plan to go check on Tom that night. Sophia feared for his safety, but Benjamin assured her he would use the same route under the road, using the creek to wash away his scent.

Sophia wasn't convinced, but Benjamin insisted, saying his other blood brother might need him right now.

"Well, at least we can all be together today," she said, "even though our family is smaller now." Tears came to her eyes. After a big group bear hug, Benjamin rolled a huge cigar for each of them.

As they sat smoking, each bear shared a tale about Oliver. These stories, along with the cigars, helped improve everyone's mood. Then, Sophia stood up and announced she was going to fix breakfast.

"I'll help you," Lucy said. "It's been a while since we've cooked together, Mom."

"Some berry cobbler would be great for dessert," Benjamin said.

Lucy glared at him. "You'll get whatever we fix," she said sternly.

"Yes, ma'am." He leaned over to James and lowered his voice. "Is she always that sassy now?"

"Yes," James whispered. "Ever since Sophia taught her how to stand up for herself, she's been wearing the pants in our household."

Benjamin remembered the day Sophia had jumped all over Oliver and James and instructed Lucy on how to keep her bear in check. As he recalled, Lucy had learned quickly.

Soon, the smell of sizzling sausage and the unmistakable

aroma of sourdough bread filled the den. "Come and get it!" Lucy yelled.

They piled their plates high and dug into their bear feast. Sophia and Lucy had made a loaf of bread for each of them. They had also prepared plenty of eggs and porridge. Benjamin was a little disappointed there was no berry cobbler to go along with it, but he ate until he was fat and happy. Then, he stood up from the table.

"Hold on!" Lucy said. "I have something else." She walked to the oven and pulled out a huge berry cobbler.

Benjamin's eyes lit up. "Lucy, you are the best sister!"

"And you're a great brother." She teared up. "I wouldn't be able to stand losing you."

After eating their fill of cobbler, Benjamin and James excused themselves to the living room.

"Ahem," Lucy said. "Mom and I are going to take a break now while you two clean the kitchen. Also, some of the cobbler spilled when it was baking, so the oven needs to be cleaned, too."

Damn you, Mom, for making a mess, was Benjamin's first thought. Then he remembered they must all help each other out. He walked into the kitchen. "Come on, James. Let's make light work of this."

"I'll clean the kitchen if you clean the oven," James said.

"Deal," Benjamin said, thinking it sounded fair.

But twenty minutes later, James had cleaned the entire kitchen to perfection and Benjamin's job wasn't even half done. "This damned oven," Benjamin said, grunting as he scrubbed. "It's all baked on so hard."

"Believe me, I know. Twice now, I've had to do that after Lucy made cobbler."

Thirty minutes later, the oven was clean, and Benjamin joined the others in the living room, which was filled with smoke. Sophia and Lucy were enjoying extra-fat cigars. *I don't even need to roll one for myself*, Benjamin thought. *All I have to do is inhale.* But he rolled himself one anyway, and as he did, the others asked him to roll one for them as well.

Soon, they were all feeling calm and happy. When the conversation turned to how much they missed Oliver, Sophia said something strange. "Tell me everything," she said. "I want to hear about what led up to Oliver's death and what happened after."

As much as Benjamin didn't want to think about it, he thought his mom should know. He told her what he and James had seen from on top of the hill. Rob and Dale fuming, calling Oliver a son of a bitch because he had killed three of their dogs, saying they were glad he was dead. Then watching as the hunters tore Oliver's belly open and yanked out his guts, lungs, heart—

"Aaaaaah!" she screamed. "Never mind, I can't hear this right now. Let's talk about something else."

Switching gears, they remembered the happy times. Coming out of hibernation and sliding down to the stream. Lucy catching the largest native trout and Benjamin picking a fight before Oliver made him apologize.

"I miss him so much," Benjamin said. He looked around at everyone smoking and chuckled. "You know, Rob called Oliver the Marijuana Bear because he weighed 420 pounds. But I think we may have become the Marijuana Family." He reminded them of the requirement to seek other means of finding joy before turning to marijuana.

"Maybe we should keep it in our systems for the next three days or so," James said. "I think we'll need it." They all thought that sounded like a good idea and agreed to wean themselves off after that.

They were so full from breakfast that when lunchtime rolled around, no one wanted to eat. At about five p.m., Lucy said she was a little hungry. "And it's James and Benjamin's turn to fix supper."

"What!" Benjamin said. "Preparing meals is a—" He was about to say it was a woman's job, knowing Lucy couldn't cut him off like she had threatened to do to James. But he didn't want to start a fight. Plus, he was learning that as part of a family, it was best to share the household responsibilities.

"Why don't we make fried fish and fried taters, James? Then we can do a berry cobbler for dessert."

James loved the idea. They both prepared the potatoes and battered the fish. Then, James took care of the frying while Benjamin fixed the cobbler, which he made with extra honey. As he placed it in the oven, he thought about intentionally spilling a little as payback for earlier.

Supper was on, and they called the sows to the table. Everyone enjoyed the fried fish and taters. Then Benjamin brought out the cobbler.

"Wow, twice in one day," Lucy said, licking her lips. "I don't think I've ever had berry cobbler twice in one day."

When they had finished, Benjamin looked at his mom and sister. "Looks like cleanup duty is yours this time. Oh, and Lucy, you'll find a nice surprise in the oven." He chuckled.

The look Lucy gave him could have sliced him in half. She stood up, walked into the kitchen, and came back a few seconds later.

"Damn you, Ben. The oven is spotless." She tried to swat the back of his head playfully, but he ducked.

"Geez! I did say it would be a *nice* surprise!"

After supper and cleanup, the bears sat in the living room and smoked. They felt calm, but they wanted to keep a certain level of marijuana in their systems for the next few days.

After several hours of smoking and talking, Benjamin announced he was going to check on Tom and Sue. James wanted to tag along, but Benjamin insisted he keep Sophia and Lucy company until his return.

Benjamin crawled through the culvert under the road the same way he had earlier. He continued across the mountain, staying about halfway up, where his scent would be harder for the hounds to pick up. Before he reached Tom's den, he checked on the young bear couple he had encountered before meeting Tom. When there was no answer to his knock, he walked in. The den was empty. *Did something happen to this couple? Will Tom and Sue be okay?* Benjamin was worried.

He felt relieved when Tom answered the door with a big smile. "Hello, blood brother! How are you doing?"

Benjamin told him about Oliver, and Tom said he was very sad to hear it. Then Benjamin asked about the young couple that lived nearby.

"That's a sad story, too. Sue and I watched them both get shot out of the same tree the day before yesterday. We heard hounds and thought they were coming for us, but really they were chasing that couple. They ran up a tree and stayed there for almost two hours. Then, the hunters showed up and shot them."

"That's terrible," Benjamin said. "They seemed really nice." As he looked around the den, he noticed all their belongings had been moved to the side. "Tom, what's going on? Why is all your stuff in one place? And where's Sue? Is everything okay?"

Sue came out of the bedroom with an armful of their belongings. "Hey, Ben! I'm here, and everything is great," she said. "After seeing our neighbors get shot, we decided to move two counties over. Bear hunting isn't allowed in that county, so our kind can grow big and old there."

Benjamin thought that was a brilliant idea, but it made him sad. "I'll miss you," he said. "When are you leaving?"

"Later tonight. It'll be safer that way, since it's illegal to kill bears after sundown. We'll both miss you, too. I can't thank you enough for helping me get my life back." He looked at Sue. "And for helping me find this marvelous sow."

Since everything was packed, they decided to lie down for a bear nap. Benjamin felt a little sleepy and said he would snooze with them if they didn't mind. They were happy for the company, even if for a short while.

But when he woke up, Benjamin had an idea. "I'll help you guys move," he said. "You have a lot of stuff to transport, and I'm sure you could use some extra paws."

Tom was ecstatic about the idea. "You're the second-best thing that's ever happened to me, Ben. Sue being the best, of course."

Benjamin gladly settled for second best, and the bears got to work. There would be no lollygagging around. They had forty-five miles to cover to reach the safe county. Once they'd each picked up all they could carry, a few items remained. Tom told Benjamin he could have the items if he wanted to pick them up on his way back.

After a long hike, they were safe inside county lines. Sue knew of a small shelter they could stay in while they searched for a good den. It was only about a mile away, and she was right: it was a small shelter. They had to leave their belongings outside while the three of them crowded inside for the night.

The next day, the bears had a quick breakfast, then made a plan to search in three different directions for a new den. They agreed to meet back at the shelter just before dark.

It was midnight by the time Benjamin came back to the shelter.

"Ben, where have you been?" Tom said. "We were worried sick. Are you okay?"

"I'm okay, and I have great news. I found a den for you! Large, spacious, very clean. Sorry, guys. It was almost dark when I found it, and I knew there was no way I'd make it back here before dark. But I was determined to find you a den, and I did. You're going to love it."

Sue was relieved that she would be getting a new den in a county that didn't allow bear hunting. At last, she and Tom could grow old together without worry.

The bears got a good night's sleep in their little shelter, and the next morning, they set off with all their belongings on the three-hour trek to the new den. When they arrived, they took a few minutes to admire their new place and have a quick snack, then Tom and Benjamin headed out hunting.

Between them, they killed three deer, two turkeys, and several possums. On the way back, Tom zigzagged and managed to run down a rabbit.

Back at the den, they were greeted by the delicious

smell of sourdough bread as they set about preparing the meat to put in the freezer.

"Give me three of the backstraps first," Sue said, "and I'll fix them for supper tonight. Y'all just relax after you get that meat in the freezer. I'll let you know when supper is ready."

It occurred to Benjamin that it had been over two days since he smoked any marijuana. He had been so happy helping Tom and Sue, he didn't have time to think about his father.

Sue announced supper was ready, and the bears sat down to eat. She had prepared a feast: backstrap of deer, possum and rabbit fried to perfection, collard greens mixed with several pounds of bacon, and a loaf of bread apiece.

"I wanted to make sure you ate well, Ben," she said. "We can't thank you enough for everything you've done for us this year."

After finishing the main course, Sue walked to the oven and pulled out three freshly baked strawberry rhubarb pies, one for each of them.

"Sue," Benjamin said after they had finished dessert, "are you trying to butter me up to stay overnight?"

"You know you're always welcome here."

He stood up. "I thank you both for the hospitality, but I'd better be on my way so I can get home before morning. I feel good leaving y'all behind, knowing you're safe. But I need to get back to Sophia, Lucy, and James."

Followed by a dark thought: *If they're even still alive.*

CHAPTER 18

Return Home

As sad as it made Benjamin to say goodbye to Tom and Sue, he at least knew they would be safe. The thought crossed his mind to move here and convince his family to come along. It would be nice to live in paradise and not worry about being killed. But North Mountain had always been home, and he had learned the old saying was true: there's no place like home.

It was a little before dark when Benjamin set out. He needed to time it just right so he wouldn't leave this county until after dark, yet still be able to cross Stone Coal Gap Road well before daybreak.

The sky was moonless and starless that evening, and by the time he arrived at the county line, it was pitch dark except for a pair of headlights approaching on the road. He waited as a truck with a dog box on it whooshed by, then hustled across the road. Since bears are nocturnal, Benjamin could see just fine.

He picked up the pace because he needed to make good time for the rest of the journey. The problem was it had been snowing, and that made traveling slower. Soon, it was clear he wouldn't make it to Stone Coal Gap Road before daybreak, so he decided to spend the day at Tom's old den so he wouldn't have to cross the road. He had to stop there anyway to pick up the items Tom had left him.

He arrived at the den after sunrise. When he walked in, the memories came back: Tom, sitting there on the day they had met, just waiting to die. Introducing Tom to marijuana, which changed his life. Outrunning the hunting dogs and leaving them stranded up in a tree. Meeting Sue, by far the highlight of that day. Pulling every trick in the book to make her Tom's even though she was determined to be Benjamin's.

All the emotions, good and bad, flowed through him. He felt blessed to have both bears in his life. *What will my life be like now without them?*

He didn't know what Tom had left for him, but he was hoping there was some food to eat. The trip back in the snow had made him hungry. He wandered into the kitchen, where he saw Tom had left him a whole yearling. He looked around a little more and found six strawberry rhubarb pies in the cupboard. *I'm in heaven*, he thought. *Thanks, Sue!*

As Benjamin cooked himself some backstrap, he decided that since tomorrow was Saturday and all the hunters would be out, he would stay put here until tomorrow night. There was no hunting on Sunday, which meant it would be safer for him and his family. It would be reckless of him to leave a scent leading up to their den.

Fortunately, he had everything he needed inside the den and didn't have to go anywhere. Outside, the snow continued to fall and cover up his tracks, making it harder for the hunters and hounds to find him.

Benjamin found some porridge, collard greens, and several pounds of bacon to go with his backstrap. He ate his fill but decided to leave the porridge for breakfast.

The delicious smells made him think of the supper Sue had cooked for them. He was really going to miss those two. When he met Tom, he gained a purpose in life. And with the death of his father came another purpose: boar of his den. Even though James would be staying with them for the winter, Benjamin still considered himself head of their household.

After he ate, Benjamin popped one of the pies in the oven. Even reheated, it tasted every bit as good as it did fresh.

He enjoyed having the den to himself, but memories of the day he met Tom kept coming back. Feeling sad, Benjamin thought about having another pie—or even all the pies—but resisted the temptation and saved them for the next day.

In the morning, Benjamin peered outside. Almost three

feet of snow had fallen, and it was still coming down. This was one doozie of a storm. Since it would probably be a week or two before anyone would be out hunting again, Benjamin decided it would be safe to head back to his den today. He had been gone for more than a week.

Before he left, he cooked some of the leftover food for breakfast. The porridge was delicious, and he was glad he hadn't eaten all the pies the night before because a warm pie was exactly what he needed right now. Sensing this was as good of a time as any to head home, he grabbed the rest of the food, along with the things Tom had left him, and started toward his den.

He trekked home in whiteout blizzard conditions. This storm was going to be one for the history books. *It's a good thing bears have a superior sense of direction or I'd never find our den*, he thought with some relief, but it was still very slow going. His plan was to get to Stone Coal Gap and hunt for deer there. If he could kill one or two, he and James could come back later and collect them.

When he finally made it to the snow-covered road, there were five deer standing along the edge. They were the easiest kills he had ever made. It was almost like hunting possums. He just walked up to them, and with one big swipe, they were dead. Even though he and James would have to make several trips to the road later, he knew they would be eating all five of those deer. This was the time of year when it was important for bears to eat a lot and get fat.

When he arrived at his den, it didn't look like anyone was home. He went inside and discovered his family safe and sound, but fast asleep.

Sophia woke up first and was surprised to see Benjamin. "I didn't expect you back today," she said. "Not with the storm of the century outside. I figured you would stay with Tom and Sue at least until the blizzard was over."

"Now that I'm the boar of the den, I feel like I need to be here," he said. "I'm about to wake James up to help me bring back the five deer I killed down at the road."

He then brought out the four strawberry rhubarb pies he had carried home. Sophia was excited and said they would have them for dessert after supper that night.

"We'll have plenty to eat for a while," she said. "Before the storm, James killed three deer, and your sister was also out fishing a lot. We wanted to be ready."

Benjamin was pleasantly surprised to hear they had prepared so well for the storm and their hibernation.

He woke James and Lucy, who were very glad to see him. "I wasn't expecting you to come back during this storm," Lucy said.

"Being the boar of the den, I had to make it back here come hell or high water. Or in this case, snow."

They both came with Benjamin to collect the deer. Three bears walking through the snow looked almost like a snowplow driving down the mountain. They each grabbed a deer and made their way back to the den.

"James and I will go back for the last two deer," Lucy said. "You've had a long day. Just relax and keep Mom company while we're gone."

Sophia asked how Tom and Sue were doing. Benjamin told her the whole story about how they moved to a new county that didn't allow bear hunting after their neighbors were killed, and how he had found them a new den they really loved. Sophia said she was happy for them.

When James and Lucy came back, they cleaned and bagged the deer to put in the freezer while Sophia cooked up fresh backstrap, smashed taters, and four big loaves of sourdough bread. The den smelled wonderful.

After the feast, Sophia told Lucy to look in the oven to see what Sue had made them for dessert. Lucy was pleased to see four of Sue's famous strawberry rhubarb pies. The smell when she opened the oven was delightful. Each of them got a pie, and there they sat, enjoying their dessert and each other's company.

For Benjamin, life couldn't be better. He just hoped they would all survive kill season.

CHAPTER 19

The Great Flood

The good news was the storm had stopped, the sun had come out, and it was a beautiful day. The bad news was there was no way to leave the den without tunneling through several feet of snow. But with a few more warm days like this, maybe they wouldn't be snowbound for too long.

They had an abundance of food in store: deer, possum, turkey, native trout, and a few rainbow trout. Also, plenty of collard greens, bacon to go with it, and porridge. Best of all, at least in Benjamin's mind, they had tons of flour and sourdough starter to make bread. On top of all that, they still had seven buckets of honey and plenty of berries for cobbler. Their den couldn't be doing better—foodwise, anyway. They all missed Oliver terribly.

The danger of being cooped up in the den was the temptation to go into hibernation early. If that were to happen, they would enter an extended hibernation where they would lose more fat and be much skinnier come spring. They had to distract themselves with board games and other family activities so they could stay energized and not drift off into hibernation. Fortunately, food was no problem, so they could continue to fatten themselves for weeks to come.

The more he thought about hibernation, the more Benjamin couldn't wait until it was over, when he could see the new cub arrivals: his new brothers and sisters, nieces and nephews.

After four days of staying indoors and putting on weight, Benjamin ventured outside one morning and found that over half of the snow had melted. Hearing the stream gurgling much louder than usual, he walked down to the bottom of the hill and was shocked by what he saw. He had seen the stream flooded before, but never like this. It was practically a river at this point.

He hiked back up to the den and was greeted by the scent of warm sourdough bread. Sophia was just setting out a breakfast of porridge, fried turkey, eggs, and bacon. After a feast, they all took short bear naps.

Benjamin was awakened by an unusual creaking sound. He had no idea what it was, so he got up and went into the living room. A small stream of water was running from the back of the den and out the front door. As the stream got bigger and the creaking got louder, Benjamin realized the den was buckling under the weight of all the melting snow.

"Everybody wake up!" he yelled. The bears came running out of their rooms, groggy and confused, but they quickly understood what was happening.

They all ran outside moments before the entire den was ripped apart and all their belongings were washed down the mountain and tossed into the raging stream below.

Their lives had been swept away in one moment of time. Everything was gone. Well, except one thing.

"I grabbed this as we were escaping," Benjamin said, holding up a deer bag of marijuana. "I figured we would need this to help us relax while we figure out what to do."

They all rolled cigars and sat down to smoke them. Gradually, they calmed down and thought about what they could do.

"What about Samuel and Angel?" Benjamin said. "Maybe we could share their den for a short period of time. At least until we can make it across the road, and then we can use Lucy and James's den until next spring when I can look for a new den for Mom and me."

Everyone was onboard with this plan, as long as Samuel and Angel would let them stay.

They agreed it would be best to show up with some food, so they turned their hike into a hunting expedition. There was still a foot of snow left, which meant they probably wouldn't find any small game, but catching a deer or some turkeys wouldn't be a problem.

Just then, they spotted the biggest buck they had ever seen standing close by. As far as Benjamin could tell, it had an eighteen-point rack that was over two feet wide. This one wouldn't be as easy as the deer he had killed earlier in the heavy snow. Even though he badly wanted to make the kill, he told Lucy it was hers.

"I won't let you down," she said, and set off to get below the massive buck. Then she charged. The deer bolted to the steepest part of the mountain and up to the rock bluffs. With the buck exactly where she wanted it, she swiped a few times with her paw, and it fell to the ground dead.

They would catch two more yearlings and six turkeys on the way to Angel's den. Benjamin thought that was enough to keep them in Angel's good graces for a few days.

Angel was happy to see them. When he didn't see Samuel, Benjamin was almost afraid to ask where he was, but he did anyway.

"He went fishing down by the pond," Angel said. "He got bored being holed up in the den for so long."

When they told Angel about their den, she didn't hesitate. "Y'all stay with us," she said. "As long as you need, but at least until you can make it across the flooded creek and the road."

Sophia let her know about Oliver being killed. Her face dropped and she told her how sorry she was to hear it. She gave each of them a big bear hug.

"We brought you some food to thank you for the hospitality," Sophia said.

"Thank you! That's a hell of a buck you have there."

"Lucy killed it herself," Benjamin said. "And for some odd reason, Lucy wants to keep the antlers to hang in her den. It's not like you can eat antlers, so I have no idea why she wants to keep them around."

The bears went to join Samuel at the pond. They knew because of the weather, Farmer Brown probably wouldn't be out, so they grabbed the last two fishing poles and headed over.

Samuel smiled and waved when he saw them. After bear hugs, they told him about the flood.

"Please stay with us as long as you need to," Samuel said. "What a crazy storm that was. Well, that means we'll need to catch a ton of fish today so we have plenty to eat."

"You're right," Benjamin said. "It's so much fun to sit on the banks and fish with the poles, but to speed things up, maybe we should all get in the pond and fish the old-fashioned way."

"That's probably best," Samuel said. "Farmer Brown will restock in the spring. Let's just catch every fish we can. The protein will fatten us up quickly, and we'll be ready for hibernation in a couple of weeks."

They all jumped into the pond and caught as many fish as they could while laughing and splashing and having a great time. They caught so many, they had to go back and get ten more baskets. It was official: they were going to be fat, happy bears.

Back at the den, they gave Angel the night off cooking, and Sophia, Lucy, James, and Benjamin fried up two baskets of rainbow trout and made fifty pounds of fried taters. Sophia discovered the freezer was full of strawberries and rhubarb, so she set about making pies using Angel's recipe—the same recipe Angel had shared with Sue.

When Benjamin smelled the pie, all he could think about was how much he missed Tom and Sue. He felt much more at ease knowing they lived in a county where they couldn't be hunted down. *Maybe someday I will move closer to them*, he thought, *but Mom and Lucy and James need me right now.*

Supper was ready. They didn't need to wonder where Samuel was because all they could hear was the snoring coming from the living room.

"You think that's bad, try sleeping with him," Angel said. "If I didn't love him so much, I would move out. That bear can snore." She woke him up and he shuffled over to the table.

"We heard you snoring over there," Benjamin said as Samuel sat down.

"What? I wasn't asleep. And I don't snore, so I don't know what you're talking about." He looked at Angel, and the piercing stare she gave him made it clear it wasn't a discussion she wanted to have right now.

After supper, everyone was stuffed. Benjamin said how thankful he was to Farmer Brown for providing them with the rainbow trout, and they all agreed. Then, feeling tired, they got ready for bed and lay down for the night.

The next morning, Benjamin was the first one awake. Wanting to visit Luna and Maverick, he left before anyone else woke up and headed down to their den.

Luna was so happy to see Benjamin, she gave him a little nose rub. As much as Benjamin liked it, he wasn't sure it was a good thing because it was giving him false hope. Of course, they were just friends and nothing more, and he would never do anything to hurt her or Maverick.

"It's great to see you, Ben," Maverick said, coming out of his bedroom. "It's been a while. What have you been doing?"

Benjamin filled them in on the loss of his dad, Tom and Sue moving two counties over, and their den being washed away in a flood. They invited him to stay for the rest of the day and have supper with them this evening. After a late supper, Maverick insisted he spend the night.

The next morning, Benjamin headed back to Angel's. When he walked out of the den, something felt strange, but he wasn't sure why. As he continued on his way, he realized what it was: the stream below was quiet. It didn't sound like a raging river anymore. *Hurray! We can probably make it across the creek now.*

When he arrived at the den, Angel was setting out breakfast while the others dug in. Benjamin told them he'd already eaten a filling breakfast prepared by Luna. But still, he couldn't resist the freshly baked sourdough bread. It occurred to him that all the honey they had at their den had been washed away, which made him sad. Worse, there was no honey to be found this time of year.

After breakfast, the bears started the trek to Lucy and James's den. The road had been badly damaged from the flood, and Benjamin didn't know if it would be fixed before the end of kill season. He crossed his fingers, thinking they might be safe from hunters for the rest of the season.

A blue object caught his eye. Could it be? Benjamin walked closer and discovered that yes, it was one of the buckets of honey from their old den, caught in some brush. Amazingly, it was still sealed, so they now had five gallons of honey. That made all of them happy.

They had been hoping Lucy's den would still be there and not in shambles after the storm, and as the bears walked up, they saw it was still in good shape. Sophia asked Benjamin and Lucy to go out and get some food while she tidied up the den.

Lucy had noticed several deep pools down at the stream that would be perfect for fishing, so they walked down. The first pool was loaded with trout, so they both dove in and came up with enough fish for two full baskets. As they walked to the next pool, Benjamin spotted another blue object several hundred yards downstream. He told Lucy to keep fishing while he went to check it out. Sure enough, it was another five-gallon bucket of honey. He rolled it back to where Lucy was.

While he was gone, Lucy had filled the last two baskets with trout, so they packed up and headed back to the den. Sophia was happy to get all the trout and honey, and she and James set about fixing a huge feast.

In a way, Benjamin thought, they were all starting over, kind of like Tom and Sue were, except those two had each other to lean on. But as he reflected on the last few days, he realized his family, too, had leaned on and supported each other, and now they had a comfortable den that Lucy and Sophia could have their cubs in later this winter.

The next morning, the bears heard something that sent

shivers up their spines. Several dogs were barking as they ran a bear on top of the mountain. Benjamin was puzzled. Had they come in from the other side? It probably didn't matter, because now, with less than two weeks left in the season, their safety didn't seem as certain as it had.

Feeling anxious, Benjamin rolled himself a marijuana cigar to calm down. Being the boar of the den was a tough business, he decided. *How did my dad do it? He never seemed to be stressed at all. Will I ever be the boar bear he was?*

CHAPTER 20

Kill Season Ends

After hearing the hounds on top of the mountain, the bears were much more careful whenever they were out. Benjamin took heart knowing kill season would be over in less than two weeks.

The weather had been warm and pretty, but their days were filled with the noise of the large machines the humans were using to repair the road below. Benjamin hiked down the mountain to see how it was coming along. The road below the machines looked good, but the destruction stretched all the way up to where their now-destroyed den was. Benjamin figured that unless a hunting group were to come in from the other side of the mountain, they would be safe for the rest of the season, but they still had to be careful not to go any higher than halfway up the mountain.

Before their den had been washed away, the bears had stockpiled plenty of food. But now their pantry was running low on supplies, so they stayed busy hunting and fishing every day.

Lucy and Sophia found success fishing in the deep holes of the stream, while James hunted the mountainside near Sophia's old den. Benjamin had been finding plenty of deer, but every time he started chasing them, he had to stop halfway up the mountain and let them go. All he was doing was burning fat when he should have been layering more on.

Desperate to get the extra protein and fat he needed, Benjamin decided to take the risk. He spotted three yearlings and chased them much higher on the mountain this time. As expected, they trapped themselves in the steep rocks. He had just killed the first one when the sound of barking dogs erupted. They were nearby and closing in quickly.

Going back to the den wasn't an option, so he bolted in the direction of Tom's old den. But the hounds were too fast for Benjamin, and they caught up. He now had two choices: fight the dogs or run up a tree. Climbing a tree was certain death, so he stood his ground.

He backed up and positioned himself against a blown-down tree, placing his ass end in the notch where the trunk met the root ball. He wasn't sure he could fight off four dogs, but the first dog made the fatal mistake of walking right up to Benjamin. That made it easy. He gave it a forceful smack and sent it flying thirty feet and headfirst into the ground. Until that moment, Benjamin hadn't realized his own strength.

The three remaining dogs were scared, staying ten feet away and trying to figure out how to get closer. Benjamin used the element of surprise and charged at the pack full speed. Terrified, the dogs turned to run, but Benjamin caught one of them with a powerful sweep of his paw and watched as it flew twenty-five feet before falling limp to the ground.

Now was his chance to escape. He ran off, hoping he could shake the dogs. But they kept pace as he ran, and as he passed Tom's den, they were five hundred yards behind and closing in. He was getting tired. *What can I do?* He searched his brain for answers. *I can't run up a tree! Unless ...*

Benjamin now knew what he had to do. If he continued all the way to the county where Tom lived, the hunters wouldn't be allowed to shoot him. He could run up a tree and sit there until the hunters called their dogs off. He wasn't sure if he had the stamina to make it that far, but he realized it didn't matter. If he wanted to live, he had to. His mother and sister needed him.

Fortunately, the dogs were also tired and not closing in as fast as they had been, so he was able to slow his pace. When at last he crossed the road that divided the counties, he figured it was safe to run up a tree. Minutes later, the dogs swarmed the tree, jumping and barking. All he had to do now was stay put until the dogs were put on their leads and pulled away from the tree. Finally, he could breathe.

The hunters showed up. "Did you see that?" one of them said to the other. "It's almost like he knew he'd be safe over here."

"Safe? He killed two of my dogs." The other hunter unshouldered his rifle. "This bear's going to die."

Benjamin tensed up, terrified. His relief had been premature.

"Come on," the first hunter said. "Put that away. We've always been ethical hunters, and that's not going to change today. Whenever we release our dogs, we know there's a risk they'll try to fight a bear and get killed."

The other hunter thought about it. Then he put his rifle away, and the two men pulled the dogs off the tree and left.

Still trembling, Benjamin slid down out of the tree. He would live to see another day.

At that point, he was only a couple of hours from Tom and Sue's den. He was hungry and tired, so he headed off in their direction, hoping he could stay with them until dark the next night.

Tom and Sue were both excited to see Benjamin and wanted him to stay at least until the end of hunting season. As much as he would have loved to, Benjamin knew he was needed at home with Sophia, Lucy, and James.

The next night, fat and happy after a day of the couple's usual hospitality, Benjamin was sent on his way with eight strawberry rhubarb pies. *That's either two apiece for our family or eight for me right now*, Benjamin thought with a chuckle. *That would be a lot of deliciousness.*

He walked up to the county line an hour after dark, just as he'd intended. As he continued toward his den, a realization hit him: *Everyone probably thinks I'm dead. Last they knew, I was being chased by a pack of hounds. Well, I'm not dead, but two of those dogs sure are.*

Benjamin picked up his pace so he could be home well before daybreak. The den was silent when he walked in. He set the pies in the refrigerator, checked the bedrooms to make sure everyone was home and safe, then crawled into bed.

It was a short night. "Oh my God, Brother!" Lucy screamed just after sunrise. "You're alive! We thought you were dead."

Over breakfast, the others were amazed as Benjamin told them how he had survived. "I know we decided not to go too high up the mountain," he said, "but I saw three deer and I had to get them. Unfortunately, I was only able to kill one before the dogs started chasing me."

"Actually, I found it and dragged it home," James said. "It's already in the freezer."

"I think possums are our best bet from now until the end of kill season next week," Sophia said. "Until then, let's all stay as low as possible. We can also fish the stream. It's still full of native trout."

Their strategy worked well, and by the last day of kill season, everyone was safe.

That morning, Lucy was up before anyone. She made her way down to the stream and had filled two baskets with trout when she heard a pack of hounds barking, coming straight up the road toward her.

The barking woke Benjamin up. When he realized Lucy was outside, his heart sank. Lucy was in serious danger. She wouldn't come back to the den because it would put all their lives at risk, and she couldn't run up the mountain because there could be more dogs. Her only option was to run away following the stream.

Benjamin estimated there were about six dogs chasing her, and they were only picking up steam. Terrified he would lose his sister today, he realized all his hopes rested on the orange ribbon. With no protection of their own, Benjamin and James stayed near the den, praying the ribbon would keep her safe.

"I'll go help her," Sophia said. "I have my ribbon."

"No, Mom, please don't go out there," Benjamin said. "You have young cubs, and they need you. Don't worry. Lucy's going to be okay. She's smart like you and powerful like Dad."

Benjamin heard a group of hunters walking up the road, along with some familiar voices. "Last day of the season, boys. Let's make it a great one."

Benjamin breathed a sigh of relief. It was Rob. Surely they would honor Lucy's ribbon.

"Sounds like the bear is staying low," Rob said. "That'll make for much easier walking. Although this road sucks. The flood really tore it up."

C3

Lucy ran as fast as she could, but after a three-mile chase, Rob's hounds caught up with her. She killed one of the dogs, but the others quickly closed in on her, leaving her with no choice but to climb a tree. She was scared to death. She had never been treed before.

At that moment, she remembered the ribbon. *I can only hope it protects me today*, she thought. *But I don't know if this hunting group will honor it or not.* She had never met Rob and didn't know it was his dogs that had chased her.

A group of hunters drew nearer. "It's treed now," Rob was saying. "It's not far off the road. Looks like we'll be killing us a bear today! As long as it's legal, of course."

As they came into Lucy's view, she could see there was a young man with them. He couldn't have been more than eighteen years old. "I'm so excited," the young man said. "I can't *wait* to kill my first bear and finally have that bearskin rug made."

"The sooner the better," Rob said. "We're going to have a long drag out along that terrible road." As he walked closer, Rob looked up at the tree and smiled. "Well, that's a nice-sized bear. Looks like a shooter. You may get your chance after all, son."

Lucy's heart pounded. *Oh no, these guys don't know about the ribbons*, she realized with horror. *I'm as good as dead.*

Still looking up, Rob stopped. "Guys, this isn't a legal bear."

"What do you mean?" the young man said. "That thing is easily two hundred pounds!"

"You're not wrong there," Rob said, "but I believe this here is Lucy."

The young man was puzzled. "Lucy?"

Rob told him about the ribbons he had given to Benjamin along with the promise not to kill his other family members. He looked up again. "This sow bear is too small to be Sophia, so it must be Lucy."

The young man looked upset, but he nodded. "Okay. I get that you made a promise, so you should honor that, I guess. I'll round up the dogs."

He had just finished tying up two of the dogs when a massive pile of bear poop splattered all over him. He looked up at Lucy and screamed, then reached for his gun.

"No!" Rob shouted. "Stop!"

"That fucking bear just shit on me!" He took aim at Lucy. Just as he pulled the trigger, Rob tackled him. It was just in time. The bullet whizzed by Lucy's head but did not hit her.

Rob was furious. "What the hell is wrong with you? You disregarded my direct order! I can tell you right now, you'll never be hunting with me again." He grabbed the gun from the young man's hands, made sure it was unloaded, then wrapped it around the tree.

"What the hell?" the young man yelled. "You just wait until I tell my dad about this. You're in big trouble, Rob."

"Oh, you won't have to tell him, because I will." Rob's face was bright red. "You know something? You're damn lucky your dad isn't here, or you would have been the tree your gun got wrapped around. I've been hunting with your dad for twenty years. We have a lot of respect for each other. And now his hotheaded punk of a son is going to come along and disrespect me? Believe me, he'll be hearing about this."

Rob shook his head and walked off. "Now get the rest of

those dogs tied up, and let's get the hell out of here."

ભ

Just outside the den, Benjamin and James heard the gunshot. In that moment, they knew they had just lost their sister and mate. Neither knew what to say to the other. Without speaking, they walked back into the den and rolled cigars for themselves. The silence told Sophia everything she needed to know. She had lost her daughter. Benjamin rolled her an even bigger cigar.

"I can't believe this," Benjamin said. "I was so sure Rob would keep his promise. I don't even want this cigar anymore. I'm so pissed off. I'm going down there."

As he turned to leave, Sophia begged him not to go. But he was determined. James insisted on going with, and the two of them headed out. Sophia sat down and cried. She had lost Lucy, and now she would probably lose Benjamin and James, too. If the hunters weren't going to keep their promise, they wouldn't hesitate to shoot if confronted.

Benjamin and James hadn't made it very far when they heard a familiar voice behind them.

"Guys! Wait up!" It was Lucy, trying to catch up.

"Lucy? Oh my God, you're alive!" Benjamin said.

James took her in his arms. "I'm so happy to see you! Where did you come from?"

"I ran home after I escaped, and Mom told me you had just left to confront Rob," she said, then told them how everything had unfolded. "I wanted to find you and—oh no, why are they coming this way?"

Rob and the other hunters had appeared on the hill, heading toward them. "Lucy," Rob called out. "This young man has something he wants to say to you."

The young man walked up to her. "I'm sorry I shot at you, Lucy," he said. "Rob has taught me a lot today, and I've learned my lesson. Never ignore orders, even if a bear shits on you, because if you lose the respect of your fellow hunters, then you have nothing."

"I'm sorry, too," Lucy said. "I didn't mean to shit on you. But the dogs scared me so much, I just couldn't hold it in anymore." Benjamin thought it was hilarious, but he waited until they were walking back before he told her that. All three of them burst out laughing, and didn't stop laughing until they got home.

That night, the bears celebrated making it safely through kill season. In just a week or two, they would go into hibernation. Right now, there were four of them living in the den. Benjamin couldn't help but wonder: how many new cubs would they be welcoming when they woke up in the spring?

CHAPTER 21

Hibernation

S ophia and Lucy were looking forward to their long, wintery naps, spending their days in the comfort of their rooms as they prepared to bed down for the season.

Benjamin and James stayed active. It was normal for sow bears to go into hibernation before the boars, so they continued to hunt and fish. For the next two days, they brought food to Sophia and Lucy so they could put on those last few pounds of fat before they fell off into dreamland.

Since they would be hibernating soon themselves, Benjamin and James fished a lot, an activity that didn't require too much energy yet provided them with plenty of protein. Because they were skilled hunters, they were also able to catch two deer and six possums without much effort. James was now over 250 pounds, and Benjamin was closing in on 300.

On the last night before hibernation, the two bears sat talking, telling their favorite stories. Benjamin loved talking about Tom and Sue. He could sense James was sick of hearing about them, but the story was important to him. Tom had genuinely saved Benjamin's life when he was depressed. And the opposite was true as well: if it weren't for Benjamin, Tom would be dead. He liked the story of Tom and Sue because of how happy they were together now, even if he had to trick them into it in the first place. Benjamin also liked to tell stories of his father, Oliver, and talk about how much the forest missed him.

James loved talking about how much joy Lucy had brought into his life. He was so thankful for Rob and all he did to prevent Lucy from being shot, because without Rob, she would be dead. Rob was a bittersweet topic of discussion:

bitter because he killed Oliver, sweet because he saved Lucy. He was willing to fight for what he believed to be right and ethical, which earned him the respect of not just the humans around him, but the entire forest.

Today, there was another topic Benjamin wanted to bring up. "James, have you and Lucy discussed cub names yet?"

"The only name we've come up with is Lucille," James said. "As you know, that's Lucy's real name. But we thought it would be best to wait until they're born and name them based on the way they look and act. Has Sophia talked about any names yet?"

"No, but I suggested Bud, and she liked that. Get it? Like a marijuana bud? It would be in Oliver's honor. Rob called him the Marijuana Bear because he weighed 420 pounds after they killed him. My mom said I have a sick sense of humor, but she does like the name Bud."

James chuckled. "It's a little morbid, but I like that name, too. I can't wait to meet Lucille and Bud in the spring." He yawned. "I'm getting sleepy, Ben. I'm going in to lay down with Lucy."

"I'm not far behind you," Benjamin said. "I'll fry us up a big basket of trout for one last protein boost."

They devoured the trout, wished each other a happy hibernation, and turned in for the winter.

☙

Benjamin's eyes fluttered open. He felt rested, but his mind was hazy, and he really had to focus to collect his thoughts.

Bud! He had almost forgotten. *Do we have ourselves a Bud?*

He jumped out of bed and ran to Sophia's bedroom. There he found three baby bears that looked to be five or six pounds apiece. Sophia was still sleeping. Benjamin knew the cubs would take care of themselves and live off their mother's milk until she woke up.

He reached down and picked one up. It was a sow with a white V on her chest. The next one was another sow with a small, white dot on her chest. *Uh oh*, Benjamin thought. *Do we even have a Bud?* Yes, as he found out: the third bear was a solid black boar. For the next hour, Benjamin sat holding his little brother, feeling close to Oliver by doing this. When Bud began to fuss, Benjamin placed him back next to his mother. Bud found a nipple and resumed suckling.

Benjamin checked on Lucy. She only had two cubs, but she and James were still sleeping, so he didn't bother them.

It was time for breakfast. As Benjamin walked into the kitchen, he was momentarily startled by Lucy's huge buck antlers hanging on the wall. He told himself not to be so jumpy, but he still wondered why the heck she wanted them up there.

He was hoping to have some bacon, but all he could find was fish. They had a *lot* of fish. Where was the bacon? He found a small amount underneath everything else in the freezer, along with a little bit of deer, but mostly fish, fish, fish. They wouldn't go hungry, that was for sure, but they would have to go out and hunt soon if they wanted much of anything besides fish. For now, he'd make do.

Since they had no eggs, Benjamin fried up twenty pounds of bacon and made an eight-gallon pot of porridge. The smell of bacon sizzling in a pan, he knew, would wake up any bear. Sure enough, he heard someone stirring.

Lucy and James came out of their bedroom holding their two new cubs. Soon, Sophia joined them with her three cubs.

Sophia let Benjamin hold Bud. "He's so precious," Benjamin said. "He even looks like a Bud."

He picked up the cub with the V on her chest. "Could we name this one Susie?" Benjamin asked, cradling her. He missed his friends Tom and Sue and wanted to name this cub in Sue's honor.

"Susie? I like that," Sophia said. She looked down at

her last cub and rubbed the white dot on her chest. "Everyone, this is Dottie."

"And this is Lucille," James said, "named after Lucy."

Sophia smiled. "She looks just like you, Lucy."

"We also have this beautiful boar," James said, handing the cub to Sophia, "with patches of white on his chest. Sophia, meet ... uh ..."

"Patches," Lucy said. "I mean, duh."

"With all those white patches on his chest, I don't know how you came up with that name," Sophia said. They all laughed.

Minutes later, the cubs were playing and running and rolling around the den like crazy. They all knew the den wouldn't be boring for a very long time.

"Do I smell bacon?" James said.

"You sure do. I got up early and started fixing breakfast, because I knew nothing wakes bears up like the smell of bacon in the morning."

"I feel like I haven't eaten in months," Lucy said. "Let's dig in!"

They ate almost all the food Benjamin had prepared and told him how delicious it was. All they had left was a gallon of porridge and a pound of bacon, so Benjamin broke the bacon into smaller pieces to give to the cubs, who were now tearing up the den.

Once Bud had finished his food, he shoved Dottie out of the way and finished hers, too. Then he went over to Patches' bowl, but Patches wasn't having it. By the time Patches put Bud in his place, Lucille had already finished her food. It would take time for Bud and Patches to figure out which one was the boss.

"What have we gotten ourselves into?" Sophia said. "These are five of the curest bear cubs, but they're going to be a full-time job. It wasn't bad with just you and Lucy. But five of these little ones in the same household may spell trouble with a capital T."

They came up with a new rule. Two of them would stay

with the cubs at all times while the other two went out to hunt and fish. That way, they could keep order in the den but also have a food supply.

Benjamin had an idea for how to get more bacon. But it was risky, he told James, because it involved sneaking onto the hog farm on the other side of the mountain. They would have to be extremely careful, or they could be shot. James thought it would be worth the risk, so they headed off.

When they reached the farm, the bears looked around and saw no one. They tiptoed into the hog lot and killed the two biggest hogs. As they dragged the hogs out of the lot, their spirits lifted. They hadn't been caught.

"Hey, you bears!" someone yelled.

"It's the farmer!" Benjamin whispered. "Let's get out of here!"

Except it didn't sound like an old man. They looked up to see a much younger man running over to them.

"What the hell are you bears doing here?" He put his hands on his hips. "I oughta go get my dad and tell him y'all killed two of his hogs."

Benjamin and James froze.

"But I won't," he said. "That bastard grounded me for sneaking off with the neighbor's daughter last night. I—" He looked behind him. "Oh no, I hear my dad coming. I'll go distract him, and y'all drag the hogs up that trail to the top of the mountain. That will be your easiest path." He looked Benjamin in the eyes. "Y'all owe me a favor for doing this, yeah?"

"Of course," Benjamin said, turning to leave.

James nodded. "Sounds reasonable."

They dragged the hogs off as fast as they could.

"Thank you for getting all this meat for us!" Sophia said when they returned. Then she frowned. "But sneaking onto a farm to kill the hogs? That's terrifying. I'm just glad you both survived."

All in all, they ended up with over a hundred pounds of bacon, four large hams, and plenty of meat for barbecue ribs. None of them had ever tried ribs, but Benjamin had seen a recipe in a magazine for "Best Ribs in the South." They removed the rest of the meat from the bone, ground it up, and added red pepper, salt, and sage to make over three hundred pounds of sausage. They were looking forward to eating well.

But Benjamin's stomach felt unsettled with worry. *What have I gotten myself into with the farmer's son?* he thought. *What is this favor he's going to ask of me?* Neither he nor James could even guess, but they swore not to tell Lucy or Sophia about it.

CHAPTER 22

Springtime with the Cubs

While the bears had plenty of hog meat on hand, Benjamin thought they could use some other types of meat, too. They were having a lot of fun playing with the cubs, but bears must do what bears must do, so he and James said goodbye to the cubs and headed out to hunt.

Possums were loaded with fat and easy to kill, so they hiked to a nearby holler, close to the stream, where they knew possums to be plentiful. When they got there, all they could see were possums. They had hit the jackpot.

After killing twenty-six possums, Benjamin told James to keep hunting while he went back to the den to get more baskets. By the time he returned, James had killed two more possums and thirteen turkeys, making it their best day ever for turkeys. Benjamin was impressed with James's hunting skills. Oliver had taught him well.

The next day, James went hunting with Lucy, leaving Benjamin and Sophia to take care of the cubs. Benjamin was most excited to play with Bud. He had an idea.

"Mom, do you mind watching the cubs while I take Bud down to the stream?"

"I think he needs another week before an outing like that," she said. "But why don't we take them outside and let them run around a little bit?"

The cubs had never been outside, and they were having a blast. At first, they would freeze up at every little noise they heard. Benjamin told them that when they saw or heard something scary, they should climb a tree to get away.

They didn't waste any time. Bud scampered up a tree right away, followed by Patches. Soon, all the cubs were up in the treetops, playing and chomping on the fresh, green leaves. Benjamin showed them how to get down, and four of them did, but not Bud. He was lying on a limb, with a full belly, snoozing away.

The other cubs were exhausted from their outdoor adventure, so Sophia took them inside to sleep. Benjamin said he would stay under the tree and nap until Bud came down.

He was awakened by a thump as Bud landed on his back, jumped to the ground, and ran away. Before Benjamin could stop him, he tore off in the direction of the stream. He was a fast little cub, and Benjamin couldn't catch him as he half ran, half rolled down the mountain. Then he jumped right into the stream and splashed around, laughing.

Sophia is going to be so mad, Benjamin knew. *But we're here, so we might as well make use of the time.* "Bud, I'm going to teach you how to fish," he said. "Come over here and—"

"No! I want to play!" He splashed Benjamin with a pawful of cold water.

Benjamin realized he was a little too young to learn how to fish, so he splashed him back. After Bud worked off some of his excess energy, they headed back to the den.

Sophia was not happy when they walked in soaking wet. "Why did you go to the stream after I told you not to? I thought we agreed not to take Bud there yet."

Benjamin tried to tell her it wasn't his fault, that Bud had taken off so quickly he couldn't catch him. But Bud sat there looking too innocent for Sophia to believe that story. Benjamin couldn't be sure, but he thought he saw a grin flash across Bud's face while he was catching hell from Sophia.

Just then, James and Lucy walked in hauling four yearling does.

"Y'all are the best," Benjamin said. "This will really help fill the freezer."

"This was Lucy's hunt," James told them. "She killed every one of these deer."

Benjamin smiled at her. "Wow, Lucy! You're really

stepping up."

"Of course I am," she said. "Look behind you. I don't see any of *your* antlers hanging on the wall." She smiled and stuck out her tongue at Benjamin.

Sophia fixed them a nice supper of fried trout, fried taters, and onions. The cubs were given their plates first. Bud was again the first to finish, but this time, Dottie finished before he could steal her food. So he went over to Susie, bumped her out of the way, and ate the rest of her fish.

Feeling emboldened, he walked over to Patches and reached for his food. Patches swatted his paw away, and a big squabble broke out. When the dust settled, Bud was the winner, and he proudly walked back and finished Patches' food. To Benjamin, it looked like Bud would be the alpha cub in the den, but he knew there would be many more fights before a true winner emerged.

Nights were also a challenge for the older bears. Even if they got a couple of the cubs to sleep, they would wake up again because the other cubs were being so rambunctious. That night, it was after one before any of them got to sleep. And at four in the morning, two of the cubs were already awake and roughhousing with each other. Benjamin started to wonder if he would ever get any rest.

During breakfast the next morning, when Bud tried to eat Lucille's food, she whipped his ass but good. He let out a high-pitched scream as she chased him away from her plate.

James clapped. "That's my girl!"

After breakfast, Sophia came around to Benjamin's idea of taking the cubs to the stream to play. She figured if they kept the cubs busy all day long, they might be able to wear them out and get some sleep tonight. Feeling tired, Benjamin said he would stay home while the rest of them went outside.

"Oh no," Sophia said. "You are not staying behind, thinking you can sleep. We all got just as little sleep as you did. This is going to be a family outing, sir."

The cubs had so much fun down at the stream, as Benjamin knew they would. They were particularly enjoying the waterslide, which was a steep bank that dropped them right into a deep pool of the stream. After a while, the cubs got bored, so the bears decided to take a walk along the main road, which by now had been repaired.

Two cars approached, then slowed down when they passed the bears. They pulled off the road and stopped, and all the people got out.

"Look at this! I've never seen so many bears before," one of them said. "Four big bears and five little cubs!" Benjamin felt like a movie star as the people stood there snapping pictures.

After walking a few more miles, the group cut up to Tom's old den. Benjamin was pleased to see it was just as he had left it.

"You know, Mom, you and I could move in here with the cubs and let James and Lucy have their den back," Benjamin said.

"But I love having the family all together," she said. "Maybe later."

Benjamin agreed, but he hoped it would be sooner than later. He knew that living in Tom and Sue's den would make him feel closer to his friends.

They cut across the mountain back to their den. Walking with the cubs had been slow going, and it was a few hours after dark when they returned home. Benjamin was ready to go straight to bed, but Sophia insisted on sitting down to a family supper so they could all put back on some of the pounds they had lost during hibernation.

Sophia and Lucy fixed backstrap, greens with bacon, and some porridge for the cubs. Benjamin and James lay down for a bear nap but were jarred awake five minutes later.

"Supper's ready!" Sophia called. As Benjamin shuffled to the table, he woke up the cubs, who were all curled up together, fast asleep. The little ones finished their food as quickly as they could, then ran into the living room to play.

The older bears were ready to turn in after supper, but none of them got to sleep until after two in the morning, and by five, the cubs were awake again. That little nap before supper was truly all they needed to power through.

"Okay, Ben, you win," Sophia said. "I'm beyond ready to move. Three cubs will be a lot easier to handle than five. I'll fix breakfast, and you can pack up our stuff to go to Tom's old den."

Benjamin was happy about Sophia's decision. While he packed, a familiar scent drifted his way. It was sourdough bread, and it smelled wonderful. All the cubs must have thought so, too, because for the first time, they marched right into the kitchen on their own, ready to eat.

Sophia had made four large loaves and five baby loaves of bread. The cubs ate half their bread with honey and the other half without. Patches liked the bread with honey best, and since he hadn't eaten any of his plain bread, Bud walked over to claim it. A fight ensued. Patches won the fight, then decided he had better eat the rest of the bread he had fought so hard for.

After breakfast, Benjamin finished packing their belongings. He left most of the hog meat with Lucy and James, knowing he could go out game hunting near Tom's den. Sophia offered to clean the kitchen for Lucy, but Lucy told her to go ahead and get moved in.

Patches and Lucille wanted to follow the others out the door, but James and Lucy held them back, much to the young cubs' dismay. They had been together so long, they wanted to stay together.

They made good time getting to their new den with the cubs and all of their belongings. Sophia cleaned up and unpacked everything while Benjamin went out hunting for supper.

He headed up the mountain, planning to find a deer and run it up onto the steep rocks. But a flock of turkeys happened along, and he was able to catch five of them, the largest being a thirty-pound gobbler with a fourteen-inch beard.

Benjamin thought about the huge antlers Lucy had hung on her wall and decided this enormous beard would go on his own wall. He was proud of it. He had never heard of a turkey that large being killed around here.

The den was clean and all their belongings had been unpacked by the time Benjamin got back. Sophia was shocked when she saw the biggest turkey. "That's a huge gobbler you got there," she said. "I didn't even know they grew that big."

He cut off the beard and hung it on the wall. "That's for Lucy to admire when she visits us," he said. "I'm going to lay down for a nap."

"Like hell you are! You're going to help me keep these monsters awake until bedtime at ten o'clock tonight."

During supper, Bud was his normal bully self and finished off both Susie's and Dottie's food. They were easy targets and gave in without a fight.

Benjamin and Sophia made sure the cubs stayed awake and played until after ten o'clock. As he crawled into bed, Benjamin smiled. They had finally figured out how to get a good night's sleep.

CHAPTER 23

Spring Becomes Summer

In the end, there was no sleep. At one in the morning, the cubs were awake and wanting to play. Sophia and Benjamin realized their trick of keeping the cubs up until ten hadn't worked. They rejoiced when the cubs went back to sleep at three, then groaned when they woke up again at six.

After breakfast, Sophia cleaned the house with Susie and Dottie, then told Benjamin she was taking the sows down to the stream.

Once they had left, Benjamin set about remodeling the den to give the cubs their own room. Bud was very interested in what his big brother was doing and wanted to help.

C3

Sophia grabbed two baskets on her way out, and they made their way down to the stream. She hoped she could remember how to fish the old-fashioned bear way. Benjamin and Lucy had been doing all the fishing for her, and other than fishing with a pole in her paw for fun, she hadn't done any serious fishing for a long time.

Susie and Dottie were having a blast, but they weren't catching anything. Sophia was a little rusty at first, but it didn't take long for her to start catching fish left and right. She filled both baskets with trout between 7 and 19 inches long and was quite proud of the biggest fish she caught, which measured 21 inches.

C3

Back at the den, Benjamin was enjoying his time with Bud, but the little guy was certainly keeping him on his toes. He would be by Benjamin's side one second and gone the next, probably trying to figure out where Susie and Dottie had gone. He wasn't a good helper, but he was trying.

Fortunately, Benjamin was making a lot of progress, and he figured he would have the new room finished by tonight for the cubs to sleep in. It even had a lockable door. Benjamin was certain he and his mother would get some much-needed sleep tonight.

Sophia came in and beamed when she saw his progress. "Wow," she marveled. "This room is looking great! I hope this means we can get a good night's sleep. Let's make sure to keep the cubs active for as long as possible."

Sophia fried up some of the fresh native trout and served it with greens and bacon. After supper, they all stayed up until midnight. Benjamin was talking with Sophia while the cubs played on the floor. When it was time for bed, Sophia took them to their new bedroom and gave them one last drink of her milk.

Benjamin stayed in the living room and rolled himself a cigarette. He and Sophia had been talking about Oliver, and he was feeling sad. The cigarette would help him feel better and help him sleep.

When Sophia came back, she asked him to roll her one, too. Benjamin rolled one more for himself, and when they were finished smoking, they went to bed.

The next morning, Sophia screamed. Benjamin jumped out of his bed and ran into the living room.

"They're gone!" she said. "They somehow unlocked the door to their bedroom and now they've run away!"

"I'm sure they're just down at the stream," Benjamin said. "I'll go down and get them."

Sophia looked around and took a deep breath. Then she nodded. "You're probably right. I'll fix us a picnic breakfast and join you in a few minutes."

Benjamin found the cubs playing in a deep pool of the

stream. But where was Bud? Just then, he popped out of the water with a fourteen-inch native trout in his mouth.

"Look, everyone!" Bud said. "It's my first trout, and I caught it all by myself!" Benjamin was proud of his little brother and happy he was learning to fish. The other cubs tried to catch some trout of their own but seemed more interested in splashing each other.

Sophia came marching down to the stream, picnic basket in paw. "Listen here, all of you," she shouted. "Don't y'all ever scare me like that again! If y'all ever leave the den without letting me know, I'll beat all your asses so hard you won't be able to sit down for a month. Hear me?"

The cubs stopped playing and looked at her. "Yes, ma'am," they said.

"Okay. Now, is anyone hungry? I brought us a picnic."

After a healthy and filling breakfast, Benjamin suggested a cross-county adventure to go see Tom and Sue and their new cubs. Everyone was excited at the prospect.

They set out through the woods and meadows, which were loaded with fresh fruit at this time of year. Between strawberries, blackberries, and raspberries, the family ate their fill. Bud was over the moon when he found blueberries higher up on the mountain. Susie and Dottie particularly enjoyed the huckleberries. By now, one thing was certain: they weren't skinny from hibernation anymore.

No one was home at Tom's den, and since they were all exhausted from the journey, they went in and took a long nap. Just as they were waking up, Tom and Sue came home. Tom introduced their daughter, Jolene, and told them two cubs had been born but only one survived.

"I'm sorry for your loss," Benjamin said.

"Thank you," Tom said. "We are, too. But it's normal for some cubs not to make it. We have our precious Jolene, and we couldn't be happier." He looked around at the other cubs. "Who do we have here?"

"This is my little brother, Bud," Benjamin said. He explained to Tom and Sue how he had come up with the name, and they laughed. "And this here is Susie, named after you, Sue. And this is little Dottie."

Sue smiled at Dottie. "She's adorable. I'm guessing the name comes from the white dot on her chest. I wish I knew y'all were coming. I would have had plenty of strawberry rhubarb pies made!"

Benjamin and Tom offered to make supper while Sue set about fixing eight pies: four big ones and four little ones. Sophia jumped in to help with the pies.

"There's something I've been saving for a special occasion," Tom said. He opened the freezer and pulled out two racks of ribs. "How would you guys like some barbecue ribs for supper?"

"That sounds wonderful," Benjamin said. "I've never tried them. But we do have some in the freezer at home, so it will be good for me to learn how to prepare them."

Tom took Benjamin outside and showed him how to put wood in the smoker and light it. Then they went back to the kitchen, where Tom cut the ribs in half. After coating them in seasoning, he took them back outside and placed them onto the racks of the smoker.

Benjamin was impressed. "Wow, Tom. I don't have a smoker. I guess I'll have to get one or build one."

Tom nodded. "I normally like to slow smoke them over a twelve-hour period," he said. "But we'll be up all night if we do that, so I'll use a little more heat to cook them faster. They won't be as good as slow-cooked ribs, but they'll still be delicious."

Supper was served at nine o'clock, a little later than the bears were used to eating, but they were happy to dig in. Benjamin took one bite of the ribs and thought he had died and gone to heaven.

The cubs enjoyed the ribs, too, but by the end of the meal, they were all covered in barbecue sauce. Sue went into the kitchen and brought out the four small pies. Fortunately, the cubs all ate their pies quickly, so there was no fighting over food. The bigger bears then sat down to eat their pies and talk while the cubs played with each other.

"Tom, we're living in your old den right now," Benjamin said. "Lucy had two cubs, and with our three, there were just too many cubs in Lucy's den, and we weren't getting any sleep, so we had to spread out."

"Tell me about it," Sue said. "Even with one cub, we had more than a few sleepless nights here, too. I had a storybook from when I was a little cub, and I started reading it to Jolene before bed. She sleeps all night long now."

Benjamin was glad Sue had found a trick that worked. *But she doesn't know how our cubs are*, he thought.

At bedtime, they decided one area of the den would be for the cubs and the other for the older bears. Sue sat down in a chair and told the cubs to gather around so she could read them a story.

"Once upon a time," Sue began, "there was a little girl whose hair was so bright and yellow ..."

Benjamin listened to Sue's soothing voice as she read. When he looked up, all the cubs were fast asleep. Even Tom was snoring. They left him with the cubs and went to their own area to sleep.

Tom and the cubs were still asleep the next morning when the others woke up at eight. Benjamin told Sophia they would need to stop by the bear thrift store to pick up a children's storybook of their own since it had worked so well at bedtime. Once everyone else was awake and had eaten breakfast, they said their goodbyes, and the family headed back to their den.

As they hiked, they came across two yearling does standing nearby, and Benjamin saw the chance to get some easy food. He told Sophia to watch the cubs while he hunted, then charged at the deer.

"Bud, stop!" Sophia yelled out.

Benjamin turned around and saw Bud running toward him. He continued chasing the deer onto the steep rocks, where he killed the first one. Bud was now right beside him, saying he wanted to kill the other one. Benjamin knew he was too young, but decided to let him have a crack at the deer before he stepped in and finished the job. Bud had so much fun with his big brother that he said he wanted to hunt with him more often.

With Bud's help, they dragged the deer back down to where Sophia and the cubs were. From there, Sophia and Benjamin hauled the two deer all the way back to the den.

Sophia recruited Susie and Dottie to help her prepare supper while Benjamin and Bud stayed outside to dress and bag the deer for freezing. After a delicious meal of ham, green beans seasoned with bacon, and some fresh sourdough bread, they moved into the living room and stayed up until midnight.

Even though they didn't have the children's storybook yet, Benjamin did his best to tell the same story Sue had told the night before. He had to make up some parts he couldn't remember, but before he got to the end, they were all snoozing.

Before bed, Benjamin suggested going to visit Caesar the next day, thinking he might have a children's book he could lend them. While they were out, they could also stop by Luna's and Angel's to spend time with their new cubs. And if they brought enough fishing poles, they could also stop at the pond along the way. He thought for sure Farmer Brown would have restocked his pond by now.

It sounded like fun to Sophia, but all she could think about was how concerned she was about bringing the cubs to the pond.

CHAPTER 24

Caesar

After breakfast, they gathered the fishing poles, grabbed two baskets, and set off. Their first stop was Luna and Maverick's den, but as soon as the stream came into view, Bud took off running toward the waterslide.

"Susie! Dottie! Come on and join me!" he yelled. The sow cubs were all too happy to run after him. Bud splashed into the pool and immediately came up with a ten-inch native trout.

They gave the cubs ten minutes to play and fish in the pool, then Benjamin told them they had a busy day ahead and it was time to go. As they headed away, a thought popped into his head: *I really need a sow to call my own. Will today be the day?*

Sophia told the cubs to keep their eyes open for berries along the way so they could bring some to Luna and Angel. They happened upon some blackberries and raspberries and spent several minutes eating and filling Sophia's first basket. Dottie started filling the second one, but Sophia wanted to save it for blueberries and huckleberries, which they soon found. The cubs ate to their hearts' content, then filled the basket.

Luna was outside her den with her two new sow cubs. She thanked them for the baskets of berries and dumped them into her baskets. She told them Maverick was out hunting and introduced her cubs: Susan, who had a white V on her chest, and Heather. Benjamin told her they were adorable and stepped closer to play with them. As he did, Luna brushed up against him a few times. *We're friends and nothing more,* he had to tell himself.

When he introduced Bud, he told Luna he was named

in honor of Oliver. When she pointed out that Bud sounded nothing like Oliver, Benjamin explained the story of Oliver's weight and the connection with the marijuana bud. She doubled over with laughter at this story and kept rubbing up against Benjamin. As much as he wanted to turn and give her a big nose rub and bear hug, he couldn't do that. *We're just friends*, he told himself again. *She's with Maverick, and they have these precious cubs together.*

A few minutes later, Maverick walked up with a large doe and waved when he saw everyone. Benjamin introduced the cubs, then told everyone it was time to leave. He felt uncomfortable with Luna rubbing up against him, and he was afraid he would say or do something that would harm their friendship. She was the most beautiful bear in the world, and he didn't want to lose her.

On the way to Angel's, the family managed to pick two more full baskets of berries. When they knocked on the door, Angel appeared with one sow cub at her side and introduced her as Liz. She was as black as coal, even her snout.

"Where's Samuel?" Sophia asked.

"Oh, he's at the pond fishing with Sam Jr.," she said. "Why don't I grab our fishing poles and we can all head down there?"

Arriving at the pond, Bud's mouth fell open in awe. "Is this the ocean?" he said. "I've never seen so much water."

Samuel chuckled. "No, this is just Farmer Brown's pond. But it's about five acres, so I can see how it might look huge compared to the small pools of the stream."

Benjamin caught a fish right away. It was a 20-inch rainbow trout, and he held it up for everyone to see. It was clear Farmer Brown had restocked his pond.

"Nice fish, Brother," Bud said. "But I'm going to catch one twice that size!" They snickered at his optimism. Ten minutes later, Bud had caught two fish, one 18 inches and the other 21 inches in length.

"I stand corrected," Benjamin said. "You're quite the fisherbear, Bud."

"I've got one!" Liz yelled as she reeled in a 19-incher. Angel caught a 15-incher a minute later.

Now it was Bud who wasn't having any luck. "That's okay," he said. "I'm just waiting for the world-record rainbow trout. I'll catch one that's over 40 inches someday." This time, no one snickered.

Before long, Samuel was ready to leave. Angel invited them all over for supper, and Benjamin said they would be over right after a quick stop at Caesar's. When Angel said she would also invite Maverick and Luna, Benjamin tensed up. He would have to keep his distance from Luna tonight.

They left their poles hidden in the brush since they would be passing by on the way back to Angel's later, and they headed off.

As they trekked to Caesar's den, Benjamin was struck by an uneasy feeling. The forest was too quiet. There were no birds chirping, no bugs scurrying about. No squirrels a-stirring or crows a-crowing. Something was wrong, but what? They continued on their way.

"Everyone stay outside," Benjamin said when they arrived at Caesar's den. "I'll go in and let Caesar know we're here."

Sophia stayed with the cubs and Benjamin walked in. No one was home. "Caesar?" he called out. He walked into the kitchen. There were a few items scattered on the floor, which was unusual. Caesar always kept his den very tidy. He turned around and walked to the door of Caesar's bedroom—and threw his paw over his mouth to keep from screaming.

Caesar's body was sprawled on the floor of the bedroom, his head resting in a pool of dark, coagulated blood. Benjamin walked closer and saw a hole, one inch in diameter, in the side of his head.

Oh my God oh my God oh my God. This can't be happening. So many thoughts ran through his mind. *What am I going to say to Sophia?*

Whoever killed Caesar had taken almost all of his marijuana. Benjamin looked around and saw only one possum bag left.

Farmer Brown can be grumpy, but he really isn't a bad guy, Benjamin recalled Caesar saying one day. *Was Farmer Brown really his marijuana supplier? Could he have killed Caesar? If so, why?*

Needing to calm down, Benjamin rolled a cigar and sat down to smoke it before going outside to tell Sophia.

"Who could have killed Caesar?" she said, tearing up. "Everyone loved him."

Benjamin explained his suspicions as he rolled her a cigar. Sophia was surprised because she had never thought of Farmer Brown as a bad person, just a man protecting his rainbow trout.

After they had finished off the possum bag, Benjamin asked Sophia to take all the cubs to the pond and fish while he stayed at the den and investigated. He was determined to find out who had killed Caesar.

As soon as the others had left, Benjamin picked up a scent. *Bingo!* he thought. *Follow this scent, and I'll find my killer.* The scent led him almost all the way to the pond, but then suddenly cut down the mountain. Soon, a house came into view: an old Victorian farmhouse covered in Virginia creeper. Farmer Brown's house.

Benjamin was nervous as he approached the porch. The house had an evil, gothic feeling to it. As soon as he walked up onto the porch, the scent he had been following disappeared, which struck him as unusual.

Before he could knock, the door opened, and the farmer's wife stepped out. "Why are you here?" she asked.

"I'm here because your husband killed Caesar," Benjamin said.

She looked shocked. "Caesar's dead? Well, it wasn't my husband. He's been right here for the last two days, sick in bed."

Benjamin didn't believe her, but he didn't want to stick around and argue about it. He asked if he could buy a deer bag of marijuana from her.

"Do you want it from the big drawer or the small drawer?" she asked.

"What's the difference?"

"The big drawer is pure marijuana, and the small drawer has ... a little something extra."

The small drawer probably held the stuff of Benjamin's worst nightmares, so he chose big drawer. He paid her for the deer bag and walked off. As he did, he found a children's storybook lying on the ground. Benjamin was sure this was the book that had been in Caesar's den, and it only further implicated Farmer Brown. He picked it up and took it with him.

Benjamin lit a large cigar as he walked back to the pond. The marijuana calmed him, but one thought consumed his mind: he needed to kill Farmer Brown. He was certain the farmer had taken their great friend Caesar from them, a bear the whole forest would soon be mourning. The more he thought about killing Farmer Brown, the more he wanted some laced marijuana. That would help him do what needed to be done.

He knew he had to chill out before meeting Sophia and the cubs, so he sat down and chain smoked four more cigars. He'd never had so much hate in his heart. When he felt calm enough to continue, he walked the rest of the way to the pond.

"I got one! I got one!" Bud shouted as Benjamin walked up. His pole bent in half. Bud dug his hind paws into the ground and held onto his pole for dear life. Benjamin ran toward him, believing he had the world-record rainbow trout on his line. But just before Benjamin could grab him, Bud was pulled right into the pond. Benjamin dove in after him and pulled him out. He set Bud on the bank of the pond, then waded back in to get the fishing pole.

"I had it, Brother," Bud said, sounding defeated. "I had the world-record rainbow trout!"

"It really looked like you did, Bud. Next time, he'll be yours."

All this excitement was just what Benjamin needed. This

was the calmest he had been since discovering Caesar's lifeless body. Soon, he had all the cubs fishing again while he talked to Sophia. He told her about the visit to Farmer Brown's house, which confirmed in Benjamin's mind he was not only Caesar's marijuana supplier, but also his killer. Farmer Brown's days were numbered, he told his mother, but he stopped short of telling her he planned to kill him. Besides, he wasn't sure he had it in him to follow through.

"We should stop by and let Samuel and Angel know about Caesar," Benjamin said. "Angel will be torn up about the loss of her granddad. I'm sure Angel will tell Luna, so I don't think we need to go to Luna's den."

Benjamin let it slip that he didn't feel comfortable around Luna, now that she was always rubbing up against him. "It probably doesn't mean anything, but since I love her, it's tearing my heart out of my chest not being with her."

"Oh, Ben." Sophia put her paw on his shoulder. "I thought that was getting easier for you."

"It's gotten a little easier over time, but when I'm with her and she brushes against me, it's all I can do to keep my paws off her."

Angel and Samuel were heartbroken. Samuel said he had noticed how silent the forest was, but he couldn't figure out why. Benjamin asked Samuel to step outside, where he told him about Farmer Brown's wife covering for him, saying he had been sick.

"I don't know, Ben. From everything I know about Farmer Brown, he's a good guy. As long as he doesn't catch you fishing in his pond, that is."

Benjamin shook his head. "But I was following a scent, and it led right to his porch. It had to be him, Samuel." He started to tell him about the book he had found.

"We're here!" It was Luna, who had just arrived with Maverick, Susan, and Heather. With all the excitement today, Benjamin had forgotten about having supper with everyone tonight.

Benjamin told them the story of finding Caesar dead.

Luna said the forest wouldn't be the same and gave Benjamin a big hug. He hugged her back. It felt like they should be together, but he couldn't tell her he had feelings for her.

After eating the delicious supper Angel had fixed, Benjamin and Sophia told everyone goodbye and took the cubs back to their den. They only got as far as the stream before the cubs jumped in and started playing, so they stayed there until midnight, letting them burn off all their energy.

When they got home, Benjamin showed Sophia the storybook he had found outside Farmer Brown's house. He told her he thought it had come from Caesar's den.

Just then, there was a knock at the front door. *Who the hell would be knocking on our door after midnight?* Benjamin thought. *I'm in no mood for company!*

CHAPTER 25

Lucifer

Benjamin picked up a familiar scent as he walked to the front door to see who was knocking. He recognized it as the smell from Caesar's bedroom yesterday. He opened the door, and it took him a few seconds to recognize the person standing there. It was the farmer's son.

"I'm sorry for bothering you so late," he said, "but I really need to talk to you about something. Remember when you said you'd do me a favor?"

Benjamin was too tired to deal with this tonight. "Listen, I've had a really long day," he said. "Why don't I come see you tomorrow?"

The farmer's son agreed, and Benjamin closed the door. He was anxious about what the favor could be. The farmer's son had saved Benjamin and James from being shot by his father, so he probably wanted something big in return. Something sinister, perhaps? *I wish I didn't owe him this favor*, Benjamin thought. *Sure, he saved our lives, but what sort of hell would he turn our lives into now? Our family has been through hell already today!*

Benjamin sat down next to Sophia, who was reading the story of Little Red Riding Hood to the cubs.

"Who was it?" Bud asked.

"It was the hog farmer's son, but I'll go visit him tomorrow to see what he needs."

Sophia finished reading the story and closed the book. The cubs were wide awake, staring at her. Now they were afraid to sleep, for fear the big, bad wolf would come get them tonight. She assured them it was a make-believe story, then turned the page to read "The Teddy Bears' Picnic." Halfway through, she looked up to find the cubs sound asleep in a pile on the floor.

Sophia and Benjamin stayed in the living room and reflected on the day. Most of the good things that had happened were overshadowed by the loss of Caesar.

"How are you doing?" Sophia asked.

"Not very well," he said. "But don't worry about me. I think I just need some marijuana to help me get through it."

"And this farmer's son who came to the door? Why would he be coming here, especially at this hour?"

Benjamin explained how he had come to owe him a favor.

"Now I'm even more worried," she said. "First we lose Caesar, then the shifty son of a farmer wants some mysterious favor from you."

After a sleepless night, Benjamin woke up to the smell of bacon and eggs in the pan and sourdough bread in the oven. For a few moments, he forgot about going to see the farmer's son today, but when he remembered, the thought turned his stomach in knots.

After a delicious breakfast, Benjamin told the cubs they needed to behave today. "I don't know when I'll be back," he said. "I need to go all the way over the mountain to get to the farm."

Sophia told him to be careful. He gave nose rubs to all and headed out the door.

After a long hike to the farm, Benjamin spotted the old farmer walking into his barn. Nearby, his son was working on his car. As Benjamin walked over to him, he could smell that same scent from the day before. *I guess it's just the way farmers smell*, he thought.

The farmer's son saw him and walked over. "I haven't introduced myself yet," he said. "My name is Lucifer. I guess you are wondering why I came by last night."

"I assume you need me to repay your favor?"

"Well, no. Not exactly. I want to help you. I heard about Caesar's murder, and as I'm sure you know, it was the work of

Farmer Brown."

Benjamin nodded. He knew.

"I would kill that son of a bitch myself," Lucifer said, "but you see, with human laws, I would be thrown in prison for the rest of my life for a crime like that. But ..."

Benjamin saw where this was going. "If *I* were to kill him ..."

"Exactly. If you were to kill him, it would be nothing more than an act of nature. A wild animal gone rogue. You would face no consequences for your actions."

"I don't know. I—"

"Listen, Ben. I get your hesitation. But I know nothing would make you happier right now than seeing that bastard dead."

"That's true," Benjamin said. "But you must know that I was already planning to kill him. Why would you want to help me?"

"Because I also know you have a heart of gold, and it would be hard for you to kill anything that wasn't food."

"You're right. It will be hard, but with how angry I am, I'm sure I can do it."

"Well, I'm going to make it easier for you." Lucifer handed him two marijuana cigars. "Smoke these right before you do it. They'll give you the mental edge you need to break down his damn door and rip his ass apart."

Benjamin was confused. "But marijuana has the opposite effect on me. It calms me down. Believe me, I've smoked a lot of it."

"Just do as I ask, trust in me, and you will kill him with no trouble."

Benjamin wanted Farmer Brown dead, so he agreed. He wanted to trust what Lucifer was saying, but he knew himself. If he smoked the cigars before trying to kill the farmer, he'd be so calm he wouldn't be able to kill a possum.

On his way to Farmer Brown's house, he stopped by the den to get his fishing pole so he could catch some fish afterward.

146

Fishing pole in paw, Benjamin approached Farmer Brown's house. The farmer had just walked inside and closed the front door. *I'm so enraged right now*, Benjamin thought. *I should go confront him now. If I smoke these cigars, I'll be so chill, I won't be able to kill him.*

But he had promised to follow Lucifer's instructions. He lit up and took a couple of puffs. This marijuana had a slightly different taste, and the smoke he blew out was purple. He liked it, but it wasn't making him calm. In fact, he was more pissed off than before. He snapped his fishing pole in half, threw it aside, and took another deep drag.

When he finished the cigar, he lit the other one. All he could think about now was how much he hated that damned Farmer Brown. His head was spinning. He finished off the cigar, then took off in a full gallop, straight through the front door of the house as it splintered apart. The farmer's wife stood in front of Benjamin, shocked and screaming. He shoved her out of the way, and she hit the floor. A pool of blood formed around her head. Fueled by his rage, he had accidentally killed her, but he didn't care.

He heard a loud noise and felt a little fly land on him. Then another, then another. Five of them. He looked to his side. Farmer Brown stood in the doorway to his bedroom, holding a smoking shotgun. He realized the flies he had felt were actually birdshot. Benjamin calmly walked toward Farmer Brown, who raised his shotgun and smashed it down on top of Benjamin's head. He didn't even feel it, but now the shotgun barrel was bent in the shape of a boomerang, and the stock had split into several pieces.

With one lightning-quick swipe of his claws, Benjamin ripped the farmer's body open, then smacked him so hard he flew into the wall. It shook the house like an earthquake. Benjamin walked over to Farmer Brown's shredded corpse, pulled his warm heart out, and ate it. Then, he ran out of the house and up to the pond and lay down in a mud wallow.

The dirty deed was done. Farmer Brown was dead.

CHAPTER 26

The Healing

Benjamin lay in the mud wallow until all the bleeding had stopped. He felt no pain, but his head was spinning. *What the hell was in that marijuana?* he thought. *It had to be laced with something. That sure wasn't Caesar's marijuana.*

He was glad that bastard Farmer Brown was dead. He had to die for what he did to Caesar. But Benjamin had never intended to kill the farmer's wife, and he felt guilty about it. None of this would have happened without the purple smoke marijuana, he was certain.

He still had some of the marijuana he had bought from the farmer's wife on his first visit. After smoking the whole bag, his head wasn't spinning as much, and he was able to crawl from the mud wallow onto the bank of the pond.

He had no idea how long he was lying there, but he had a dream he was with Luna, and they were raising a beautiful family together. He wasn't sure what was real and what wasn't anymore.

A bright light appeared, and the prettiest bear he had ever seen was standing over him. It looked like Luna. Was he dreaming? Were they together now? He was too groggy to tell the difference between fantasy and reality. What about Maverick? He didn't want to do anything to harm their perfect family.

"You're the most beautiful bear I've ever seen," Benjamin said. In his dreamlike haze, he gave her a huge bear hug, rubbed her nose, then smacked her on the ass. "I'm Benjamin. What's your name?"

"You crazy thing, you know who I am. I'm Luna."

Benjamin was stunned. *Is this real?* "I'm having the wildest dream right now," he said.

"Are you okay, Ben?"

"No. I smoked something terrible and now I'm having a weird dream. I remember killing Farmer Brown's wife by accident. I just shoved her. I didn't mean to kill her."

Luna rubbed her paw on his arm. "It's okay."

"But then I killed Farmer Brown, who deserved to die. He shot me and smashed his shotgun over my head. So I ripped his body open, threw him against the wall, and ate his heart."

Luna looked at him for a few moments. Benjamin knew she was appalled at his actions. He was appalled at himself for killing an innocent person. Surely Luna would never want to speak to him again.

"Did it taste good?" she asked.

Benjamin smiled. "So good."

"You've been through hell and back, Ben." She gave him a big hug and told him she'd always be his friend. "Can you make it back to our den? I'll nurse you back to health."

Once they had made it back to the den, Luna sent Maverick to tell Sophia about what happened. Benjamin was worried about Bud. Even though he was his younger brother, Benjamin loved him like a son.

"Let's get you cleaned up," Luna said. "That mud wallow stopped the bleeding, like it was supposed to, but it will probably start again when you wash off. Why don't you shower while I run out to my herb garden. I need to get some yarrow to stop any bleeding and some goldenseal to prevent infection."

After Benjamin's shower, Luna placed the herbs on his wounds, then wrapped bandages around the herbs to help him heal. "You need to eat something," she said. "I'll make you some spinach with bacon. The spinach will help raise your iron level since you lost so much blood. You also need to drink plenty of water to rehydrate. We are so lucky you didn't die." Luna went out to collect a basket of spinach from her garden.

Benjamin's entire body was in pain. He was also depressed because of what he'd accidentally done to the farmer's wife. But he was grateful to Luna for helping him through it. *She truly is the best friend a bear could have,* he thought. *And she's right. I'm damn lucky to be alive.*

He knew he would need a lot of marijuana to control the pain, but he was running out. He had asked Maverick to stop by Farmer Brown's house and get all the marijuana out of the big drawer. He didn't tell him what was in the small drawer, though. He was guessing it was the same stuff Lucifer had given him. All he knew was the purple smoke had altered his mind. Once he felt better, he would go talk to Lucifer and ask him what the hell was in that marijuana.

After smoking a couple of cigars, the pain was easing up. Benjamin told Luna to roll one for herself. She said she didn't want to because she wasn't in any pain and didn't need one. Benjamin was proud of her for keeping the promise they had all made to Caesar.

Sophia burst into the den. "Oh my God, Benjamin, I thought I had lost you." She gave him a big bear hug. Benjamin screamed out in pain. She apologized for hurting him.

"It's okay," he said. "You just wanted to give me a hug. Oh, and here come my siblings!" Susie, Dottie, and Bud were all happy to see him. He told them they would no longer have to worry about fishing at Farmer Brown's pond, but he didn't say why or give any details.

He asked Luna to roll him another cigar. She said they were out of marijuana, but that Maverick would be back soon. All the cubs were eager to help Benjamin, especially Bud. Benjamin was grateful to have so much help, and he was especially grateful to Luna. If she hadn't found him at the pond, he might be dead now. He was feeling less groggy, but without any marijuana, the pain was getting worse.

Maverick came back with a huge bagful. Benjamin had never seen so much marijuana, but he knew they'd be supplied for quite some time. He asked if it had come from the big drawer, just to be sure. Maverick said yes and rolled a cigar for Benjamin. After smoking it, he was in much less pain.

Benjamin wanted to make sure no one would ever get ahold of the evil marijuana. As soon as he felt better, he would go to Farmer Brown's house, take all the laced marijuana out of the small drawer, and put it in a safe spot.

When suppertime came, Sophia and Luna told him to rest while they fixed the meal. Luna said the herbs she was cooking with would help the healing process. As soon as he stood up to join them at the supper table, a sharp burst of pain caused him to fall to the floor.

Luna and Sophia ran in and helped him back onto the bed. "You silly goose," Luna said. "You are staying in that bed for the next few days, and you're not getting up until you're fully healed."

"Yes, ma'am," Benjamin said, and thanked them for helping.

Luna brought his supper: a whole deer backstrap, a large bowl of spinach with bacon, and two loaves of sourdough bread. "Everything is high in iron," she said. "You'll be feeling better in no time." *A bear could get used to this kind of pampering,* Benjamin thought. *Especially from such a beautiful sow.*

They stayed with Luna and Maverick all week. Every day, Sophia would take the cubs to the pond to pass the time fishing. But now that Farmer Brown was dead, there was no one to restock the pond. Knowing it would take several years for any new fish to get to keeper size, they agreed to limit their fishing to no more than one fish per bear per day, with a twenty-two–inch size limit. That way, they could continue to fish at the pond, which was more fun than fishing in the stream.

Every day, they would bring back one or two fish. The largest one was twenty-five inches, but Bud kept saying the world-record trout was still out there and insisted he would catch it. They believed him.

Benjamin was in less pain with every passing day. Soon,

he was able to get out of bed and walk into the living room and kitchen. But he was still weak, so Luna insisted he lean on her while he moved about the den. He didn't mind that at all. In fact, he was feeling more comfortable being around her, even when she rubbed up against him. But he still had to keep telling himself they were just friends.

After a week, he was able to go outside with Luna's help. She stayed close to his side to make sure he was okay.

"Why don't we venture down to the pond, Luna? Everyone's down there today."

"That's a lot, Ben. Are you sure you're up to it?"

"I think so. If I get tired, I can sit down and rest."

The trip to the pond was exhausting, but they made it without stopping. Susie ran over right away and showed him a 23-inch trout she had caught. So far, that was the only keeper. Bud's pole was bent like he had a nibble, so Benjamin walked over, but Bud told him it was only the very large minnow he was using as bait.

"I have a big one!" Dottie screamed. The fish on her line was jumping all over the place and doing acrobatics. She pulled and pulled and finally managed to reel it in. At 28 inches and 10 pounds, it was quite a big rainbow trout, but not a record setter.

The action slowed down, and for the next hour, no one got any bites. As Benjamin lay there, he drifted off, only to be awakened minutes later.

"I got the world record!" Bud shouted. This time, he had braced himself against a tree to keep from being pulled in. The huge trout he had on the line was out of the water more than it was in. For over half an hour, he battled with it. Finally, Bud succeeded in wearing it out, and he hauled it up onto the bank. It was a remarkable 44 inches long and 38 pounds.

"Nice going, Bud! That's a world record for sure. It'll be a delicious supper tonight," Benjamin said.

"Oh no," Bud said. "I had so much fun catching that monster fish, I want to throw it back so someone else can do battle with it." Benjamin was proud of his little brother for thinking of other bears like that.

As they walked back to Luna's den, Benjamin told the bears he had recovered enough that tomorrow they would be able to go back to their own den. But tonight, they would have one last feast together.

As excited as Benjamin was about going back home, there was something he was dreading: meeting Lucifer again.

CHAPTER 27

Rest Before Meeting Lucifer

The next morning was bittersweet for Benjamin. They were finally going home, but that meant he had to leave his great friend Luna.

They enjoyed a nice breakfast before saying goodbye. Benjamin was almost back to normal now, and since he only needed about four cigarettes a day, he left half of the remaining marijuana with Luna and Maverick. They agreed to continue living by Caesar's rules and to give some, at no charge, to any bear in need.

On their way home, the bears stopped by the stream because the cubs were anxious to go fishing. After only an hour, Bud had caught fifteen native trout, Susie nine, and Dottie eight. They were practically masters of fishing now.

Their den was a mess when they walked in. "Looks like some raccoons found their way in while we were gone," Sophia said. "Cubs, give me a hand cleaning up, please. Benjamin, why don't you take a break and relax. You must be exhausted."

It was true. The journey to their den had been about five times as long as his painstaking trek down to the pond the other day, and he was beat. He was also in pain, so he lit up a cigar.

As he smoked, the pain melted away, and he reflected on recent events: Lucifer knocking on his door at midnight. Smoking the laced marijuana and killing Farmer Brown the next day. Being shot at close range. He wasn't mad about any of it, though, just glad that Farmer Brown was finally dead.

He hadn't forgotten about the small drawer, either. One day soon, he would go over and retrieve the contents of that drawer. He had the perfect hiding spot for it, too. No one else would ever know of its evil existence.

He had just fallen asleep when there was a loud knock on the door. Sophia went to answer it.

"If it's Lucifer, tell him I'll be over in about a week," Benjamin said. But instead of Lucifer's voice, he heard Tom's. He perked up and told them to come in.

Tom, Sue, and Jolene walked into his bedroom. "We missed you," Tom said. "We just wanted to stop by and visit."

"Strawberries are everywhere this time of year," Sue said, "so I made a hundred strawberry rhubarb pies. I brought you half of them because I know how much you like them."

That made Benjamin very happy. He asked Sophia to take the hog ribs out of the freezer so they could feast. He didn't have a smoker, but Tom said that with some flat rocks and red clay mud, he was sure they could make one that was better than anything they could buy.

Bud wanted to watch them build the smoker, so he followed Benjamin outside. As they worked, Benjamin told Tom about everything they'd been through lately.

"After we found Caesar dead," he said, "I went to see Lucifer, who gave me two cigars—"

"Wait a minute," Tom said. "Lucifer? You mean the devil?"

"No, this is just the hog farmer's son." He told Tom the whole story: smoking the laced marijuana with purple smoke, breaking down the front door, being shot five times by Farmer Brown, then killing him and eating his heart. Benjamin paused and tears rolled down his cheeks. "I accidentally killed his wife," he said. "I didn't mean to. She had done nothing wrong. But I had no control after smoking that laced marijuana. I didn't know my own strength, and I killed her."

Tom was in shock. "My God, Ben. You have truly been to hell and back since I saw you last."

"Bud, I'm sorry you had to hear all that," Benjamin said, realizing he had told the story in front of his little brother for the first time.

"I can handle it," Bud said. "I'm growing into a big bear

now. I'm just glad you're okay and that damn bastard is dead."

"Bud! You may be a big bear, but not big enough to be using that language yet."

"Sorry, Brother. I'll wait until I'm older."

Soon, they had built a beautiful, functioning smoker. Benjamin knew of an old, dead apple tree they could use for firewood. Tom told Benjamin to stay and relax with Bud while he went to gather some wood. When he came back, they built the fire and let it bake the red clay until it hardened.

Bud pointed at the fire. "Look, Ben! Purple smoke!" He laughed his head off at his own joke.

They went inside and joined Sophia and Sue, who were chatting while the cubs played with each other on the floor. In the kitchen, they seasoned the ribs. Benjamin's mouth was watering remembering how tasty and tender they were last time. Since they weren't in a rush this time, they could cook them slower and make an even more delicious batch.

Back outside, they placed the ribs on the racks in the smoker. By now, all the red clay had hardened into brick. They had even fashioned a damper to allow them to adjust the heat. They set it at the perfect low and slow temperature.

"You couldn't have picked a better time to come by," Benjamin said as they watched the smoker.

"I figured you could use the company. How are you feeling, by the way?"

"I'm in some pain but not as much as before," Benjamin said. He lit a cigarette and took a drag. "It's amazing how fast this stuff takes the pain away."

The smoker seemed to be working well, so the bears went back into the den, where the smell of sourdough hit them. Sophia and Sue told them to relax while they finished preparing the food. Benjamin smelled spinach, which he liked, but since he had been eating it every day, he was getting bored of it. As much as he would have loved some fried taters, Luna had ordered him to eat one or two servings of spinach every day.

Every thirty minutes, Benjamin and Tom stepped

outside to baste the ribs. *Good God Almighty*, Benjamin thought. *These ribs are smelling and looking good.* Once they were done to falling-off-the-bone perfection, supper was served. The ribs were to die for. Sue then heated each of them a strawberry rhubarb pie in the oven for dessert.

Tom and Sue stayed for the next week, and they went to the pond to fish almost every day. The minnow Bud was using was almost as big as the fish everyone else was catching, but he was hoping to face off with the world-record rainbow trout again. Tom could hardly believe it when Benjamin told him about Bud catching that fish.

As the others fished, Benjamin pulled Tom aside. "Would you mind coming with me to Farmer Brown's house? It's not far from here, and there's something I need to take care of." Tom said he would, and they set off.

On the way over, Benjamin told him about the two drawers. "Maverick already emptied the big drawer," he said. "But I need to get rid of whatever evil marijuana is in the small drawer. I don't ever want this forest to go through the same hell Samuel and Maverick put us through."

"Are you going to destroy it by throwing it in a fire?" Tom asked.

"No," Benjamin said. "I have a special hiding spot where it will always be kept safe." Tom said he thought burning it would be a better idea, but hiding it was better than nothing.

They walked up to the old Victorian farmhouse. "This is a creepy-ass place," Tom said. Benjamin agreed.

Inside, they found the marijuana drawers. The big drawer was still open from when Maverick had emptied it. The small drawer had a padlock on it, but one smack of Benjamin's paw broke it right off. The drawer was stuffed full of possum bags, and he noticed the laced marijuana had a different color than the marijuana he was used to smoking. He gathered up all the bags, and they headed back to the pond.

The cubs had caught four rainbow trout, and now they were jumping in the water to play. Bud wanted to join them, so he asked Tom to keep an eye on his fishing pole. Benjamin told the cubs to go to the other side of the pond to play so they wouldn't scare the fish over here. Minutes later, Tom's pole bent in half. As he struggled to reel the fish in, Bud saw what was happening and came over to watch. The fight lasted for thirty minutes.

When Tom finally brought it in, Bud looked at him and grinned. "Looks like you and me are the only ones who know how to catch the world-record trout, Tom."

Tom gave Bud a fist bump, then unhooked the massive fish and released it for others to enjoy in the future.

"Sue, Jolene, and I will have to head home tomorrow morning," Tom said as they hiked back to the den. "But it's been really great spending the whole week with my blood brother." He added that he had found two other dens, if ever they decided to come over to his county. "It's a safe harbor from bear hunting, as you know."

"Living there would be wonderful in so many ways," Benjamin said. "But I think our home is here."

After supper, they sat up and talked for half the night. The cubs were having a great time playing until Sophia told them it was time for bed soon. Sophia took out the storybook and sat the cubs down to listen. Sue asked where the book had come from, and Sophia told her that Ben had found it outside Farmer Brown's house, believing it to be Caesar's.

During story time, Benjamin walked away and showed Tom where he was hiding the laced marijuana. He told him it would always be safe because it was a hiding spot no one knew existed.

"After you leave tomorrow, I'm going across the mountain to see Lucifer," Benjamin said.

Tom looked concerned. "Do you want me to go with you? After everything you've told me, I don't trust that guy."

"No," Benjamin said. "It's just the farmer's son. He's harmless. I'll be fine."

CHAPTER 28

Unearthing Lucifer

The next morning after breakfast, the bears said goodbye and parted ways. It had been a good week. Having Tom's family around really helped Benjamin during his recovery, and he was also happy to have a smoker now, so he could barbecue ribs whenever he wanted. Plus, they needed the company after experiencing the horror of Caesar's murder.

Benjamin was happy that Farmer Brown had gotten what he deserved, but he was still in distress knowing he had killed the farmer's wife. Fortunately, he still had plenty of the farmer's marijuana to help him deal with the guilt he was feeling.

When Benjamin told his mother he was going to see Lucifer, she was concerned. "I think you should heal more before making the trip over the mountain to see him," she said.

"This is something I've been needing to do for a while now," Benjamin said. "But don't worry, I'm feeling up to it."

"You've always taken your responsibilities seriously," she said. "We'll be hoping for the best."

Bud said he wanted to come, but Benjamin told him he was needed at home to keep his sisters in line. That made him very happy. Bear hugs were given all around, and Benjamin headed out the door.

After hiking over the mountain and down the trail on the other side, Benjamin arrived at the farmhouse. He stayed low and hidden at the edge of the woods, even though there was no one in sight. Except for the crowing of roosters, clucking of chickens, and mooing of cows, everything was quiet.

At that moment, a young woman walked up to the

farmhouse and knocked on the door. Lucifer answered, and she stepped inside. Benjamin thought it must be Lucifer's girlfriend. He remembered Lucifer being upset at his father after he was grounded for sneaking off to see her. Through the windows, Benjamin could see them moving into the living room.

One of the windows was open, so Benjamin made his way over and crouched under the windowsill. Again, he picked up that familiar scent from the day Caesar was murdered. Feeling brave, he lifted his head just enough to peer inside.

"Ann, I'm so glad you're here," Lucifer was saying. "We never get to see each other because of my stupid dad. But I think I'm falling in love with you."

"Aww, Lucifer. You're the sweetest guy ever, and I'm falling in love with you, too. Maybe someday I could be the farmer's wife?" She batted her eyes, then sat down on the couch. "Speaking of your dad, where is he?"

"Don't worry about him." Lucifer sat down next to her and kissed her. "He's not here right now."

As they kissed, they whispered into each other's ears. It was hard to hear, but Benjamin assumed they were talking about how much they loved each other.

"I want you," Lucifer said. "Right now."

"Please, Lucifer, take me now. Before I change my mind." She took her blouse off and unhooked her red lace bra. Lucifer suckled on her breasts, much like a bear would drink milk from its mother.

She moaned. "I've been saving myself for the right man, and that's you. Let's do it." She ripped his red flannel shirt off, exposing his muscular chest, then unzipped his blue jeans and pulled them off. She sat on top of him, and the two began to move in rhythm with each other.

Benjamin had never witnessed humans making love, but it was quite different from the way bears did it. *I think I like the human way better*, he thought. *Then: What am I saying? I've never even been with another bear*. He had seen his parents do it before, but it was nothing like this.

When they were finished, they lay with each other on the couch for a short while before Lucifer drifted off. As he slept, Ann got up from the couch, put her clothes back on, and walked into the other room. Moments later, a bone-chilling scream erupted. Benjamin heard footsteps as she ran into the next room. Another earsplitting scream. He couldn't imagine what was going on.

Lucifer woke up. "Ann? Ann, are you okay?"

She was crying. Benjamin walked around to the back of the house so he could get closer to where she was. Luckily, that window was also open. Lucifer had just come into the room.

Ann was shaking and sobbing. "Your dad. He's ... dead, Lucifer. I saw him lying dead on the floor. And then I came in here and now I see ... your mom. Also dead. What the hell is going on?"

Lucifer didn't seem disturbed. He tried to put his arms around Ann, but she threw them off.

"Don't put your hands on me right now," she snapped. "Why aren't you upset? Did you know your parents were dead?"

Lucifer backed off and sat down on a chair in the corner of the room. "Yes," he said. "Yes, I knew."

She raised her voice. "And you weren't going to fucking tell me this when I first got here? Who even are you? What the hell is going on here?"

From his hiding place under the window, Benjamin had the same questions. He remembered Tom saying he didn't trust Lucifer. Now, Benjamin was second-guessing his own judgment. *How could my instincts have been so bad?*

"Tell me everything, Lucifer," Ann said. "Right now. If you want me to ever have anything to do with you again, I need to know everything—and I mean everything—about how they died."

"Okay," Lucifer said. He closed his eyes for a few moments, then opened them. "I hated my dad. I hated him because he wanted to keep us apart. He told me you were way too good for me and said he would never let us be together. Every day, I hated him more and more."

Ann sank down onto the bed.

"Also, I had big plans for this farm, which he didn't approve of. I wanted to make some serious money. Fuck the pigs. Fuck the cows. I wanted to be like Farmer Brown and grow marijuana for a living. But my dad said no way. He said this has been a hog and beef farm for three generations now, and he would never change that. It made me so damn mad that he wouldn't let me follow my dreams. The difference between me and Farmer Brown is that he mainly sold plain marijuana that wasn't laced. But he did keep one small drawer full of marijuana laced with PCP. He'd only sell it to select customers, and at a huge premium. He knew it could be harmful, but the high prices helped keep his farm afloat. He had a big heart and would give away his marijuana to anyone who really needed it, like if they were depressed or in pain. The only time he didn't have a huge heart was if he caught someone fishing in his pond, taking his trout. He loved the pond. He loved taking his wife there to sit and relax and fish. But big heart or not, I needed him dead."

Ann stared at him, still trembling. "Why?"

"Because with Farmer Brown out of the picture, my marijuana farm would have a much better chance of succeeding."

"So you killed him."

"No. I couldn't, because that would be murder, and if I was caught, I'd go to jail for the rest of my life. So I came up with a plan. The first step was to kill Caesar."

"Who the hell is Caesar?"

"He was a bear that sold marijuana to other bears. Since he—"

"Bears smoke marijuana?" Ann looked confused.

Lucifer ignored her question. "Since Caesar was just a bear, it wouldn't be murder, just a fine and a slap on the wrist if I was caught. From there, I walked to Farmer Brown's house, knowing the other bears would follow my scent there and think Farmer Brown was the culprit. I even took a children's storybook and placed it outside his house. Then, I went back the way I came, jumped into the stream to hide my scent, and followed the stream a ways before I got out and sat against a tree, soaking wet. I figured it wouldn't be long until a bear came along to kill Farmer Brown. That wouldn't be murder, just a violent act of nature. That's when Benjamin—he's another bear—came by. Except Benjamin didn't kill him, he just bought some marijuana off the farmer's wife. I wanted to make sure he knew that Farmer Brown had killed Caesar, so later that night, I went to his den."

Benjamin was getting angry listening to Lucifer's story. He felt betrayed.

"Benjamin said he would come see me the next day, and that's when I gave him my special blend of marijuana, which was laced with PCP, cocaine, and LSD. That's the one with the purple smoke. I have eight blends altogether, like orange, which is laced with PCP, and green, which contains highly concentrated fentanyl. Anyway, Ben smoked the purple stuff and went completely out of his mind. He couldn't wait to kill Farmer Brown."

Lucifer stood up and walked toward Ann. She stood up from the bed.

"That brings me to good old Dad," he said. "He had to die, Ann, so that we could be together." He reached his arm out to touch her.

"Get your fucking hands off of me!" She swatted his arm away. "I'm in total shock right now. I don't understand any of this."

"It's actually pretty simple. I gave Dad my special green blend, with the fentanyl. After a few puffs, he was gone. And then I—"

"Never touch me again!" Ann shrieked. "You're the fucking devil!" She grabbed her things and ran out of the house.

As Benjamin stood up to leave, he knocked over a flower planter.

"Hey! Who's out there?" Lucifer yelled.

Benjamin took off in a sprint and ran up the trail without looking back, not knowing whether Lucifer had seen him.

A few minutes later, he heard Ann crying. She was sitting on a rock just off the trail. When she saw Benjamin coming toward her, her eyes widened. Shakily, she stood and started backing up.

"It's okay," Benjamin said. "I'm a friendly bear. My name is Benjamin. I just saw everything that happened. I'm so sorry you got involved with that devil. Can I walk you home?"

Ann relaxed a little. "Thank you, but no. I can't go home now. Not like this."

"Come back to our den, then. You can meet my mom and my little brother and sisters. They're a lot of fun."

Ann thought that was better than sitting on a rock in the woods, so they set off on the trail together.

When they arrived, Sophia was surprised. "Who is this?" she said. "We've never had a human in our den before!" She looked more closely at Benjamin. "You look horrible, Ben. I can tell something is wrong. What's going on?"

"The way I feel right now, I can't talk about it," he said. "I've just learned the most disturbing news of my life." He went straight for the marijuana and rolled two huge cigars.

"Well, I'm here," Sophia said, "whenever you need to talk. Can I do anything to help you two right now?"

"Would you mind rolling us eight more cigars? I think between the two of us, we're going to need it."

She looked at him for a few seconds. "You're not going to do anything drastic, are you?"

"It's too hard to talk about now, but I promise I'll tell you all about it tomorrow."

But tomorrow, Benjamin knew, was the day it must happen. The forest was in grave danger, and it was up to him and Ann to save it by sending the devil back to hell.

CHAPTER 29

Sending Lucifer to Hell

After a sleepless night, Benjamin told Bud to take the cubs outside for the morning. "I want to see how well y'all can survive by yourselves," he said. "Bud, I'm putting you in charge of Susie and Dottie. I'm giving you a pack of matches, so any game you kill or fish you catch, you can cook. You can't come back until noon. You've all grown up a lot, so I know you can handle this."

"Okay," Bud said. "I accept this challenge, but I know you're just doing this to get rid of us so you can talk with the adults. I don't know what happened with Lucifer yesterday, but it must have been really bad."

"You're right, Bud. We all need to talk. But I know you and your sisters can pass this little test."

Sophia saw the cubs off, then turned to Benjamin. "All right, I don't have a clue what's going on. I couldn't sleep last night, and I know you couldn't either. You were up rolling cigars every hour or two. You weren't even like this after being shot five times by Farmer Brown. I'm not here to judge you, I just want to help you get through whatever happened yesterday. And you've always been firm on not bringing humans into our den, not even Rob or Dale!"

Sophia turned to Ann. "I truly feel for you, Ann. It broke my heart to hear you crying all night. I know you're not any sort of threat to us, or Ben wouldn't have brought you here. But I'm here to help you, too."

"Thank you, Sophia."

"Even though I was hurt yesterday, Ann was devastated," Benjamin said. "So I think it would be easier if I told this story." He looked at Ann, and she nodded.

"I went to Lucifer's house yesterday to let him know I had done the deed of killing ..." He thought of the farmer's wife and tears formed in his eyes. "Killing Farmer Brown. But I also wanted to find out what that marijuana was laced with."

Benjamin told Sophia about how Ann had discovered the dead bodies of Lucifer's parents, and how when she confronted him about it, he admitted to killing them.

"But what makes this so terrible is that Lucifer was the man Ann thought she'd be with forever," Benjamin said. "So one minute she's in love, the next minute she finds out her lover is the devil."

Ann was sobbing Benjamin handed her a tissue and asked if she wanted him to stop telling the story.

"No," she said, dabbing her eyes. "It's good to talk this out. But then we have to come up with a plan. Lucifer must die."

He went on, telling Sophia that Lucifer had murdered Caesar in a scheme to get Benjamin to kill Farmer Brown.

"As it turns out, Farmer Brown was actually a good guy. He just didn't like anyone messing with his trout. Knowing what I know now, I feel so bad about killing him. Lucifer is pure evil. I agree with Ann. We need to go and kill him now."

"As much as I want to see him dead right now," Ann said, "I think we should take a few days to clear our minds and make a plan before we send him to hell. We need to come up with a way for him to die at his own hands."

"This ordeal shouldn't have ever happened," Sophia said. "I support both of you through this. Would it be easier if I took the cubs to stay with Lucy and James while you work through your plans?"

Benjamin and Ann agreed it would be easier not having the cubs around. At noon, when they came back from their survival adventure, the cubs were excited to hear they were going over to stay with Patches and Lucille.

Once she and Benjamin were alone, Ann laid out the plan she had in mind. Then, they spent the next three days going through it again and again, practicing their roles, and thinking about it from every angle until it was absolutely airtight, or so they hoped. To celebrate—or to go out with a bang in case their plan failed—Benjamin wanted to get all his friends and family together for a picnic at the pond the next day.

When he and Ann woke up the next morning, they went to Lucy's and told them to grab their fishing poles. The next stop was Luna's den, then Angel's. At each stop, he introduced Ann but only said they had become friends due to circumstances beyond their control.

At the pond, everyone was having a good time. Benjamin had packed a huge picnic basket for everyone to enjoy. Bud sat in his favorite spot with a twenty-inch minnow lure on his hook, hoping to reel in the world record again. The other cubs were using worms or small minnows, and they had already caught three keepers. But they soon got bored and skipped over to the opposite side of the pond to play. Bud went to join them, and asked Ann to keep an eye on his fishing pole, letting her know she just might catch the world-record rainbow trout.

While the cubs were gone, Benjamin and Ann told the older bears they had worked out a plan to kill Lucifer.

"Lucifer?" Angel said, eyes wide. "You mean the devil?"

Sophia spoke up. "I can tell you that this man is the devil himself. From what I know, he has done terrible things, and killing him will make the forest safer."

Benjamin told the bears he couldn't say too much right now but assured them he would let them know more when the time was right.

The groups headed back to their dens, except Lucy's family, who came over to stay at least until Benjamin and Ann had completed their mission. They had a nice supper that night, and Ann even made blueberry pies for dessert.

The next morning, Benjamin and Ann weren't hungry. Even though they were confident in their plan, they still had nerves. After smoking a cigar each and taking four more for the road, they said goodbye to everyone.

Ann freaked out when she saw the farmhouse, so

Benjamin gave her another cigar. The plan was for Benjamin to stay outside until she gave the signal for him to come in.

"I'll be watching," he said, "and if anything goes wrong, I'll be there for you."

Ann walked up to the front door and knocked.

"Ann?" Lucifer said when he opened the door. "What are you doing here?"

"I was angry at you, Lucifer. But I thought about it, and I really love the idea of being a rich marijuana farmer. I had saved myself for you, and that night, I made a commitment to you. I'm not ready to fully be with you yet, but if everything goes well, I will be totally committed to this relationship."

"Oh, Ann. I thought I'd lost you forever. Please come in. Since we're going to be farmers together, I have something to show you."

CB

Lucifer led Ann into the living room and gestured at a large piece of furniture.

"This is my marijuana cabinet," he said. "It can store up to twenty different types of laced marijuana along with the supplies to make each one."

He opened it up to show Ann. Inside were bins of different sizes, each containing its own type of laced marijuana.

"And here is everything to lace it with," he said, pulling out some PCP, cocaine, LSD, ketamine, and two different concentrations of fentanyl. He also showed her the additives he used to give each type its own color of smoke. "I've started making them already, as you can see, and I labeled each bin with a color."

"I love how organized you are, Lucifer," Ann said. "I believe this may work out for us."

Lucifer kissed her, which made Ann want to puke, but for the sake of the plan, she let him. Lucifer smiled.

Ann smiled, too. This was going better than she had

expected. "You've got me steamed up," she said, pretending to fan herself. "I think I need a little fresh air, Lucifer. Don't move. I'll be right back."

ᙏ

Ann came outside and stood there for a minute or two, then disappeared back inside. That was Benjamin's cue. He waited ten minutes, then walked up to the house and knocked on the door.

Lucifer answered. "Well, hello, Ben!"

"Hey, Lucifer." He looked at Ann. "Who's this over here?"

"Ben, meet my girlfriend, Ann."

"Hello, Ann. What happened, Lucifer? I thought your dad didn't approve of her."

Lucifer stared at him for a few moments. "Oh yeah, well ... he's changed his mind."

"Listen, I need to talk to you about Farmer Brown." He glanced at Ann again. "I mean, alone."

"Ann's my girlfriend, Ben. Anything you want to talk about, you can talk about in front of her."

"Okay then. Well, when I went over to kill Farmer Brown, I first saw his wife, who said her husband was not the one who killed Caesar. I didn't believe her, so I killed her. Then, Farmer Brown came in and shot me five times, and I went after him, but I passed out before I could kill him. Anyway, he nursed me back to health, then told me that you, Lucifer, had set him up. He said it was *you* who dropped the book outside their house."

Lucifer shook his head as he listened to Benjamin. "None of that is true."

"Well, he said he was at Caesar's making a delivery that day, and he saw you kill him, even though you didn't see him. Of course, we all know Farmer Brown is dead now. That's because I was so angry at him for shooting me that I killed him and ate his heart. But here's my question, because I've been thinking about what the old man told me. *Was* it you who killed Caesar?"

"No! Farmer Brown lied to you." He turned around. "Ann? I think Benjamin needs a little marijuana to calm down. Get him a green one, if you will. That should help him relax. And get us some of the white smoke ones."

Ann walked to the cabinet to prepare the cigars. She knew exactly what to do. In Benjamin's cigar, she used the pure marijuana plus an additive for green smoke, but no fentanyl. Then she prepared two with white smoke for herself and Lucifer, except to Lucifer's cigar, she added a double dose of the highest concentration of fentanyl.

"By the way," Benjamin said. "What was in that purple smoke marijuana, anyway? That was some good stuff."

"Oh, that had some PCP, LSD, and cocaine. I also—"

"Here we go." Ann walked in and handed out the cigars. Benjamin lit his and took a draw. Green smoke rose as he exhaled.

"Lucifer, my sweetie," Ann said, "can you please light mine for me?"

He lit Ann's cigar, then his own. A smile spread across his face as he watched the green smoke swirling around Benjamin's head. "You did real good, Ann. Real good. He should be relaxed very soon here."

Benjamin took another drag and fell to the floor. Lucifer beamed. His scheme had worked. He had killed Benjamin.

Ann looked at Lucifer. "Let's both take a big drag," she said.

Lucifer breathed deep. Exhaled. And again. Then he fell to the floor.

He looked up, eyes half open. "Ann," he croaked. "What have you done?"

"I'm sending you to hell, you fucking bastard."

Lucifer's eyes closed, and he stopped breathing.

Benjamin stood up and smiled. "Great work, Ann. Your plan worked perfectly."

"Yes," she said. "I knew I had to remain strong, but truthfully, I wanted to puke from the second I walked in the door."

CHAPTER 30

Reflection and Tranquility

Benjamin asked Ann if he wanted him to walk her home. She said she needed some time before she went home and talked to her parents about what she had done, so Benjamin invited her back to the den.

They used the walk back to talk over what had just happened. They needed time to heal from what Lucifer had done to both of them. They were sad for what he had taken from them, but they felt at peace now that the deed was done.

Back at the den, Sophia was relieved to see them. At the same time, she was still worried about them and had a lot of questions. They told her they weren't up for answering questions yet and would need a little time to heal mentally.

Sophia and Lucy prepared lunch while Benjamin and Ann each had a cigar. Soon, the den smelled of fresh sourdough bread, fried country ham, green beans, and potatoes. Adding to this was the aroma of warm berry cobbler from the oven.

Despite the sorrow in their hearts, Benjamin and Ann both had feelings of inner peace. But Ann, he knew, would need more time to heal. Her dream was to be a farmer's wife, helping to raise chickens, cows, and pigs. That was what had drawn her to Lucifer in the first place. But Lucifer had cruelly pulled the wool over her eyes, blinding her to what a terrible person he was. And in the end, she had given up her innocence to the devil.

Benjamin felt regret and sorrow for killing Farmer Brown and his wife. Only time would lessen his pain. The big mistake he had made was not thinking everything through. Now that he thought about it, he realized the scent he had followed to Farmer Brown's house didn't go all the way up to the porch. And every time he had gone to Lucifer's farm, he smelled the same scent but didn't make the connection. He had been so blinded by the hate in his heart after losing Caesar, that his mind, in its need to blame someone, made Farmer Brown the killer no matter what anyone said. He should have listened to what his nose was trying to tell him. He could have prevented all this from happening. And he would have, if he didn't have so much hate for Farmer Brown in the first place. He knew the guilt would plague him for some time.

He and Ann had one more cigar before lunch. After lunch, the older bears sent the cubs outside so they could talk to Benjamin and Ann about how they had killed Lucifer.

"Ann, that was a brilliant plan," James said after they had told the story. "And kudos for following through even though it made you sick."

"I second that," Sophia said. "You're such a strong person to be able to control your emotions well enough to pull this off."

Ann nodded. "Thanks. I wanted to puke the whole time I was in the house. And when he kissed me, I really thought I would. It wasn't easy to hold it together, but I wanted him dead, so I didn't have a choice."

Lucy chimed in. "You took the devil out of this world, Ann. You're the real hero. You made our forest so much safer."

The rest of their day and evening was quiet, but the next day, they invited Luna's and Angel's families to stroll to the pond. As the families walked, Benjamin and Ann shared the details of all that had happened.

For Benjamin, it felt good to be in nature with friends and family again. In fact, he was much more at peace than the last time they had converged on the pond. It brought him great relief to know that Lucifer, the devil in the flesh, was dead. He would still need marijuana for a few more days, but he'd wean himself off soon.

The cubs caught several keepers—none of which were world records, sadly—but threw them right back. Their freezers were already full of food, so they didn't feel the need to end the lives of any trout today. All they wanted was a nice, peaceful day, and they got it. The forest was already feeling safer and more tranquil, Benjamin thought. But still, knowing chase season was approaching worried him.

The next morning, Lucy and her family went back home to their den, while Benjamin, Sophia, Ann, and the cubs went to visit Tom. Benjamin couldn't wait. He and Tom were the best of friends, and he loved spending time with him. Bud loved Tom, too, especially after they bonded over that world-record trout.

The trees along the way were full of acorns again this year, and they ate as many as they could while they walked. With all that food, they would be fat and happy this fall.

Tom was starting a fire in his smoker when they walked up. "Look who's here!" he said, smiling. "Looks like I'll have to get more ribs out for everyone. Who is this you have with you?"

Benjamin introduced him to Ann. "I'll tell you more about her later," he said. "But it looks like we came on the right day. Love me some of Tom's barbecue ribs!"

They walked inside, where Sue was preparing food for supper. She was surprised to see them.

"I hope you don't mind us stopping by," Sophia said. She introduced Ann as Benjamin's friend.

"Nice to meet you," Sue said. "I'm just fixing some fried taters and onions."

Ann asked if she could help, and Sue gladly accepted the offer.

In the living room, Susie had found the children's storybook. She opened it up and read "Three Little Kittens" aloud to all the cubs except for Bud, who was outside helping with the barbecue.

Supper was a feast for all. Afterward, Benjamin and Ann told the story of Lucifer again. It was healing for them to talk about it, and they both hoped it would help them get back to their normal selves, if that was even possible.

Ann talked about how she had allowed Lucifer to take

her innocence because she thought they had a future together. But after finding out he had killed his own parents, she realized she didn't know him at all. He was only what she wanted him to be and what he wanted her to think he was.

Benjamin told of his own ordeal, how Lucifer used him as a pawn in his scheme to kill Farmer Brown. When Tom and Sue learned that Lucifer was Caesar's killer, they were shocked.

Tom looked at Ann. "So, what happens now?"

"I need to tell my family about this," Ann said. "I'm sure my mom, dad, and brother are worried about me because they know nothing yet. But I haven't been able to face them since this all happened."

"For now, why don't we relax a little?" Tom said. "I know of a nice catfish pond nearby." The bears were excited about the idea, so they packed up and headed out.

Tom didn't have enough fishing poles for everyone, so they had to share. But the fishing was so good that they managed to load up four baskets of catfish before it was time to go back to the den.

After they left Tom's den the next morning, Ann announced she was ready to go talk to her family. "Will y'all come with me, please?"

"Of course we will," Benjamin said. "We're here for anything you need."

"When we get there, try to stay hidden until I warn my parents that a family of bears will be coming into their home."

They stayed at the edge of the woods while Ann went inside. A few minutes later, she came out and walked over to them. "Okay, we're ready. My mom passed out when I told her I had made friends with a family of bears, but she said you can come in."

"Well, I've seen everything now!" Ann's mom said. "My daughter can truly make friends with anyone. I was afraid she was dead. Lucifer's older brother, Dominic, came by to check on Ann. He had found a murder-suicide scene at their house. Apparently, Lucifer murdered his parents, then took his own life."

Benjamin and Ann looked at each other.

Ann's mom went on. "I know his dad didn't approve of Ann, but that seems a little extreme. Dominic told me they had found high levels of fentanyl in all their bodies. Ann, I was so afraid you were somehow caught up in all this."

"Actually, Mom, I was." Ann looked at Benjamin again, then told the story. "Lucifer did kill his parents. But he also killed Caesar, a well-known bear, then tricked Ben into killing Farmer Brown. He took my innocence, knowing I loved him and would do anything for him. When Dominic found the murder-suicide scene, that was only half right. There was no suicide." She looked at Benjamin again. "It was Benjamin and I who killed Lucifer by giving him marijuana laced with fentanyl."

Ann's parents were in shock. Her mom came over and hugged her and they cried together. "I can't believe this happened to you, Ann. What a true-life nightmare."

"I hate that bastard," she sobbed. "I saved myself for the one I thought I would spend my life with. I don't know if I can ever be with another man, the way I feel now."

"No one else needs to know the true story," her dad said. "If it's believed to be a murder-suicide, then it shall remain that way." They all agreed with this.

"Thanks for coming by, everyone," Ann said, drying her eyes. "I appreciate the moral support. I didn't know how my mom and dad were going to react." She looked at her parents. "No offense. I can see now that you're here for me."

Benjamin told her she was welcome to visit anytime, and she assured them she would. "You're welcome here anytime, too, you know."

Ann's mom laughed. "And I promise I won't pass out next time."

Over a nice meal at the den, Benjamin talked about how happy he was that life was starting to get back to normal. After supper, he sat in the living room and lit up a marijuana cigarette. *From now on*, he thought, *I'll only need an occasional smoke.*

As he relaxed, his mind again turned to chase season. He knew it was coming up, but when he looked at the calendar, he saw it would be starting in just a few days. The horrible prospect of having to run from hounds and worry about his family and friends made him shudder.

He rolled himself another one.

CHAPTER 31

Training Season and Maverick

hase season, the bears' second-most hated time of year, had arrived. After a filling breakfast, Benjamin had no sooner stepped outside than he was greeted by the unnerving sound of barking dogs. He could tell they were across the road and over near Luna and Maverick's den. He could also tell it was a pack of eight or so. *Are they chasing Luna?* Worried for his friend, Benjamin ran off in the direction of the noise to see if he could help.

The barking only grew louder as the hounds picked up the scent. Now they were crossing Stone Coal Gap Road and heading up the ridge he and Sophia lived on. Moments later, Benjamin caught sight of Maverick sprinting through the trees. The hounds weren't far behind. *Maverick needs to stop and fight the dogs*, was all Benjamin could think. Instead, Maverick continued to run as the hounds closed in on him.

Benjamin ran down and intercepted the pack, smacking the last three dogs good and hard as they ran by. Stunned, they turned around and headed back to the road. But the others were still chasing Maverick. Benjamin didn't think he could catch up with them in time to help.

The dogs closed in on Maverick and ran him up a tree. Voices drifted from the top of the mountain. "That was a great run!" one of the hunters said. "I hope the first day of kill season goes that well," said another.

By now, Benjamin was only a few hundred yards below Maverick and the dogs. Maverick was fifty feet up in a big oak tree, and five dogs were jumping and clawing at the base of the tree, barking with every breath.

The hunters arrived. "Good dogs," one said as he petted

the hounds and put them on their leads. "You do that during kill season, and y'all will be having prime rib for supper."

Once the hunters had shuffled off down the mountain, Benjamin ran over to the tree. Maverick was shaken up, but at least he was alive. "Thanks, Ben," he said. "I saw you smack those dogs that were chasing me. You're so much braver than I am. I'm too afraid to turn around and fight them, so I just keep running."

Benjamin shrugged. "I don't know what to tell you, Maverick. If you want to live through kill season, you'll have to learn to fight dogs. Once you run up a tree, you're a sitting duck. If this were kill season, you'd be dead right now."

Benjamin was worried about Maverick and knew it was only a matter of time before this would happen again, which was why he felt the need to give him such a stern lecture.

The very next week, it happened again. Benjamin heard the hounds in Maverick and Luna's area and hurried over to see if anyone needed help. This time, the dogs were chasing not just Maverick, but also Luna, Susan, and Heather. As Maverick ran, he kept straight while Luna and the cubs made a sudden right turn into some thick laurel and pines. Some of the dogs kept going after Maverick, but the others followed Luna and the cubs.

Just as the dogs caught up with Heather, Benjamin jumped in and smacked one of them halfway down the hillside, where it lay motionless, probably dead. The other two came toward Benjamin. He charged them and swatted the first one so hard, its head nearly popped off. His next swing wounded the last dog, who decided he didn't want to fight anymore and ran off.

Luna was crying. "Thank you, Ben. You saved my Heather." The sound of dogs barking ferociously in the distance confirmed Maverick had been treed.

"It's just training season now," Benjamin said, "but I'm scared that Maverick's not going to make it through kill season."

"I know," she said. She wiped tears from her eyes.

The dogs were quiet now as the hunters led them away. But Benjamin knew that any minute now, they would discover the dogs he had killed.

"Let's get out of here," Benjamin said. "I'll come to your den. I'm sure that's where Maverick is going after this, and I need to talk to him."

Maverick arrived back at the den an hour later. Benjamin was furious. "What the hell happened, Maverick? Why didn't you stay and protect your family?"

Maverick looked down. "I guess I thought all the dogs would follow me," he said.

"I *know* you thought the dogs would follow you, because you *always* think you can outrun them. How the fuck is that working out for you?" Benjamin took a deep breath and tried to keep from shouting. "Do you realize Heather would be dead right now if I hadn't come to fight your fight? How do you think Luna would feel without Heather? As the boar bear, *you* are responsible for your family. Your family should always be in *front* of you while you stay back to fight the dogs off."

Maverick was upset at himself. "You're right. I'm just not good at protecting myself and others like you are, Ben. I see now that the hounds will always outrun me, and I have to fight them to stay alive and protect those I love. I'll try harder next time."

Outside, the hunters were shouting. "That damn bear killed two more of my dogs!" one screamed. "I will *make sure* he dies next time we tree him. I don't care what season it is. He is dead. I'll take great pleasure in shooting that son of a bitch and leaving him to be picked apart by the buzzards."

Maverick glared at Benjamin. "See, Ben? See what fighting gets you? Now they think it was me who killed their dogs, and they want to kill *me*."

"What I'm saying is that if you stand up and fight, Maverick, then you won't need to run up a tree, and they'll never know which bear it was who attacked and killed their dogs."

Maverick sighed. "Yeah, I guess you're right. I will fight

next time. And I'll make sure my family is in front while I stay back to fight the dogs. My family is the most important thing in the world. Truly, I would be lost without Luna, Susan, and Heather."

ଔଓ

The next time the hounds chased Maverick and his family, they stayed together for about half a mile before Maverick told Luna and the cubs to run ahead and cross the road.

"I'll stay here and fight!" Maverick yelled. He found a blown-down tree with an exposed root ball, which he thought was the perfect place to do battle with the hounds. This time, there were eleven dogs, and they had no fear of Maverick. Two of them jumped toward him, and with one vigorous swipe of his paw, Maverick sent both dogs flying twenty-five feet back. One was injured, and the other was dead. Three more attacked him, and one by one, Maverick pulled the dogs toward him and finished them off with his powerful jaw. The remaining six dogs stayed back, but they had him trapped. He charged a few times, but the dogs were too far away for him to catch one.

In the distance, trucks approached. He had to get out of there. He charged again, and this time, he managed to smack and kill one of the dogs. *Bang! Bang!* Shots fired. He ran up the mountain as bullets whizzed by his head.

"That bear is as good as dead!" one of the hunters yelled, picking up his radio. "Attention all hunter groups! There is a bear killing all of my dogs. Any hunter who sees this bear, please kill it on the spot."

Maverick had escaped his first successful fight not just with his life, but a little more confidence as well. For the rest of chase season, Maverick did a great job of protecting his family. Still, he tried his best not to kill any more dogs so as not to anger the hunters.

ଔଓ

Benjamin was proud of how Maverick had stepped up to protect Luna and the cubs. He'd been so busy lately, but now he wondered when it would be his turn to find a mate and have a family of his own. For right now, he just hoped they would all be able to survive the hounds and hunters come kill season.

Soon, they would have to think about how to fatten themselves up for the winter. The acorns were now falling. They had two huge cornfields—without farmers—they could gorge themselves in. This fall, there would be plenty of food to make them very fat and very happy.

CHAPTER 32

Putting On Weight

The bears celebrated the end of chase season with a picnic at the pond. Now that Farmer Brown was dead, they knew they were in no danger. But that also meant the pond would never be restocked, so to make sure there would always be fish to catch, they agreed not to keep any trout they caught. There were plenty of native trout in the streams to keep their baskets full. Meanwhile, the rainbow trout would grow to mammoth size over time, which was great news for Bud since his favorite thing to do was fish for the world-record rainbow trout.

The fishing had noticeably improved, which felt bittersweet to Benjamin. On the one hand, they were regularly catching fish that were 28 inches long. The best one measured 30 inches and eighteen pounds. On the other hand, Benjamin was still distraught over what he had done to Farmer Brown and his wife.

They had their lines in the water for two hours before it was time to dig into the food they had brought. As the others gathered on the picnic blankets, Bud was still patiently waiting on his record trout. He didn't even care that everyone else had caught way more fish than he had. "Big bait equals big fish" was his motto, and he would wait as long as necessary.

Their picnic was more of a potluck, where everyone contributed. Luna had brought fried turkey and smoked turkey legs. Sophia had made twenty loaves of sourdough bread, and since they were out of hog ribs, Benjamin had fixed two hundred pounds of barbecue deer ribs. Lucy had prepared turnip greens mixed with twenty-five pounds of bacon. Angel had baked a variety of pies and cobblers, and she had also tried her hand at coconut cake. That snow-white, fluffy cake was everyone's favorite at the picnic.

After that wonderful feast, everyone was stuffed. Since it was a beautiful evening with a full moon coming up, the bears decided to stay at the pond and sleep under the stars—a decision that was met with cheers from all the cubs.

"I can fish all night long!" Bud said. Some of the cubs grabbed their poles, too, while the others played together near the water.

The sky was packed with stars, the air had a slight nip to it, and the trees were gently swaying. The older bears were glad to have a quiet evening with friends and family as they talked softly well into the night. Around two a.m., the quiet was shattered.

"I've got the world record here!" Bud yelled. The monster fish was thrashing about, and with no other sounds in the dead of night, the splash of every flip and flop was practically deafening. Every so often, a glint of pink flashed when the moonlight hit the fish at just the right angle.

It took Bud almost forty-five minutes to wrestle that trout onto land. It certainly looked bigger than his last one, although they had nothing to weigh or measure it with. The fish's long, hooklike jaw told them it was male.

A little before sunrise, the bears strolled down to Farmer Brown's cornfield, knowing it was safe to enter. Completely undisturbed, they gorged themselves until they could eat no more, then took a bear nap in the middle of the tall cornstalks. It was a bear's paradise. With as much free corn as they wanted this year, they had it made.

When they woke up, some of the bears didn't feel like walking all the way home. They talked it over and agreed that Lucy and her family would stay with Luna, while Benjamin, Sophia, and the cubs would stay at Angel's. They kept this arrangement for the next three weeks.

This time of year, their lives consisted of eating corn and stuffing themselves with the countless acorns now littering the forest floor. Along with regular meals of backstrap, turkey, greens and bacon, sourdough bread, and other favorites, the bears were able to put on weight much faster this year than last.

They headed back to their dens to settle in and get ready for kill season. On the day before the season started, Benjamin announced he was going to check on Ann to make sure she was okay.

When he arrived at Ann's parents' house, Benjamin was told she had moved out. She and her best friend from high school had moved in together on the farm. Dominic, Lucifer's brother, had come by and given Ann the deed to the farm, saying that while he had never wanted to be a farmer and had no desire to keep the farm, he knew Ann had always dreamed of that life.

Benjamin was surprised that Ann would feel comfortable in the house where Lucifer had murdered his parents. But as he soon found out, the house had been reduced to a pile of ashes. Seeing smoke coming from the chimney of the mother-in-law suite, Benjamin walked down and knocked. A young woman in pajamas opened the door, took one look at Benjamin, and screamed.

"Alice? What's wrong?" Ann came running over. "Alice? What—" She saw Benjamin and grinned. "Ben! Alice, it's just Benjamin, the bear I told you about. Ben, this is my best friend, Alice."

"Hi," Alice said, giving a slight wave. "Sorry, I'm just not used to seeing bears at the door."

"Well, come in," Ann said. "Alice is my high school friend, and we've gotten much closer after the Lucifer ordeal. She was right by my side through it all. Now we're living the farm life, and I'm so much happier."

"I see the farmhouse burned down. Did you …"

"Yes. I wanted to destroy anything that reminded me of that devil. So, the day I was handed the deed, Alice and I came over here with ten gallons of diesel fuel. I didn't want to set foot in the house, so Alice went in and poured the gas all over. I lit some newspaper on fire and tossed it inside. Then we stepped back to watch the house burn until there was nothing left. You should've seen it. There was a whole rainbow of color coming up from the living room area. We had to make sure we weren't in the path of the smoke so we didn't inhale any of that nasty stuff."

Benjamin told her how happy he was that she had purged Lucifer from her life.

"Ben, would you like to join us for supper?" Alice said. "We've got some ribs smoking out back on the patio."

Benjamin enjoyed a delicious meal with the farmers, then said he had to get back to the den because tomorrow was the first day of kill season.

As he walked home, he thought about Maverick. Most of chase season had been a nightmare for him and his family. He had stepped up his game toward the end of the season, but Benjamin had doubts he could keep that up.

What would tomorrow hold for everyone? What about the next five weeks? Would that group of hunters be shooting every bear they saw as revenge for killing their dogs? There were simply more questions than answers.

But Benjamin was sure of one thing: *I lost my dad last year*, he thought. *I'd better not lose any more of my family and friends this year.*

CHAPTER 33

The Most Devastating Day

The hunters were out before daylight, their hounds fiercely sniffing for the slightest hint of a bear. Minutes later, the dogs opened up barking. Somewhere on the ridge where Luna and Maverick's den was, they were in hot pursuit.

Benjamin slipped outside so he could be ready to help any bear in need. For a few minutes, he listened. There were two packs of dogs: one had already stopped a bear and was in an intense fight with it. But the other group of hounds had already crossed the road and were now chasing a bear up the ridge that Benjamin was on.

He caught sight of the bear they were chasing. It was Luna. That meant the other bear was probably Maverick. If so, he had done a good job of getting half the pack off of Luna. But Luna was going to need Benjamin's help.

Luna had her orange ribbon on, which might help save her, but only if it was Rob's hunting group that was chasing her. If it was the group that was angry at Maverick for killing their dogs, they probably wouldn't honor the ribbons.

Benjamin took off toward Luna as the dogs gained on her. He wanted to cut the dogs off, but they were still a good distance from him. Luna stopped and turned around to fight the hounds. Cornered against the rocks, the dogs moved in on her. She smacked them hard several times, but they kept coming at her and grabbing her fur with their paws and teeth. "Please, Luna, don't run up a tree," Benjamin said to himself.

He snuck up on the dogs from behind. They were so busy attacking Luna, they didn't know he was there. Within seconds, he had killed two of the dogs and injured three. The five remaining dogs ran off, and Benjamin realized they were heading toward his den.

He bolted back to the den, afraid for Sophia and the cubs. Bud was standing outside the den as Benjamin ran up. "The dogs are chasing Mom!" he said.

"Okay, Bud. Where are Susie and Dottie?"

"They're inside, crying. We're so worried about Mom."

Benjamin ran after the barking dogs as fast as he could. Moments later, the dogs stopped, and Benjamin knew Sophia was fighting with them. Then the chase was on again, but now there were only two dogs chasing Sophia. She had escaped more than two dogs before, so Benjamin was hopeful she would be able to get away from them.

High on the mountain, the dogs stopped again. Benjamin didn't think he could get there before the hunters did. Perhaps Maverick would see what was happening and jump in to save Sophia. If not, all Benjamin could do was hope his mother could get out of there before the hunters showed up.

To Benjamin's great relief, he heard Rob and Dale talking back and forth on the radio. *That means she might be okay*, he thought. *They'll honor the ribbon.* The dogs weren't barking anymore, which was another good sign.

Just then: *Bang! Bang! Bang!*

His heart sank. He knew Sophia had been shot.

"Dale, get the hell up here!" Rob said over the radio. "I shot a bear, but I didn't kill it, and now it's trying to kill me. I'm out of bullets! Come quick!"

She was still alive. With renewed hope, Benjamin tore off to see if he could still help his mother. But now, he had twenty dogs behind him. No doubt other hunting groups had added their dogs to the mix. It was the largest pack of dogs he had ever seen, and they were bearing down on him. Benjamin turned around and fought some of the dogs, but he was only able to get rid of four dogs before he was forced to take off again. That left him with no option but to abandon Sophia and hope she would be okay. All his instincts told him to climb a tree, but he knew that meant certain death, so instead, he ran up into the steep rocks and managed to lose the dogs.

By now, he was at least four miles from Sophia. But he didn't want to give up. He sprinted down from his perch and ran toward where he had last heard the dogs. There he found Sophia, chasing Rob around a tree. She was alive!

Benjamin started toward them. Just before he could yell his mother's name, *Bang!* Sophia dropped to the ground and didn't move. He looked to his left, where the gunshot had come from. There was Dale, lowering his gun and running over to Rob.

"Thanks for saving me," Rob said. "I shot that bear three times, but I just wasn't in position for a good shot. And I didn't even see that orange ribbon until after she started chasing me around the tree. But you know what, it doesn't even matter. That damn bear killed and injured so many of our dogs today."

They walked over to one of their injured dogs. "He's alive, but barely," Rob said. "I need you to carry him out while I try to find the other one."

Dale scooped the dog into his arms and headed down the mountain.

Benjamin was furious with Rob and Dale. Thanks to them, both his parents were dead. He was devastated. Even though he was now fully responsible for Bud, Susie, and Dottie, he wasn't sure he had the strength to take care of them.

At least he had been able to save Luna. And he was proud of Maverick for beating back at least half of the dogs that were chasing Luna. But he felt lost. How could he get his life back?

He didn't know. But somehow, he would have to.

CHAPTER 34

Losing Himself

After the hunters dragged Sophia's body away, Benjamin sat down in the spot where she had been killed. It was a freezing cold, rainy, and windy night, with trees swaying and some even falling over. When daylight broke, ice hung thick on the branches.

Benjamin still hadn't moved when Maverick found him just before dark. "Ben, are you okay?"

Benjamin just stared straight ahead. He couldn't think. "My life is over," he said. "I can't go on without my mom. She's been my rock ever since I lost my dad."

"Ben, if you want to—"

"This is your damn fault, Maverick!" Benjamin shouted. "*Your* fault that Sophia is dead. I should kill *you*. I know I'd feel better if I did."

Maverick stayed calm. "I fought half the dogs off so Luna would be able to survive. Then I went to check on her. She said you helped her."

Benjamin nodded.

"Thank you for helping Luna, Ben. That was a real blessing." He took a deep breath. "Yesterday, Luna and I heard the dogs chasing Sophia. At first, we didn't know who they were chasing, and by the time we realized, the hounds were too far away for me to help. We were afraid to leave the den last night, but this morning I left to check on everyone, thinking no hunters would be out in this weather. I went over to your den. The cubs were worried about you and Sophia, so I took them back to our den and told them I was coming to find you. Ben, I am so sad that Sophia died. But it's good to see that you're okay."

Benjamin couldn't control his anger. "Okay? *Okay, Maverick?* Do I look okay? I am the furthest thing from okay right now. I wish I was the one who died instead of Sophia."

"I know this is hard on you, but your siblings need their big brother now more than ever. Somehow, you must pull it together for them."

Benjamin knew that, but he wondered how he could help them when he couldn't even help himself. He'd been depressed before, but this was different. This time, it was his mom. He wanted to kill everyone and everything right now. He wanted to kill Rob and Dale, too, along with anything else in his path.

"Come home to our den," Maverick said. "Everyone is there, and they can't wait to see you. They just want to know you're okay."

The bears were relieved to see Benjamin walk in. Bud jumped up. "Is Mom dead?"

"Yes, Bud. She is. She fought as hard as she could, even after being shot by Rob three times."

"I thought Rob said he wouldn't do this to her."

"He said he didn't see her orange ribbon. But he also said it wouldn't have mattered because she had killed too many of their dogs."

Tears flowed from Bud's eyes. "I see why Rob would be angry, but I'm going to miss Mom."

"We all will, Bud." Benjamin told the bears he needed some time alone at the other den. "Bud, you're in charge of Susie and Dottie while I'm away."

"I'll make you proud, Brother."

Benjamin was trying to be brave and hold it together in front of the others, but the truth was he had never been so broken. He had no idea how he would get through this. But he knew he wouldn't be able to help anyone else unless he had some time to heal.

CHAPTER 35

Depressed

Benjamin lit up a cigar the second he got back to his den. One wasn't enough, though. The pain was unbearable. Soon, he was chain smoking cigars, but the marijuana was hardly helping his intense sadness.

He didn't know what to do. *I wish Tom were here*, he thought. *Maybe he could help me in the same way I helped him. But he's two counties away, and I can't even think about making such a long trip right now.*

Then he remembered the laced marijuana. He had never wanted to use it because he didn't want to end up like Samuel and Maverick, wreaking havoc on the forest. But a cigar or two might make him feel better. At the very least, it wouldn't be as bad as the purple smoke marijuana.

He retrieved his stash from the secret hiding spot and rolled himself a cigar.

Almost instantly, he flew out of his mind. He left the den and marched through the forest, killing every deer, rabbit, squirrel, and possum in his path. But not for food—he got pleasure from murdering them and leaving a trail of carcasses in his wake. He was still in pain, but the thrill of each slaughter kept his spirits up.

Benjamin went back to the den after the killing spree. *I need to calm down*, he thought. *I need to control myself. I'm all Bud, Susie, and Dottie have now. They will need their big brother to teach them how to survive.*

Still mad as hell and very depressed, Benjamin lit up a few regular cigars to quiet his nerves. He had to be there for his siblings. They needed him more than ever right now.

After a sleepless night, Benjamin got up and stepped

outside, only to be greeted by barking dogs over near Maverick and Luna's den. He knew he'd need to help. But in his current state, he couldn't even help himself. Unless ...

He pulled out some laced marijuana from his secret hiding spot and rolled two cigars. He smoked one and took the other with him, then ran down and crossed the road without a care in the world.

The dogs were chasing Maverick. He didn't see Luna anywhere and didn't hear any other dogs, so he figured she was safe. Driven by anger, Benjamin ran toward Maverick and the hounds. Already, the dogs had bayed Maverick twice, and each time, he continued running. He had probably covered five miles of mountainous terrain by now. From what Benjamin could hear, the dogs had caught up with him again, and he was now up a tree. If Benjamin didn't intervene, Maverick would be killed.

There was a huge pack of dogs at the base of the tree, barking, snarling, jumping. Benjamin thought someone new was hunting in this area today because he didn't recognize any of the hounds. With no fear, Benjamin strolled toward the tree and gave a loud whistle. Thirteen dogs stopped what they were doing, looked at him, then ran over and attacked him.

Benjamin's first drug-fueled smack sent one dog forty feet down the hill. They wanted more, so Benjamin continued to kill one dog after another. He was bleeding from their bites and scratches, but he felt no pain. The last three dogs turned to run, but he chased them down and didn't leave a single one alive.

Maverick slid out of the tree and walked over. "Thanks, Ben."

"You damn coward! Learn to fight your own damn fights. I can't even think about my own fights, much less yours. I can't keep saving your fucking ass. If it weren't for this marijuana, the hunters would have killed you already. Now get your cowardly ass back to your den."

Maverick looked at him more closely. He could tell something was off, but didn't know what.

Luna came running up. "Ben! Oh my God, thank you so much for saving Maverick's life."

Benjamin exploded. "Maverick is no boar bear! He will end up getting killed, and maybe you and Susan and Heather will, too."

Luna frowned. "What the fuck is wrong with you, Ben? I know you're hurting, but why the hell are you being so mean to us? It's like you've been smoking laced marijuana."

"Well, Luna, you've never lost your damn mom before. And maybe I am smoking laced marijuana. What the fuck are you going to do about it?"

"Don't you see, Ben? I heard about all the animals you killed last night. It's like having Samuel and Maverick on the loose again."

"Y'all are both lucky I don't kill both of you right now."

"If you've ever cared for me," Luna said, "please go back to your den. Smoke some regular marijuana to calm down. I've always seen you as a superhero, Ben. But today, I see a villain."

"I'm sorry, Luna. I've been in so much pain." Benjamin turned around to leave. "I will go and smoke some regular marijuana, but I make you no promises. I don't even know what I might do one minute from now."

CHAPTER 36

Sunday Fun Day

Benjamin returned to his den, his head spinning in circles. He was mad at himself for using the laced marijuana and terrified of who he was becoming. But he was still so depressed. He didn't know how he would survive the loss of his mother. He had lost Oliver on the first day of the season last year and Sophia the first day of the season this year.

He'd also lost himself. *I lost myself by turning to the laced marijuana,* he thought. *I swore I would never use it. Why did I bring it home with me?* Still, he didn't want to dispose of it. Maybe later, but not yet.

Benjamin lit up a large cigar of regular marijuana. It had always helped in the past, but never had the pain cut this deep. As he sat there in self-pity, he realized he hadn't eaten since his mother's death.

He walked to the kitchen and fixed some backstrap, greens and bacon, and sourdough bread. The smell of the bread reminded him of Sophia, and tears ran down his cheeks as he ate. He forced himself to eat the rest of his supper.

Benjamin had been focusing so much on his mental pain, he only now realized the dogs had shredded his precious black coat. With no herbs to treat himself, he would get a huge infection, if he didn't already have one. He needed Luna. She could nurse him back to health again. Even though he still felt weak, he was pretty sure he could make it to her den.

After dark, Benjamin set out for Luna's. He took a deer bag of regular marijuana with him, and without knowing why, also brought a possum bag of the laced stuff.

He stumbled into their den. "Oh my God!" Luna said. "I didn't realize your injuries were that bad. I was so mad at you for being mean I didn't stop to think that you're not immortal. I have some fresh herbs to help with your infection. Also, we need to get you eating spinach twice a day again. Go shower, and I'll prepare some yarrow to stop the bleeding."

The bleeding was much worse than he had realized. As he showered, red rained down the drain.

The last thing he remembered was turning the shower faucet off. Twelve hours later, he woke up, covered in bandages. Luna told him she had heard a loud thud from the bathroom and found him on the floor. With Maverick's help, she had brought him into the bedroom.

"I put yarrow on all your wounds, then I bandaged you up with oregano, garlic, goldenseal, echinacea, and more yarrow. With all that, you smell good enough to eat!"

"Maybe so," he said, "but I really need a cigar right now."

Luna went to get his marijuana. "Ben?" she called from the other room. "Is it the deer bag or the possum bag?"

Benjamin froze. *Oh no! I forgot I had the laced marijuana!* "Deer bag, Luna! Only the deer bag, please!"

Thirty seconds later, Luna came into the room and held up the possum bag. "What the hell is this, Ben? Is this the laced shit you smoked the other day?"

He sighed. "Yes."

"Why did you bring it? Either way, you can't have it anymore. I'm going outside to burn it." She stormed out of the room and left the den.

For the next several days, Luna, Maverick, and the cubs kept Benjamin company. He was still depressed over losing his mother, but the marijuana helped with both the mental and physical pain.

On Wednesday night, Lucy and James brought the cubs over to check on him. They had stopped by his den, and when they didn't find him there, they came to Luna's. Benjamin told Lucy about what had happened to Sophia, and she was heartbroken. Luna was an awesome friend with great nursing skills, but what helped Benjamin the most was having Lucy and her family around to help him laugh again.

After several days in the den, Benjamin was feeling antsy. It wasn't in his nature to stay put, and he had the constant urge to venture out and roam around. But he knew he had to heal, and spending time with his family was helping with that. He decided the best day to leave would be Sunday, since the hunters wouldn't be out.

On Sunday, they planned a family trip to the pond. The pond had always been one of his favorite places to go, and with the passing of Farmer Brown, they no longer had to worry about being shot. But what he liked best about the pond was watching Bud sit there at the edge of the water, tirelessly waiting for the world-record trout to bite again.

With a few baskets of food and fishing poles for everyone, they set out. On the way, they stopped by Angel and Samuel's den to invite them to come with. They had been laying low for several days, with plenty of food in the den, and they had no idea Benjamin had been mauled by dogs and Sophia had been killed by hunters.

While Angel, Luna, and Lucy opened the picnic baskets, Bud ran straight to his favorite corner of the pond with his twenty-inch minnow. Benjamin and Samuel sat together, watching the cubs fish.

"Do you ever miss using laced marijuana?" Benjamin asked.

"No," Samuel said, then took a few moments to think. "Before I got together with Angel, yes, I missed it, but my heart told me it was wrong, so I refrained from using it. It was hard at first, but with Angel in my life now, I never think about it anymore. Why do you ask?"

"I'm asking because not only did I use it before I killed Farmer Brown, but after losing my mom, I used it again because I was hurting so badly. All it did was make me want to harm the forest and kill people and animals. I was using it when I killed all those dogs and saved Maverick. What's interesting is, after being mauled by the hounds, I didn't even feel pain. I haven't used it since then, but I can't get it off my mind."

"Do you still have any left?"

"I had a full possum bag, but Luna burned it the other day." Benjamin didn't mention he still had more back at his den.

The cubs ran around to the other side of the pond to play. As usual, Bud wanted to join them, so he left Benjamin in charge of his fishing pole. Moments later, Bud's pole doubled over. Benjamin lunged forward and grabbed it. The fish was thrashing about, jumping out of the water and flipping like it was in a circus. It put up a good thirty-five–minute fight before Benjamin had it on the bank of the pond. He was proud of his catch, but prouder still that he had not once thought about any of his problems while fighting this beast.

He wished every day could be a Sunday, but sadly, tomorrow was Monday, another chance for the hounds to come and hunt them down. They talked about it and came up with a survival plan. They would make sure to store at least a week's worth of food in both Luna's and Angel's dens. Then, they would burrow deep inside the dens and hopefully be safe for the coming week.

The day at the pond was just what Benjamin needed. But somehow, he knew this inner peace wouldn't last long.

CHAPTER 37

Dottie

For the next week, the bears stayed in Lucy and James's den. Benjamin loved spending time with his family, and the cubs loved roughhousing with each other. Bud was enjoying his time, too, but he kept asking to go to the pond. Each time, Benjamin would tell him they needed to stay put in the den until Sunday, when there would be no hunters out. "All right," Bud would say in his best disappointed tone.

Occasionally, Benjamin would poke his head outside to listen for hunters or dogs. He could hear trucks driving along Stone Coal Gap Road, but the dogs weren't barking. Their strategy of staying deep inside the den was working, he thought. So far, the dogs hadn't picked up their scent.

On Sunday, when they could safely leave the den, the bears headed out to forage for food. Since the cornfields were mostly bare, they had to find acorns, which were only scattered about at this point. But to pack on weight before hibernation, what they really needed was meat. Fortunately, there were plenty of deer and possums to hunt. The cubs went around to their favorite places to catch possums, while James, Maverick, and Samuel hunted for deer and turkeys.

They also needed bacon and ham, so Benjamin decided to walk over to Ann and Alice's farm to ask them for a large hog. He asked Lucy if she would like to join him, and she jumped at the chance. She had been cooped up long enough.

Together, they departed on the long trek to the other side of the mountain.

 og

Down in Possum Hollow, Lucille was having a blast. She had already killed fourteen possums and a rabbit. Bud was nearby looking for big game when he spotted a monstrous buck. He estimated it to be twenty-one points and thirty inches wide. Following his instincts, he ran it up into the steep rocks, just the way he always did. But this buck wasn't going down without a fight, and he rammed his antlers right into Bud's shoulder. The sharp pain and bloody mess only unleashed Bud's fury. He charged the massive buck, instantly killing it.

Lucille had seen the whole thing. She ran over to him. "Bud, are you okay?"

"Hell yeah, I'm okay. Look at this buck, Lucille! His antlers are going in my den."

"But your shoulder, Bud." She pointed at the bloody wound. "That looks nasty. We'd better get you to Luna's den."

Luna told Bud to get in the shower while she got her herbs together. She was glad she had stored so many herbs this year. They were being put to good use.

Once Bud was cleaned up and bandaged, he thanked Luna for taking care of him. "Now I'm ready to do battle with the world-record rainbow trout again!"

Luna chuckled. "Okay, but not until everyone is back from the hunt."

Patches had gone hunting with Heather and Susan, and as the day wore on, Susan was getting more and more frustrated. Because those two were giggling so much, all their prey was fleeing before they could catch it.

"Quiet down, you two!" Susan finally said. "We can't even get close to these animals before they run off."

Heather snapped back. "Why don't *you* shut your damn mouth, Susan?"

While Susan fumed, the other two were having a great time together, laughing and flirting the whole time. Patches thought Heather was a wonderful, beautiful bear, and Heather felt the same way about Patches. Even after they all came back home empty-handed, the giggling continued.

Sam Jr. and Susie also went hunting together, and Sam

wasn't shy at all. He told Susie she was the prettiest bear in the woods and that he liked her a lot. Suddenly they lost interest in hunting and decided they would rather get to work starting a family. "That would be better than hunting any day," Susie said. They made their way over to Caesar's old den, where they could be alone.

Across the mountain, James, Samuel, and Maverick had run across a herd of twenty-four yearlings and does. They knew the deer population was higher this time of year, but they didn't know there would be this many. After running them up into the steep rocks, they were able to catch eleven of them. It was a successful hunting trip, but they knew it would take several trips to bring all the meat back.

Not far from the den, Dottie and Liz had paired up to hunt big game together. They wanted to prove to the others just how well they could hunt. Right away, they found two does and the chase was on. But the does weren't cooperating. Instead of running up the mountain, they were running across it. The bears couldn't let the does win, so they kept chasing. At last, the does made the fatal mistake of running up into the steep rocks, where Dottie killed one and Liz killed the other. Now they had to drag these animals back to the den, but the chase had brought them much farther from home than they realized.

That was when they heard the barking. It started out far away, but it sounded like the dogs were quickly approaching. Dottie and Liz looked at each other. "Why are there dogs?" Dottie whispered.

"I don't know! It's Sunday. There's no hunting on Sunday."

Dottie's eyes swelled with fear. "We need to get out of here, Liz."

They ran off toward the den, hoping to find the boars and get help. But the hounds were too fast, and they caught up with Dottie, who was left with no choice but to climb a tree. *It's illegal to kill a bear today*, she thought. *They're probably just chasing.* The dogs crowded around the base of the tree, snapping their jaws and barking at full cry.

Liz ran as hard as she could to find the boars. She saw Samuel and the others hauling their deer toward the entrance to the den.

Not sure what to say, Liz just shouted. "Dottie is treed! Dottie is treed!" They looked at each other, dropped their deer, and ran toward her. Liz turned around to lead the way back.

When the tree came into view, it was still one ridgeline over. Maverick recognized the dogs. They were from the pack that had come after him several times during chase season. He and Benjamin had already killed several of them. All he wanted to do now was finish them off.

Two hunters showed up. "Yeah, it's a cub, maybe eighty pounds," one of them said into his radio.

"Those fucking bears have killed so many of my dogs this year," came the snarling response. "I know today is Sunday, and it's a cub, but I want you to *kill that damn bear* and leave it there to rot."

Bang! Dottie fell out of the tree and hit the ground. The dogs sailed in on her, mauling her for several minutes until the hunters clipped on their leads and took them away. Liz and the other bears stood there, shocked and horrified by what they had just witnessed.

They carried Dottie back to the den. The other bears were devastated. Luna was especially worried about Benjamin, knowing he had just lost his mom. Now his little sister was dead. How much more could he take?

 C୪

On the other side of the mountain, Benjamin and Lucy were sitting with Ann and Alice, who had just given them two large hogs. Ann had gone outside earlier to shoot them, hang them, and pull the guts out.

"We really appreciate this, Ann," Benjamin said. "We should probably be leaving soon."

"I'm so glad you stopped by," Ann said. "We'll load up the hogs in our truck and bring them over to you. We can't go all the way to your den, but we could meet you on Stone Coal Gap Road and you can take them the rest of the way."

At the side of the road, they only had to wait a few minutes before Ann pulled up in her truck. They unloaded the hogs, thanked Ann, then set about dragging the hogs back to the den.

It was slow going with the hefty animals. They weighed at least eight hundred pounds, three times what either bear weighed. They had to take several breaks along the way, but the journey was otherwise enjoyable and filled with banter. Lucy remarked on how late it was already and said it was too bad they wouldn't make it to the pond. Benjamin wondered if Bud had caught his world-record trout today.

Outside the den, Luna was crying. "I have horrible news to tell you," she said. "Dottie is dead."

Benjamin dropped to his knees. Lucy put her arm around him.

"It was the hunters who were after Maverick during chase season," Luna said. "The ones who swore they would kill every bear they saw."

Bud walked over and hugged Benjamin. Tears flowed. The pain was unbearable, but the anger Benjamin felt toward *those fucking poachers* was unlike anything he had ever experienced. They would pay.

CHAPTER 38

Revenge for Dottie

It was a bitterly cold, sleepless night for Benjamin. His heart had been ripped out of his body, and he had already finished his deer bag of marijuana. His thoughts raced all over the place. *I must get a grip on my feelings so I can protect the cubs. I must remain calm. And I must get more marijuana.*

It was the laced marijuana he really wanted, but he knew he had to use regular marijuana because Bud and Susie would need him. The journey back to his den to get more would be dangerous because he would have to cross the road, but it was necessary.

When he told Luna this, she begged him not to go.

"I have to, Luna. But I promise I will only get regular marijuana."

Luna sighed, knowing she wouldn't win this battle. "Please be careful, Ben. Keep your eyes out for that awful group of hunters. No, not hunters. Poachers."

Benjamin took his usual stealth route, passing under the road by way of the culvert, then staying in the creek to hide his scent. When he was just about at his den, a truck rumbled by on the road. He hoped the hounds wouldn't pick up his scent, but moments later, barking erupted and the dogs were set free. They weren't after Benjamin, though. They were headed straight toward Luna's den.

He had to do something, and fast. But what? All he could think to do was rush into his den and grab four cigars from his secret hiding spot. He smoked the first one as fast as he could. Now he was ready to mix it up with *those fucking poachers*. It was time to get his revenge for Dottie.

Moments later, Benjamin was back at the road. It was amazing how fast he could move after smoking the laced marijuana. He looked around: there were four hunters standing in the road and three trucks parked on the side.

"That damn bear ain't gonna get away from us today," one of them said. "The two guys who got here at dawn are already on top of the mountain. Our hounds will run that bastard bear right up to them."

Benjamin was terrified to think about which bear the hounds would chase. *Will any of my family die today? I've had too much loss already. I can't handle any more.*

Benjamin estimated there were twelve hounds running up the mountain. They seemed to be close together, not spread out, as though they were only chasing one bear. He would worry about that later.

Right now, it was time to end these poachers' lives. But first, he lit up one more cigar and sat down on a rock to smoke it. Then, he stood up and charged the group as hard as he could. He smacked the first hunter he came to. The forceful blow took his head right off, and blood flew everywhere. The other hunters turned around, only to see their friend's head sailing through the air. It hit one of them in the chest, and he instinctively reached his arms out and caught it. Holding his friend's head in his arms, he looked up at Benjamin and screamed at the top of his lungs.

He dropped the head, and they all ran to their trucks to get their guns. Benjamin almost laughed at how cute they were thinking they had a chance. One hunter already had his gun, so Benjamin walked up to him and slashed his abdomen open. The motion of his paw sent the intestines flying everywhere, landing mostly on his truck. To finish the job, Benjamin plunged his paw into the poacher's chest, pulled out his warm, fresh heart, and swallowed it whole.

A fly landed on his right shoulder. *Bang!* He'd been shot. Benjamin took off at full tilt toward the shooter, who shot again but missed. Terrified, the poacher turned and ran, shit streaming out of his pant legs with every stride. Benjamin caught up and sliced the man in half with one swipe of his claws. The top half flew straight into the last poacher and knocked him down.

Benjamin had him right where he wanted him. He walked over, bit the guy's foot off, and worked his way up from there. The next ten minutes of shrill, desperate screams from his prey only made the meal more delicious. He saved the heart for last, then collected the other two hearts and devoured those as well. He was finding poachers' hearts to be a delicacy.

On the way back to Luna's den, Benjamin rubbed some dirt in his gunshot wound to stop the bleeding. It wasn't that bad. He just hoped everyone back at the den was okay.

Luna saw him coming and ran to him. "Ben, I'm so worried about Maverick. The hounds were coming for us and Maverick went down to confront them. He ran straight up the mountain so they would leave us and follow him."

Benjamin's heart sank. He knew there were two poachers up there. "I have to go and help Maverick."

Luna stopped him. "You're bleeding. Let me put some yarrow on your wound at least."

After Luna bandaged him up, Benjamin lit one more cigar. He knew this wasn't over yet.

"Is that the laced marijuana?" she asked.

"I'll tell you everything later. But right now, I need to go help my blood brother."

Benjamin tore off and sprinted up the mountain. With his head in a psychotic spin, he was ready for the poachers. The dogs were now stopped on top of the mountain, about a mile away. He just hoped he could get there on time.

Bang! Bang! Bang!

That was it. His blood brother was dead. He slowed down and approached the scene quietly so the poachers wouldn't hear him coming.

Crouched over Maverick's body, the poachers ripped his guts out while the dogs pulled on his fur. One of the poachers stood up and turned around, but before he could say anything, Benjamin whacked his head, and his brain exploded everywhere.

The second poacher looked up at Benjamin, trembling. "Oh my God, I'm going to die."

Yes you are, Benjamin thought, spotting his gun lying near a tree. He walked over, grabbed the gun, and bent it around the tree. As Benjamin turned around, the dogs jumped all over him, biting, clawing, pulling. He calmly swatted them away and took them out, one at a time, until they were all dead.

The poacher had disappeared. Fortunately, he had left Benjamin a long trail of shit that he followed for two hundred yards. Even though Ben was full after eating the last poacher, he was determined to eat this one, too. When he caught up with him, Benjamin ate slowly as he sliced the man's flesh bit by bit. He saved the two hearts for last.

Now, he had to go tell Luna that Maverick was gone. He shuddered when he thought of how she might react. He just hoped the forest was safer now with the poachers dead.

CHAPTER 39

The Aftermath

"He's dead, isn't he?"

Luna had been waiting at the front door for Benjamin to return.

Benjamin nodded. "I'm afraid so."

"I'm going to miss him," Luna said, tears rolling down her cheeks. "He died trying to protect us. If the dogs had found us in the den, it would have been horrific. You may have been harsh with him, but it gave Maverick the bravery to confront those dogs and fight for his family. That means you saved a lot of lives today, Ben."

Benjamin was still angry. "If those poachers didn't already have two men on top of the mountain, Maverick would have fought off all the dogs and been right back here with you. I was—"

"Ben, right now, we need to get you cleaned up. You shower and I'll get my herbs to nurse you back to health. You can finish telling me the story tomorrow, okay?" She smiled. "I'm starting to think you use my shower more than I do."

"After you get me bandaged up," Benjamin said, "I'm going out. I have to do something with Dottie's body."

When he came back to the den, he realized how miserable he felt. He just hoped he could push through until he could get more marijuana.

The next morning, Luna's den smelled wonderful. The aroma of freshly baked sourdough bread, bacon and eggs sizzling in the pan, and ... were those cinnamon honey buns?

"You named it all," Luna said, flipping the eggs. "How did you sleep?"

"Much better than I thought I would," Benjamin said.

"I didn't think I'd sleep at all."

Luna asked him to wake up the cubs. He gently shook Bud, Susie, Susan, and Heather awake and gave each one a big bear hug as they opened their eyes.

"Ben, that's so sweet of you to give everyone a hug," Luna said. She had been standing behind him the whole time. "We all need this more than ever right now."

He turned around and gave Luna a hug, too.

After breakfast, they decided to take the cubs to Angel and Samuel's den so they could play together. They also needed to deliver the devastating news to Samuel that his son was dead. They felt it would be safe to go on the short hike since Angel's den was only halfway up the mountain.

Samuel was heartbroken. "How did it happen?"

"He was defending our family when the poachers shot him," Luna said. "He died a hero." She gave Samuel a long bear hug.

"Luna, can I talk to you?" Benjamin said. "Let's go back to your den so I can finish telling my story from yesterday." Samuel and Angel told them to take as long as they needed.

Back at Luna's den, Benjamin told her the entire gruesome story, from smacking the first poacher's head off to slowly eating the last one. Luna's jaw was on the floor. She couldn't believe what she was hearing. "Oh, and I almost forgot," he said. "I ate all their hearts for dessert."

"Oh my God, Ben, you are my hero for killing those poachers and their dogs. They won't ever bother us again. And—"

Benjamin lifted his paw and turned his head slightly. "Do you hear that? Something is going on outside."

They left the den and saw vehicles with flashing lights down on the road. "It's the police!" Benjamin said. "I'm going to get a closer look."

"Not without me."

They walked down together, stopping about two hundred yards from the road to watch and listen.

The Conservation Police had found the horror scene.

Uniformed officers milled about while their search dog sniffed around. "It looks like we have a bear that has gone on a killing rampage here," one of the officers said into his radio. "We have three bodies in varying stages of dismemberment. And ... get ready for this. All their hearts are missing."

Luna leaned over to Benjamin. "I thought you said there were four poachers," she whispered.

"Remember, I ate the fourth one," he said.

As the officers talked, they agreed they needed to find the rogue bear that had done this and destroy him.

Benjamin looked at Luna, worried. "This sounds bad," he said. "Really bad."

One of the officers followed the search dog as it sniffed its way over to a tree that had blood splattered on it. Lying next to the tree, in a pool of blood, was Dottie, exactly where Benjamin had placed her.

"Guys? Come take a look at this!" The other officers walked over. "This changes the whole scenario. Looks like we had three poachers who shot this young cub illegally. The bear was just distraught because the poachers had killed his family member." They all nodded in agreement.

"I think it goes without saying that we need to close Stone Coal Gap for the rest of the season," another officer said. "That way, all the bear families can heal from this horrid ordeal. Also, this particular bear needs time to calm down, because if a hunter approached him now, we'd have a repeat of this." He motioned toward the carnage. More nodding.

Benjamin winced. "Oh boy. That last poacher's not sitting very well with me." He ran off into the trees and vomited. "I need more marijuana," he said when he came back. "Let's go to my den and get some. I'm in a lot of pain, physical and mental."

"Okay. But I want you to show me where that laced marijuana is, because we are going to destroy it once and for all."

"Deal," Benjamin said. "I've caused enough harm by smoking it. I agree it's time for it to be destroyed."

They were hardly through the front door when Luna grabbed him, gave him a huge bear hug and a nose rub, then led him to the bedroom. They stayed in bed together for several hours.

"It feels so good being with you like this, Luna. I've always had feelings for you, even before you and Maverick got together. But I was afraid you didn't feel the same way."

"There has never been any bear like you, Ben. I didn't really want to be with Maverick, but I didn't think you wanted to be with me like this."

Benjamin got up and asked Luna if she would like to smoke with him. She said yes, but not before they destroyed all the laced marijuana. They took the stash from Benjamin's secret hiding spot and burned it outside.

After that, they rolled two cigars and settled down in his bed to smoke them. That night, they were awake more than they were asleep, working on starting their own family.

In the morning, Luna smiled at him. "I'm so happy right now," she said. "But there's one problem. Since I just lost Maverick, will anyone approve of us being together so soon after it happened?"

CHAPTER 40

Preparing for Hibernation

After a passionate night together, Benjamin and Luna headed over to Samuel and Angel's den. It was time to fill them in on the events of the past few days, although they were a little nervous about how they would react.

When they arrived, Benjamin asked the cubs if they would like to go off by themselves and fish at the pond.

Samuel was shocked. "Are you out of your mind, Ben? We're still in the middle of hunting season!"

"I'll explain everything that's happened," Benjamin said. "But for now, trust me when I say that hunting season has been canceled."

Luna chimed in. "It's true. We heard it from the Conservation Police themselves. The road is closed until after hunting season, and both mountains are closed for bear hunting."

"But what about those damned poachers? They'll do whatever they want," Samuel said.

"You don't have to worry about them anymore," Benjamin said. "I'll explain everything later. The cubs don't need to hear the gory details."

Samuel held his arms up. "Okay, y'all. I believe you, but I'm so confused right now."

As soon as the cubs had left, Benjamin told the story. The laced marijuana, the disemboweled poachers, the dead hounds. And the best part: the hearts. When Benjamin finished talking and looked around, everyone was staring at him, mouths agape.

James broke the silence. "Laced marijuana, you say?" He laughed. "I think I need me some of that."

"No! No, you do not," Samuel said. "That is some bad stuff. Ben, we have to get rid of it all. It makes you do things that will haunt you for the rest of your life."

"It's all gone," Luna said. "I made sure of that."

Benjamin continued with his story. "After the horrific killing of Dottie," he said, "I went and dragged her to the side of the road and left her lying there for the police to find, hoping they would realize they were dealing with poachers and wouldn't be so anxious to hunt me down and kill me."

"That was brilliant," Angel said. "But I know that had to be hard on you, placing your little sister's body down there."

"It sure was. Luna, would you like to walk with me? I want to see if the police left her lying there."

Dottie was still there, lying next to the blood-splattered tree. Benjamin scooped her up and carried her back to Luna's den. "I want to bury her here," he said. "But let's get everyone together first."

"We left out a big part of our story," Luna said as they walked back to Angel's. "The part about you and me getting together. I think we need to let everyone know."

Back at Angel's den, the cubs came home and said they had a great time fishing. Benjamin figured Bud would have been trying for the world record again. "Did you get any bites, Bud?"

He looked disappointed. "No, but I tried."

Luna put her paw on Benjamin's arm. "I'll tell the rest of the story, okay?"

Benjamin nodded.

"Ben and I have something to say to everyone." Luna looked around the room. "Ever since I was a small cub, I've had eyes for Ben. I never thought he wanted anything more than friendship with me. Well, it turns out he felt the same way. We didn't know this until last night, and ..." She took a deep breath. "Well, we may have started a new family!"

All the bears broke out in smiles and congratulated the new couple.

The families had brought home so much meat from

their hunts on the day Dottie was killed, they didn't need any more game. But Lucy said she would take all the cubs to the stream and fill several baskets with native brook trout.

"Y'all, I have something to show everyone," Bud said. "With the loss of Dottie, we haven't been able to think about much else lately. But guess what I killed on Sunday?" He produced the antlers of the huge buck he had killed. "Twenty-four points and thirty-three inches wide, y'all! This will be hanging on my wall forever."

"I believe that's the biggest buck ever to be killed in the state of Virginia," Samuel said.

Benjamin congratulated Bud, then brought up another pressing topic of discussion. "Lucy and James, I'll be moving in with Luna soon, so would you like to move into Caesar's old den? That way, all three dens would be just over a mile apart. I know Caesar would have wanted that."

They loved the idea, especially James. "With the mountain closed to hunters," he said, "there's no better time than now to start moving into our new den!"

Samuel and Angel said they would be glad to help.

"Before anyone leaves," Benjamin said, "we all need to go down to Luna's den to bury Dottie. I want to have y'all there to pay respects to my beautiful sister."

With all the bears standing in a circle outside Luna's den, Benjamin picked Dottie up and laid her at the bottom of a deep depression in the ground. He scattered some small rocks over her body, then gathered a few larger stones to place on top. The others joined in and helped, and soon they had a mound of rocks about a foot higher than the ground. Bud had lashed two sticks together, perpendicular to each other, and he placed this in the ground next to where Dottie's head was.

After the burial, Benjamin and Luna decided to take all the cubs to visit Tom and Sue. They ate as many acorns as they could on the way over. Even though acorns were getting harder to find, they were all full by the time they got to Tom's, which was good because it was well past suppertime.

Tom and Sue were beyond surprised to see them.

Benjamin told them hunting season had been canceled, so they had felt safe making the trip. He also told them that he and Luna were a couple now, with a family possibly on the way.

When Benjamin told them about their recent losses, Tom and Sue were crushed.

"But I'm happy you finally found your sow," Tom said. "Are you sure you don't want to move over to this non-hunting county?"

"I think we're good for now," Benjamin said. "We don't have to worry about hunting until next year, and we have all our dens laid out very close to each other. But I'm sick and tired of all the death, so we may consider it next year." Tom was happy to hear this.

After two days of fun with the families, Benjamin announced it was time to go. He wanted to visit Ann and Alice and let them know about recent events. They said goodbye to Tom and Sue, who were sad to see them leave.

Ann and Alice were happy to see them, but also surprised, given that Benjamin and Lucy had visited just a few days ago.

"It was right after we saw you that the horror started," Benjamin said. "We lost Dottie that day, and we lost Maverick shortly after that." He told them the reason they were out today was that hunting season had been canceled, so they didn't have to worry.

"I saw that on TV," Ann said. "The Conservation Police made a statement about hunting season being canceled, but they never gave a reason."

"There's more news," Benjamin said. "Luna and I are a couple now, and we might be having cubs!" Ann and Alice were happy for the new couple, and they asked them to spend the night. Benjamin said they would love to.

"Looks like you'll be having a baby yourself, Ann," he said. "When you turn sideways, I can tell you're starting to show." Ann winked.

The next morning, Benjamin moved into Luna's den.

They had already moved most of his belongings, but they would need to make another trip to get the rest.

"I'm going to burn all the regular marijuana I have left," Benjamin said on the way back to his den.

"No, Ben. Don't do that. I'll add it to my herbs, because you never know when it may be needed. I know you feel great now, but if you're ever injured, you may need it to soften the pain."

She was right. Ever since they had rubbed noses, Benjamin had been on cloud nine. But he agreed that having some marijuana on hand still wouldn't hurt.

They finished moving Benjamin's things, then headed over to Angel's, where they learned that James and Lucy were already set up in Caesar's den.

"But we need to find another den for Patches and Heather," Angel said. "They might be raising a family soon. If that's the case, they can stay with us here through the winter, but we'll still need to find them a den after that."

With the den situation figured out, it was time for each of the families to return home and get ready for hibernation. They had plenty of food to last until then, with enough to spare for when they woke up in the spring.

The big question was how many new cubs would they have come spring? And would Ann be having a son or a daughter? They would have the answers soon.

CHAPTER 41

The Awakening

Benjamin was the first to wake up. He looked at the beautiful bear lying next to him and felt blessed to have Luna in his life. He was groggy after the long sleep but excited to see their new cubs. He gave Luna a gentle shake.

It took Luna a few moments to wake up. "It feels like we just went to sleep," she said. "Oh my God! Something is moving over here."

Lying next to her were two adorable baby cubs. The first had snow-white fur and looked like a polar bear. Luna picked her up and cradled her. She had a pink nose and pink eyes. "She's so precious," Benjamin said.

The second cub was all white, too, except he had black around his eyes and ears, black legs, and a black stripe that ran up and over his back, connecting one front leg to the other. Benjamin loved their new family, but he told Luna he had never seen bears that looked like this before.

"I have," Luna said. "I've heard tell of white bears in the north. They're called polar bears, except they don't have pink eyes and pink noses. Did you ever see that polar bear on TV? I think his name was Coca-Cola."

"That's a cute name," Benjamin said. "We can call her Cola for short."

Luna smiled. "What about our little boar? He looks just like one of those panda bears from China."

"Pandy!" Benjamin said. Luna loved that.

With their cubs named, Benjamin and Luna gave each other a big bear hug and rubbed noses.

The other cubs were stunned at the sight of the new arrivals. "What the hell is this?" Bud said, pointing at Cola's pink nose and Pandy's black stripe.

"Watch your language, Bud. Yes, they are unique, but they are part of our family."

"I've seen bears like them before!" Heather said. "In the storybook we read from every night. A polar bear and a panda bear."

"That's what they look like," Luna said. "But they are black bears just like us. Cola is albino, and Pandy is piebald."

"Well, I love my new brother and sister," Susan said, giving them each a hug.

After breakfast, the family went outside for a stroll. The sky was clear with only wisps of white, and the trees swayed gently in the breeze. Hints of green were showing up on the bushes.

Cola and Pandy darted around as fast as they could, exploring and touching everything they saw. Fortunately, they ran as fast as the older bears walked, so there was no danger of the new cubs running off.

They saw Angel and Samuel outside their den, enjoying the beautiful spring day, and walked over to say hi.

"Good morning," Samuel said. "I thought y'all were going to sleep 'til summer. We've been up for almost a week now."

Angel gasped. "Luna! Are those my grandcubs? They are so beautiful!"

"Aren't they?" Luna said. "This here is Coca-Cola, but we call her Cola. And this is Pandy."

Angel handed Cola a slice of sourdough bread with honey on it. When Pandy saw that, he decided he wanted it, and a rough fight broke out. Benjamin broke them apart and made them apologize to each other, but Cola now had a small streak of red running through her snow-white coat.

Their next stop was Lucy's. No one was stirring, so they let themselves in. Snoring filled the den: a big snore, a medium snore, then a baby snore. Pandy bolted straight into the bedroom and jumped on top of James.

"Who's this little black-and-white fella?" James said,

rubbing his eyes. "This must be Sam and Susie's little guy."

Luna laughed. "No, James! This is Pandy, your new nephew. And this is Cola, your niece."

James was excited. He went around the den and woke up the others, leaving Sam Jr. and Susie for last. Sam said he wanted to wake her himself. Susie opened her eyes and stretched, then looked down to find her baby sow snuggled up with her. She was as black as coal with a light-tan muzzle.

"That's the sweetest thing I've ever seen," Sam said.

Susie wasn't sure what to name her, so Benjamin suggested Suzanne. Susie loved the idea.

With three new cubs in their extended family, the bears were excited to enjoy spring. Their first outing was to the pond to do a little fishing. When Cola saw her Uncle Bud put the twenty-inch minnow on, she was so transfixed that she stayed right next to him the whole time he was fishing. Bud didn't mind. He told her he always fished for the world-record rainbow trout.

"I want to catch him," she said.

"You have to be able to fight, though. By this fall, you might be big enough to hold on to the pole if he bites." Cola grinned, happy to have something to look forward to later in the year.

Benjamin sat off to the side, thinking. He missed the bears that had passed away, but he wasn't depressed about it anymore. Having Luna in his life had made him very happy and changed his life for the better. Tom had said the same thing about Sue after Benjamin set them up.

He missed Tom and Sue. He really wanted to visit them, but it was a long trip, and it would be at least a month before Pandy and Cola were big enough to make the journey. The thought of living in Tom's county, where hunting was outlawed, was more appealing than ever. He never wanted to lose Luna. Benjamin made a mental note to scout for dens in the area next time they were out there.

Just before dusk, they packed up and headed back to their dens. It had been such a great day with family. As they walked, Benjamin reveled in feelings of love for his unique son and daughter. He knew they would be the talk of the forest soon.

After supper, Benjamin sat down and read Little Red Riding Hood to Cola and Pandy. Cola was scared the big bad wolf would get her. Benjamin told her there were no wolves in Virginia, only coyotes.

"Don't be scared, my precious daughter," he said, carrying her to bed. "I will always be here to protect you." He tucked her in, and she was sound asleep in no time.

The next morning, Benjamin took the cubs to the stream to teach them how to fish for native trout. As expected, it took twice as long as usual to get there because Cola and Pandy wanted to explore and play as they walked.

At the stream, Bud dove in right away and came up with a seventeen-inch native trout. That made Cola squeal with excitement, and she dove in after him. They played together, splashing around and having a blast.

Pandy walked over, looked at the water for a minute, then gently dipped a toe in. He pulled it right back out. When Cola saw this, she got out, snuck around behind him, and pushed him in. Then she lost her balance and fell in after him. When Pandy got over his shock, he realized it was a lot of fun being in the water.

Susan jumped in to fish with Bud, and together they caught a basket full of gorgeously colored native brook trout. For Benjamin, today was the perfect way to spend time with his family and reflect on his new life with Luna.

Benjamin and Luna spent the next two weeks teaching the cubs how to hunt possums. At first, Cola and Pandy were hesitant to kill the animals, and they would just smack them around a little instead. Each time, Luna had to make the kill for them. But they quickly got the hang of it, and soon, Pandy was able to kill every young possum he saw. Benjamin told them it was all part of learning how to be a bear.

Later that spring, wild fruit popped up everywhere. Cola and Pandy went around devouring as many strawberries and blueberries as they could get their paws on, but the problem was they were eating more than they were putting in the baskets. And they were good at making a mess of it, too. Cola was starting to look like an American flag, with red and blue splotches all over her white fur. Bud joked that all she needed now were some stars and stripes.

Benjamin told the little cubs that Luna would make berry cobbler later if they could fill the baskets. When Cola and Pandy tried the cobbler later that night, they thought it was the best thing ever.

Benjamin also thought they should learn how to hunt big game. They were too young to do it themselves, but he at least wanted to show them how it worked. Benjamin found a large doe and two yearlings and chased them up into the steep rocks, where Luna and the cubs waited. They watched as Benjamin demonstrated how to kill the animals.

Pandy got excited. "Wow! I want to hunt now. That looked like fun!"

"Give it a few months," Luna said, "and you'll be able to hunt on your own."

Cola was less enthused. "I don't know," she said. "My beautiful white coat would just be covered in red." She did a twirl to show off her fur, and they all laughed.

"That's what the shower or the creek is for," Luna said.

Over the next couple of weeks, Benjamin and Luna continued training the cubs. They were growing quickly. Soon, they would be ready to make the long trip to see Tom and Sue. Benjamin was excited about the possibility of moving there.

Before they left, they took the family for a picnic down at the pond. Bud went straight to his usual spot and cast his twenty-inch minnow into the water. Cola, who was a little bigger than the last time they had done this, sat beside him.

"When are we going to catch that world-record rainbow trout, Uncle Bud? Tell that fish to bite!"

Bud wanted to be a good uncle, so he obliged. "Bite, fish!" he yelled.

The pole bent in half. "Give me the pole!" Cola yelled.

Good luck, Bud thought as he handed her the pole, remembering his first time with this fish. Cola held on to the pole for dear life, her hind legs fighting for purchase as she skidded closer to the water. Seconds later, she was in the pond.

Then the show began. Cola kept her front paws on the pole and her hind paws on top of the water as the enormous trout pulled her around the pond. The other bears watched in amazement as she waterskied in circles. The trout was showing off, too, jumping out of the water, into the water, and doing flips. Cola probably did fifty laps around the pond before the trout swam into shallow water, stopped, and turned on its side.

The other cubs ran over to move it into deeper water, but the old fish was tired, and it died before they could do anything.

Cola turned to Bud. "I'm sorry I killed your world-record trout."

"That's okay, we were all laughing so hard watching you waterski. That was incredible!"

Benjamin remembered seeing a fish hanging on the wall at Lucifer's farmhouse, and he told Cola that perhaps Ann could help them preserve it. That way, Cola could keep it on her wall to remind her of the day she caught it.

Ann was impressed with their catch when they saw her later that day. "That has to be a world record!" she said as she measured and weighed it. "Fifty-one inches long and seventy-two pounds."

Benjamin introduced her to Pandy and looked around for Cola, who had wandered off.

"Ann, I was telling the cubs that humans have a way of preserving fish," Benjamin said. "Do you know anything about it?"

"It's called taxidermy," she said. "And I would be happy to—"

At that moment, Cola sprinted through the living room, chasing the cat.

Ann smiled. "Did I just see a polar bear run through

the house?"

"That's Cola. She's albino, so she does look like a polar bear. And Pandy is piebald, which is why he looks like a panda bear."

"I've seen a piebald deer," Ann said, "but I didn't know a bear could be piebald. You have such a beautiful family."

Benjamin noticed her bulging belly. "How are you holding up, Ann? When are you due?"

"In less than two weeks." She grinned. "Big news, by the way. Things have changed for Alice and me since y'all went into hibernation. We're married now!"

Benjamin congratulated them and told them about the birth of Suzanne and other family news.

While Alice placed the rainbow trout in the freezer, Ann invited the family to stay overnight. "I'll take the fish to the taxidermist tomorrow," she said. "But tonight, I want to watch these two baby cubs play some more. They are so cute!"

Ann and Alice fixed a delicious supper, and they all enjoyed a nice evening together. As they were saying goodbye the next morning, Benjamin told Ann they would be gone for a few weeks, visiting Tom and scouting out some new dens for everyone.

"We want to move out there before next fall," Benjamin said. "I can't handle any more deaths in the family."

"Be sure to stop by on the way back," Ann said. "I'll have the fish back from the taxidermist by then, and you can meet my new baby, too."

Benjamin had never seen a human baby before. It would be one of the highlights of the year.

CHAPTER 42

The Search for Dens

Benjamin would have loved to be there when Ann gave birth, but he needed to find at least four dens to make sure everyone he loved would be safe in the coming years. He never wanted to live through the terror of another kill season. Although he was very happy now that he had Luna in his life, the sadness of losing three members of his family often weighed him down.

Since the cubs were bigger now, the journey to Tom's was a little faster. They feasted on berries as they walked but were still able to fill two baskets for Sue. Benjamin couldn't stop thinking about strawberry rhubarb pie, hoping Sue would be making some.

When Tom opened the door, he took one look at Cola. "Is that an American flag bear?" he said.

Benjamin laughed. "No, it's just a polar bear that loves berries." He introduced the baby cubs to Tom.

"Where are the strawberry rhubarb pies?" Cola said. "I heard Sue's pies are the best." Tom said she was right about that and promised they would be chowing down on some later.

Luna and Susan went inside to be with Sue, while Benjamin stayed outside with Tom and the other cubs. Tom was building another smoker that was even larger.

"Tom, if it would be okay, we'd like to stay with you for a couple of weeks while we look for dens in the area," Benjamin said.

His eyes lit up. "Really? That's terrific! I'm so excited you finally decided to move here."

"I can't live through any more hunting seasons after all the tragic loss I've experienced. Now I know how important a sow is to a boar bear."

Tom nodded. "I couldn't agree more. It would kill me to lose Sue. And again, I can't thank you enough. She was yours, but you made sure she was mine."

He finished sealing the smoker with red clay, then asked the cubs to gather a few small limbs for kindling. When they came back, he threw the kindling in and looked at the cubs. "Okay, who wants to light the fire?"

"I will," Pandy said. "But you may need to help me." Tom was happy to show Pandy how to do it. He explained how to keep the heat low and increase it as the clay dried.

Benjamin just hoped Tom had plenty of ribs to barbecue while they were there. Otherwise, he would need to make a trip to Ann's again.

"Supper's ready!" Sue yelled. They went inside and were greeted by the smell of roasted turkey, dressing, green beans and potatoes, and freshly baked sourdough bread. After savoring the delicious meal, Sue opened the oven door.

Cola's pink nose perked up. "What is that heavenly smell?"

"Just my famous strawberry rhubarb pie!" Sue said, placing large pies in front of the older bears and small ones in front of the young cubs.

Cola finished her pie in record time and asked for seconds.

Luna glared at her. "Coca-Cola, don't be asking for more pie. It's rude."

"It's okay," Sue said. "We have plenty of pie." She went into the kitchen and brought Cola another one.

As the cubs played together after supper, Benjamin talked to Tom about his den search. Tom knew of two suitable dens less than a mile away. Benjamin told him that was helpful, but they would need more. They agreed to check out the two dens tomorrow, decide who would take them, and worry about finding the other dens later.

"Before we leave in the morning, I'm going to put some ribs in the smoker," Tom said. "That way, they'll be ready when we get back for supper."

When Benjamin woke up the next morning, Tom was already outside with the ribs and Sue was fixing breakfast. One by one, the others woke up, and after breakfast, they set off to check out the new dens.

The first den was very large and comfortable, and it was only half a mile from Tom's. The den was divided into different sections. One of the sections had multiple shelves and drawers that Luna thought would be perfect for her herbs.

"This is our den," she said.

"One down, three to go!" Benjamin high-fived her.

The next one was only a quarter of a mile away. It wasn't as big, but it was still cozy. Benjamin thought it would be perfect for Susie and Sam Jr., who had a smaller family.

It was a short day, but Benjamin was happy they had secured two dens. He hoped the other dens they found would also be close by.

They smelled the ribs before they even got back to Tom's den. Benjamin was excited to try them. He could tell Tom was getting better at making ribs every time he did it—at least that was what his nose said. Sue had fixed two full buckets of fried taters to go along with the ribs. Between the ribs, which were falling off the bone, and the mouthwatering side dishes, it was one of the better feasts in recent memory.

"Who's ready to go fishing?" Tom said. Bud was the first to jump up. They fished half the night, filling six baskets with catfish. None were particularly large, but some were up to twenty-four inches long.

It took the bears two days to find the next den. Bud found it after searching around in the laurels, and it was less than half a mile from Susie's new den. But it was a little bigger, so they decided it would be ideal for Lucy and James. Now they had three dens all within a mile of each other, and only one more to find.

For the next week, they searched high and low. They found several that would be good for rabbits, but nothing large enough to house a growing bear family. Knowing they would be leaving in a few days, Benjamin was prepared to postpone the search and share dens for the time being.

That evening, the bears enjoyed a picnic at the pond. They had planned to fish, but Cola and Pandy said they were tired of fishing. So when they found an old soccer ball lying nearby, they were thrilled. Pandy kicked it as hard as he could, and it sailed over some trees and landed in a pine and laurel thicket. They ran off to look for it.

The other bears could hear limbs cracking and snapping as the cubs trudged into the thicket. Then, Pandy's voice: "Found the ball! You guys, there's a very big den in here!"

Benjamin ran over, but he couldn't see the den, much less get through the thicket. The baby cubs were the only ones small enough to get in there. He knew they would have to clear the vegetation, but since it was so late in the day, it would have to be tomorrow.

Luna was so excited they had found the fourth den, and even more excited it was located at the pond. She said she might be willing to trade in her perfect herb den for lakefront property.

The next day, they brought handsaws and sickles to clear the brush from around the den. Cola and Pandy were excited to show their discovery to the rest of the bears. But the thicket was so dense that clearing it was slow going and tiring. Benjamin couldn't figure out how even tiny Cola and Pandy had been able to slip through it and find the den.

As dusk fell, they could just see the outline of an entrance, but they were only halfway through the thicket. They would have to come back tomorrow after a good night's rest.

At noon the next day, they finally had the brush removed from around the entrance, and it was big enough that a large bear could get through comfortably. Inside were five large rooms and a smaller one.

"I love this," Luna said when she walked into the smaller room. "With a few changes, this would be an even more perfect herb room. Also, how wonderful would it be to sit at the entrance and look out over the whole lake—er, pond?"

Benjamin agreed. He told Luna they could take this one and give the first den to Angel and Samuel.

They spent the rest of the day clearing more of the thicket. As they worked, Benjamin told Tom how much he hated the thought of leaving the next day, even though he knew they'd be back soon.

"Here's an idea," Luna said. "We can have two homes, a summer home and a winter home. In the summer, we can go back to our old places, then spend the winters here with Tom and Sue."

"Great idea," Benjamin said. "Better yet, you could also have a summer home with us, Tom. Just come back and stay in your old den!"

Tom and Bud were both excited about this plan. Tom because he would be able to spend time with his friends, and Bud because of how much he loved fishing in the rainbow trout pond.

After a good night's sleep, they set off and told Tom they would be back in about a week with some of their belongings.

Although the road ahead was long, Benjamin planned to stop at Ann's along the way. He wanted to see her new baby, the one the devil had fathered.

CHAPTER 43

Ann's Baby

As they walked, the bears couldn't stop talking about their upcoming move. Luna was still over the moon about their place on the pond. Bud was far from sad about it himself, but Benjamin was concerned his little brother would never sleep with the amount of time he would spend fishing over there.

As they walked up to Ann's front door, Benjamin heard panting and screaming coming from inside. He knocked, quietly at first, then louder.

"Come in!" Alice yelled.

Ann was lying on the floor, legs spread as wide as they could be, moaning, yelling, and breathing rhythmically. Benjamin had no idea what was going on.

"She's in labor, y'all," Alice said. "She's getting ready to give birth!"

"I know what to do!" Luna said. "We need boiling water and towels. I'll go get them."

Benjamin asked if there was anything he could do.

"Hold my hand," Ann said. "That will help me while Alice delivers my baby." Her moans were getting more frequent.

"Her water has broken," Alice announced. Benjamin still had no idea what was going on.

Waaaaaaaa! Waaaaaaaaaaa! Benjamin thought that must be the sound baby humans made when they cried.

Alice lifted the baby into Ann's waiting arms. "Ann, I want to introduce you to our little baby boy."

"Uh oh," Ann said, giving a weak smile. "We only came up with girls' names."

Luna walked back in with the boiling water and towels. *You're just a little too late*, Benjamin thought. *Ann's baby boy is already here.* Ann rested the baby on her bosom. Her eyes were heavy, and she fell asleep as the baby suckled.

Alice turned to them. "Y'all, I have never been so glad to hear someone knocking on the door. I was scared to death, and you made this much easier for me."

A few minutes later, Ann opened her eyes. "Luna, I was going to name our daughter after you. One night, the perfect name came to me: Luan. It has Chinese origins and refers to the moon."

"Just like me," Luna said. "I'm named after the Roman goddess of the moon. Luan sounds like a lovely name, even if you had a boy instead of a girl."

"That was so cool to watch!" Bud said. "I've never seen anyone giving birth before."

"That may have looked cool," Ann said, "but oh my God, I have never felt such pain before. It was worth it, though, so Luan could be here with us."

They stayed for the next two days to help Alice take care of Ann and Luan. At one point, Cola and Pandy crawled into Luan's crib, and they all snoozed together.

Now that Ann felt better rested, Benjamin told her they had found four perfect dens and would be moving to Tom's county. "We'll keep our dens here so we can visit in spring and summer," he said, "but for our safety, we'll be two counties over in fall and winter."

"I'll come see your new dens when Luan is a little older," Ann said.

Luan had stolen the bears' hearts, and none of them wanted to leave. But Benjamin knew they had a lot to do and Tom would be expecting them, so they packed up and got ready to go.

"Bud, before you leave, go into my bedroom and look at what's in there for you," Ann said.

"Oh, wow!" came Bud's voice from the bedroom. "It's my world-record rainbow trout, and it's just as beautiful as the day we caught it. The plaque says, 'Bud, Benjamin, Tom, and Cola caught me.'"

The next morning, all the bear families met at the rainbow trout pond. This time, Bud was using the same bait as everyone else. They were catching fish left and right, and Bud said he was having fun but would always miss fishing for the world record.

They fished until late afternoon, then everyone headed back to their dens to get packed and decide what they would take and what they would leave behind.

After a restful night, everyone was packed and ready to travel. The bears were excited to see their new dens, but no one was as excited as Luna. Benjamin was sure the forest was confused seeing four families of bears walking along with all their belongings, and he laughed to himself at the thought.

After telling Tom they had arrived, the families went to see each of the dens and drop off their things. The first den was Angel and Samuel's, followed by Susie and Sam Jr.'s, then Lucy and James's.

Everyone seemed to love their dens, at least until they got to the last den, which Benjamin and Luna had already claimed. Of course, they all wanted the pondfront property for themselves. Still, they were appreciative of the hard work Benjamin and his family had done to find dens for them, and it made them feel better to know they would be having many family outings at the pond no matter who was living there. But now, it was getting late. After a long day, the bears were ready to retire to their dens.

The next day, dens were tidied up and plans were made for a party at the pond later. It was a relaxing evening, and the bears caught so many catfish. No one was surprised when Bud reeled in the biggest one, which was thirty inches long. It was a long way from the world record, but he knew it would happen one day. After fishing, Cola, Pandy, and Suzanne played together, swimming from one end of the pond to the other.

The next day, Tom went from den to den helping the

families build their own smokers. At the pondfront place, the plan was to build two: one for Benjamin's family and a larger one for parties with all five families. Everyone was so happy about their new dens and living arrangements. For Benjamin, though, the greatest happiness came from no longer having to be worried about hunters come winter.

After Tom left, Benjamin drifted off in his chair as he sat there fishing. Soon, he fell into a deep sleep and dreamed he was knocking on the door to Ann's house, just as they had the other day. Ann was lying on the floor, moaning and panting. Alice was saying Ann's water had broken, except she kept saying it over and over again, each time sounding more frantic. The moaning and panting got faster and louder until it reached a fever pitch and Ann screamed out. Calmly, Alice pulled the baby out and laid it onto Ann's bosom. Benjamin took one look at the baby and stifled a scream.

Benjamin woke up, terrified. Luna was beside him. "You were having a nightmare, Ben." She rubbed his arm.

"No. It was real. We were at Ann's place, just like the other day. But this time, when Luan was lying on Ann's chest, he looked up at me. His eyes were bright red, Luna, and he had two bright-red horns coming out of the sides of his head."

About the Author

Dale Thacker is a seasoned bear hunter, firefighter paramedic, and avid outdoorsman from Troutville, Virginia. He and his wife, Judy, have been married over forty years and live with their many pets, including the love of their lives, a black teacup poodle named CoCo. Dale's grandson, Landon, is in the Boy Scouts and becoming a bear hunter himself. In addition to hunting, Dale also loves fishing, camping, hiking, and enjoying the great outdoors.

More from Dale Thacker

Be sure to check out *Tales of a Bear Hunter*, Dale's debut work and #1 Amazon bestselling memoir.